Praise for Joan Smith

"Smith knows how to devise a slick and intelligently crafted plot and her book moves along at a cracking pace."
—*Sunday Telegraph* (London)

"Smith brings much-needed freshness to the academic mystery. . . . [She] is a tidy, streamlined, and clever prose stylist. She also manages to use sexuality in ways English writers seldom do: as both a weapon and a source of salvation."
—*Booklist*

By Joan Smith
Published by Fawcett Books:

MISOGYNIES
A MASCULINE ENDING
WHY AREN'T THEY SCREAMING?
DON'T LEAVE ME THIS WAY
WHAT MEN SAY

WHAT MEN SAY

Joan Smith

FAWCETT CREST • NEW YORK

A Fawcett Crest Book
Published by Ballantine Books
Copyright © 1993 by Joan Smith

All rights reserved under International and Pan-American Copyright Conventions. Published in the United States by Ballantine Books, a division of Random House, Inc., New York. Originally published in Great Britain in 1993 by Chatto & Windus Limited.

Library of Congress Catalog Card Number: 93-46501

ISBN 0-449-22297-7

Manufactured in the United States of America

First Ballantine Books Hardcover Edition: June 1994
First Ballantine Books Mass Market Edition: June 1995

10 9 8 7 6 5 4 3 2 1

Nunc iam nulla viro iuranti femina credat,
nulla viri speret sermones esse fideles.

CATULLUS 64

That's it—from now on no woman should listen to a man who claims he loves her.
In fact, if she's got any sense, she won't believe a word he says.

CATULLUS 64

1

"THEY'RE ALL *BURNT*." THE BOY PULLED A gargoyle face and pushed away the paper plate Loretta was holding out to him.

"They're not burnt, it's just that the grill's very hot—it makes black lines when you put them on. Look, they're all like that." She pointed to the neat row of hamburgers, blotting-paper pink and curling at the edges, cooking on the grill. "Haven't you been to a barbecue before?"

The boy, a sandy-haired child of nine or ten in a garish Ninja-turtle T-shirt, ignored the question. "They're not like that at McDonald's."

"Aren't they?" Loretta had been to McDonald's once in her life and felt in no position to argue. Dumping the rejected plate on the table in front of her, she used her forearm to push her hair out of her eyes and wished she had brought something to tie it back from her face. She hadn't believed the previous evening's weather forecast, with its confident prediction that heavy overnight showers would give way to bright sunshine, but this was one of those rare occasions when it was spot-on. She had long ago discarded her jacket but there was no escape from the stinging heat of the gas-fired barbecue and she could feel her dress beginning to cling between her shoulder blades. Loretta thought anxiously about how much it would cost to dry-clean, distrusting the "hand wash, cool iron" instruction on the reverse of the size-12 label. She should never have worn a new dress on such a muggy day, especially not this dark-blue silk which she had been able to afford only because it was on sale—and was that a grease stain she could see near the hem? She bunched up the cloth, scratched ineffectually at it and then realized that the surly boy had not moved away.

"Changed your mind?" she asked hopefully, nudging the plate towards him. On closer inspection she saw that the burgers had acquired a penumbra of animal fat; Loretta was quite hungry herself, but it occurred to her that these shrivelled apologies for meat were enough to make anyone a vegetarian.

The boy's attention had wandered to a group of older children arguing over a frisbee further down the lawn. Loretta hoped he would go and join them but after a while he turned back, a wistful expression on his face. "You got anything else?"

Loretta bit her lip, deducing from his avid glances at the frisbee players that he was clumsy at games, unpopular with other children, or both. "Why don't you go over there," she suggested in a friendly voice, "look, where Bridget's standing, and someone'll give you a bagel."

"What's a bagel?" His voice was flat, uninterested.

"It's a sort of—it's a kind of bread roll with a hole in the middle. You eat it with cheese and smoked salmon . . ." As she spoke, Loretta realized that this was an even less attractive offer to a ten-year-old than her stripy hamburgers. "Wait a minute. What about these?"

2

She rummaged in a box under the table and came up with a packet of crisps.

"They chilli?" He twisted his head sideways in an attempt to read.

"Um—no. Salt and vinegar." Loretta hadn't known you could get chilli-flavored crisps.

The boy twisted his face into another bizarre expression of rejection. "I only like Bovril and chilli."

"Bovril *and* chilli? Oh, I see. Let's have a look." Loretta knelt and took packets out of the box one by one. She was supposed to give out a packet of crisps with each plate of hamburgers but she had forgotten their existence until a moment ago. "Sorry, they're all salt and vinegar. Go on—try them."

He shook his head emphatically and Loretta's patience finally wore out. "Well—that's it, then. I haven't got anything else."

He thrust his hands in his pockets and slouched off, disappointment radiating from his hunched shoulders. Halfway across the lawn he dropped this act, veered off to chase the frisbee and was shouldered out of the way by a larger boy. Loretta sighed and wondered where his parents were.

"Trouble?"

She turned to see Stephen Kaplan, a politics lecturer she knew slightly, watching her with amusement. He was short, dark and intense, and they had become embroiled in a fierce argument over the resignation of Mrs. Thatcher, an event Loretta celebrated with an impromptu party at her house in Oxford, the last time they met. She was surprised to see him at Bridget and Sam's house-warming party, not on political grounds but because she had the impression Bridget found him less amusing these days.

"Just a bit of consumer resistance." She tried to put

3

the dinner-party argument, which had struck her as childish and embarrassing even when it was going on, out of her mind. "I can't compete with McDonald's, apparently. Or do I mean Burger King?"

Stephen smiled and looked superior. "Anyone can see *you* don't have kids. Burger King is—" He gestured downwards with his thumb. "McDonald's, now . . . Rachel had her birthday party there last month. Ten overexcited kids, balloons, sticky drinks . . . prepubescents' heaven. Can I get you a drink?"

Loretta nodded gratefully at this unexpected offer and held out her empty plastic beaker. Stephen, she noticed, was drinking from a proper glass. "Something nonalcoholic. I think I'm starting to melt."

"Orange juice? Mineral water?"

"Mineral water. Oh, and do you have any idea of the time? Someone's supposed to take over from me at two o'clock."

He glanced at a watch equipped with sufficient hands and dials to time an Olympic race. "Ten to. I wondered if you were stuck with that thing all afternoon." He nodded towards the barbecue. "Did you volunteer?"

"Well, not exactly. Sam had a sort of rota . . ."

Stephen looked smug. "He tried to sign me up for something but I promised Jane I'd keep an eye on the kids. I've been in Warsaw for ten days and she says it's my turn."

Loretta had never met the Kaplan children, a boy and a girl, so she had no idea whether they were among the half-dozen youngsters on the lawn or inside the house. Stephen evidently wore his parental responsibilities lightly, beginning an anecdote about Lech Walesa and someone Loretta had never heard of—Wakowski or Wachowski, some name like that—as though he had the entire afternoon to himself. Loretta listened to him skeptically, recalling a dismissive remark by her most recent lover, a history lecturer, to the effect that Stephen's Polish contacts were merely a bunch of Poujadists without political access or influence. Of course, Joe was inclined to sneer at anyone who might be construed as a potential rival, which was one of the reasons Loretta had ended their relationship, but his parents were Polish, he spoke the language fluently and his friendships with KOR intellectuals went back a decade.

Stephen finished his story and waited for Loretta to laugh. She had not really been listening and managed only a thin smile, after which they lapsed into awkward silence.

"Well—" Stephen looked at his absurd watch again, though it was only five minutes since she had asked the time. "I'd better see about this drink."

Loretta watched him set off for the house. Its unusual name, Thebes Farm, had prompted a nervous joke from Bridget when she first produced the estate agent's details, something about the surprisingly short distance between Thebes and Jericho, the latter being the area of Oxford in which Loretta lived. Troy was only four or five miles up the road, Bridget added, referring to an imposing farmhouse of that name in Somerton; this bit of Oxfordshire was a veritable map of the ancient world. The geography lesson was intended, Loretta guessed, to cover up Bridget's anxiety about her announcement that she was about to move to an isolated farmhouse half an hour's drive from the city center, thus putting an end to their old habit of walking round to each other's houses when the mood took them. Although her own first reaction was dismay, Loretta joined in the joke, such as it was, by adding to the list Nineveh Farm on the road from Oxford to Nuneham Courtenay.

Bridget and Sam were so proud of their singular address that they had commissioned a local artist to provide a sketch of the house for their writing paper. The drawing was only slightly fanciful, showing a solid, double-fronted house with a barn standing at right angles to it; the artist had used her imagination on the barn, which was actually rather dilapidated and booby-trapped, when Loretta last looked inside, with rusting farm machinery of unknown provenance.

The house itself had flagstone floors in all the downstairs rooms, and Loretta thought wistfully of the cool, shady interior. She was rather sick of hearing about the floors, which had been painstakingly lifted, cleaned and replaced by Bridget and Sam's builders in an operation which, in terms of expense and effort, seemed to be on only a slightly smaller scale than the renovation of the Piazza della Signoria in Florence. Loretta had not seen the final result until an hour or so before the party, when Sam showed her into a drawing room straight out of *The World of Interiors*: smooth, dove-gray flags, brilliantly colored kelims, and two scroll-end sofas newly upholstered in deep-yellow velvet. Even if she had been invited to sit down, Loretta would have been reluctant to disturb their shiny tautness, but the occasion did not arise. Sam had given her a lightning tour of the ground floor before leading her into the kitchen and asking if she'd mind slicing and dressing a gargantuan quantity of boiled potatoes. Loretta wished now that she had given in to the temptation to nibble as she whizzed up mayonnaise in a state-of-the-art food processor, instead of assuming that there'd be plenty left when she escaped from the hamburgers.

"Hello, how are you?" Loretta greeted Audrey Summers, Bridget's former next-door neighbor in north Oxford, without enthusiasm. Loretta suspected that Audrey disapproved of her, a suggestion Bridget denied in such a half-hearted way as to convince her of its accuracy. She certainly didn't want to be trapped into making polite conversation with her across the hamburger stall, and she was relieved when Audrey returned her greeting and kept going, cool and unapproachable in a Liberty-print skirt and jacket.

"Jack! Jack—why don't you bring a bottle?" A woman's voice drifted up from the orchard at the bottom of the garden, vainly trying to attract the attention of a man striding towards the house with a tray of empty glasses. Loretta turned to look at her, watching as she smilingly acknowledged that Jack hadn't heard and went back to breast-feeding a small baby. She had not seen the dark-haired woman before, nor any of the other adults forming a companionable group about her under the trees.

The garden was, according to the estate agent, one of the "glories" of Thebes Farm. It was large, south-facing and triangular in shape, at its widest in front of the house where it was laid to lawn. Like the house, it was raised well above the level of the road and was further protected by a high wall. A narrow gate, reached by half a dozen deep stone steps, provided the sole access from the road so that anyone arriving by car had to turn off and drive round the back of the house into the old farmyard. Loretta's hamburger stall—actually a scarred pine table covered with a thick paper cloth—had been set up parallel to the wall, just in front of a newly planted herbaceous border. Facing her, on the far side of the lawn, was the barn which featured so prettily on Bridget and Sam's notepaper.

The dark woman and her friends were at least twenty-five yards away and it was only when one of them turned in her direction that Loretta realized they

7

were not all strangers after all. The woman in the green skirt or shorts was Janet Dunne, an art historian who lived in Park Town; Loretta had been placed next to her at Bridget's final dinner party in Woodstock Road. A couple of weeks later she had seen Janet on "The Late Show," taking part in a very solemn discussion on the work of a sculptor whose one-man show, consisting almost exclusively of nude male torsos, had been threatened with prosecution for obscenity. Janet's attempt to lighten the proceedings with a joke—something about the penis not standing up well to such close scrutiny—had so infuriated another of the guests, a thuggish Glaswegian poet, that he leaped to his feet and hurled abuse at her in an increasingly impenetrable Scots accent. Janet's spirited attempt to defend herself, on the grounds that the sculptures had more to do with their creator's personal anxieties than art, had been drowned in the ensuing uproar and the item ended early. Loretta had begun writing a sympathetic note, including a variation on the old joke about the penis being only a phallic symbol, but the phone had rung or someone had come round—whatever the reason for the interruption, she had never sent it.

She peered up and down the garden, hoping to spot Sam Becker and tell him she'd had enough of his hamburgers and wanted to circulate, but she could not see him. She guessed he was in the house, uncorking more bottles—people seemed to be drinking freely, perhaps because of the heat—or getting the puddings out of the big fridge she had observed in the kitchen. There was no sign of Bridget, either, even though she had been helping to dish out food the last time Loretta looked. She wondered, again, whether Bridget was all right; she had been upstairs when Loretta arrived that morning, taking no part in the party preparations and appearing only as the first guests drove into the yard so there was no chance of speaking to her alone. Loretta had been slightly miffed by this until Bridget stopped to greet her, lifting a pale, tired face which suggested the party was too much for her at this stage in her pregnancy. Either that, Loretta concluded, or she'd had a row with Sam.

The latter thought came into her head not because of any evidence that Bridget and Sam were on bad terms—on the contrary, he had seemed solicitous and fond as the party began—but because Loretta was feeling uncomfortable about her own relations with Bridget. Their last meeting, over lunch at a wine bar in Little Clarendon Street a couple of weeks before, had been marred by a rare argument; the episode was so unusual, and so unsettling, that she had tried to explain it away as a side effect of Bridget's condition. Bridget had arrived in an odd mood, joking with the waiter as she ordered mineral water instead of her usual glass of red wine and entertaining Loretta with a satirical account of the antenatal class she and Sam had recently attended, but she looked and sounded preoccupied. Loretta, still unsure of the new boundaries imposed by her friend's marriage, was trying to think of a tactful way of asking what was wrong when the waiter returned with their main courses, fish cakes for Bridget and kedgeree for Loretta.

Bridget cheered up at once, asking Loretta's advice on names for the baby as she finished her first mouthful of food. "I mean, I don't want to land her—him—with something that's going to sound dated or embarrassing." Bridget listed some of her own wilder inspirations, then pulled a face in answer to Loretta's question about Sam's preferences. "Howard, can you imagine it? Howard Becker—"

9

"Becker? You mean—it's going to have Sam's name?" Loretta was too astonished to conceal her reaction.

"Well, I don't think those double-barrelled things really work . . ." Bridget hacked at her fish cake, avoiding Loretta's eye.

"Neither do I, but what's wrong with Bennett?"

"I haven't been pressured into it, if that's what you're thinking," Bridget said crossly, making Loretta think she had. "It's all very well theorizing, but when you're actually faced with . . . If you must know, it means a lot to Sam."

This, from a woman who had been outraged by her younger sister's decision to change her name when she got married the previous year, was more than Loretta could bear. "I'm sure it does. I'm sure it's meant a lot to men throughout the ages, which is why—"

"Oh, for God's sake, Loretta, spare me the lecture. Can't you see it's personal?"

"And that isn't political, all of a sudden?"

They glared at each other, unused to confrontation and uncertain how to deal with it. When the waiter removed their plates, Bridget refused his offer of pudding and announced she had to dash, thrusting a ten-pound note into Loretta's hand to cover her share of the bill. They had spoken on the phone since, feeling their way back towards the old, easy companionship, but the sense of constraint had not entirely disappeared. Bridget's suggestion that Loretta arrive early at the party had raised her hopes of a quiet talk, but in the event she had spent the time in the kitchen, listening to Sam's enthusiastic description of his plans for the top floor of the house.

"The best woman."

"Sorry?" Loretta looked up in surprise, realizing too

10

late that someone, a man who looked faintly familiar, was talking to her.

"We met at the wedding—you were the best woman. You made a great speech."

"I'm glad you liked it. It didn't go down too well with Bridget's parents."

"Older people often are traditional. You had a nice touch, livened the party up no end. That place they got married—it was the pits."

Loretta smiled. The Oxford register office was a first-floor room in the Westgate Center, a dreary indoor shopping arcade, near a branch of C & A. It had slightly more charm, but not much, than a doctor's waiting room, and the guests hurried out after the ceremony to find themselves confronted with the frankly inquisitive stares of half a dozen middle-aged shoppers who had stopped to see the bride. Bridget, taking advantage of the unseasonally warm spring weather in a halter-neck dress and Loretta's gold Italian sandals, was an obvious disappointment and they soon drifted away. Her parents, whose pleas for a church wedding, a Pronuptia dress and bridesmaids in pastel polyester had been swept aside, were left to pose unhappily for photographs with their slightly pregnant daughter, her new American husband and Loretta. They were even denied the consolation of meeting Sam's mother, who lived in Boston and was unable to come to England at such short notice. Instead, she sent flowers and a conventionally worded telemessage.

"Christopher Caesar," said the erstwhile wedding guest, holding out his hand. "I don't think we were introduced."

"Loretta Lawson." He had a lean, serious face, with high cheekbones and dark hair parted in the middle—good-looking in a very un-English way. Loretta would

11

not have been surprised to discover that he worked out at a gym and drank only mineral water.

"Bridget's talked about you," he was saying. "You teach English, right?"

"Yes, but not at Oxford. And only part-time." She hesitated, her cheeks growing warm. "The rest of the time I write books." She felt uncomfortable talking about her writing, especially with strangers, so she added quickly: "I'm a lecturer at London University, one of the newer colleges. I have an office near the Post Office Tower, if you know where that is."

"How'd you know Bridget?"

"Oh—" Loretta and Bridget had been in the same women's group around the time Loretta left her husband, a journalist called John Tracey. She was not normally reticent on the subject, but it occurred to her that she had no idea whether Sam knew about this bit of his wife's past, or how he would feel about it. "We've known each other for years," she said vaguely, "it must be at least ten. What about you? I assume you're a friend of Sam's?"

"We work for the same company," he said, and began to talk about a joint project between CES—Loretta had never quite got over her astonishment that the initials stood for Computo Ergo Sum plc—and the university engineering department.

She nodded politely from time to time, understanding enough about computers to work her own word processor and nothing more. Bridget, usually as technologically illiterate as Loretta, had developed a baffling interest in the subject in December, suddenly talking knowledgeably about macros, megabytes and even logic bombs; then she introduced Loretta to Sam, and all was explained. Christopher Caesar's account of ways to use computers to simulate aircraft wear and tear, instead of destroying expensive engines, left Loretta terminally bored and she looked down, hiding a smile at this silent pun, then realized he had stopped speaking.

"Would you like a hamburger?" she asked quickly. "Everyone's allowed two, though there hasn't exactly been a rush . . . Shit!" The flat pink circles which had been sitting harmlessly on the grill last time she looked were now reduced to black, misshapen nuggets. An acrid smell hovered about them, a pungent combination of singed meat and fat-spattered charcoal.

"You know how to turn that thing down?"

"I suppose you just . . ." Loretta bent and fiddled with various knobs at the back of the barbecue. "This looks like the gas supply . . . yes, I've got it."

"Why don't I take over for a while?" He picked up the fish slice and used it to lift the charred hamburgers onto a plate. "You look like you need a break."

Loretta stared at him for a moment, then seized her bag and slid out from behind the table before he could change his mind.

"Whoa—just missed your dress."

She turned and saw that she had almost collided with Stephen Kaplan, who was holding out a plastic cup.

"Stephen—thanks." Flustered, she took the cup and sniffed the reddish-gold liquid inside. "What *is* this?"

"Some sort of fruit juice. Mango, passion fruit and persimmon—one of those unlikely combinations. They've run out of mineral water and I didn't think you'd want tap."

"Really?" Loretta was surprised by this admission of the low quality of the local tap water. It was often cloudy and there had been several incidents of contamination since privatization, but she would not have expected Stephen to acknowledge either problem. "I thought you were all for privatization."

"I am, but it's early days yet. You can't wipe out years of socialist neglect overnight." He seemed on the verge of launching into a speech, then apparently thought better of it. "How's your book selling?"

"My book?"

"A biography, isn't it? Some authoress."

Bridget had once claimed, when challenged by Loretta over her friendship with Stephen, that she liked his dry wit. Loretta had never seen any evidence of it, merely an ill-mannered tendency to mock anything he disagreed with. She reined in her irritation and said crisply: "Edith Wharton."

"Of course. Jane's got some of her books but I can't say I've read them . . . Don't you think those green covers have become a bit of a cliché? I suppose you're getting lots of lovely royalties?"

"Not yet. Though the paperback is doing quite well." Loretta's royalty statements so far had been a disappointment, but her literary agent assured her it was only because the system was slow to cough up. Loretta hoped she was right.

"You're doing another one, aren't you? Bridget said something about it, not a biography this time."

In the distance Loretta saw Janet Dunne getting to her feet, brushing twigs from a pair of baggy green shorts and sliding her feet into sandals. Stephen only wanted to hear about her new book so he could make silly jokes about it; she flashed him a dismissive smile and began edging away. "Stephen, would you excuse me, there's someone I have to . . . Thanks for . . ." She held up the cup of exotic fruit juice, moving sideways so she did not see Sam Becker until he slipped a proprietorial hand under her left elbow.

"Loretta—you having a good time?" He was wearing wire-rimmed sunglasses, Ray-Bans she thought, and his straight fair hair fell boyishly onto his forehead. The first time they met, six or seven months ago and in the depths of winter, this striking combination of blond hair and permanently tanned skin had made her think of the Beach Boys—not the balding, middle-aged men she had recently seen on television, but the carefree, party-loving surfers of the mid-sixties. She had recognized the incongruity of the comparison as soon as she made it, for Sam was in his early thirties, too young to have experienced the Summer of Love, and had no connections with the West Coast.

He was waiting for her reply. "Yes—lovely party," she said formally, suppressing her annoyance over the hamburger stall.

Sam squeezed her arm. "Glad you could make it. It mattered to Bridget, you being here."

Loretta bridled, disliking his habit of speaking on Bridget's behalf. "I haven't had a chance to exchange two words with her, as a matter of fact." She thought of their brief meeting that morning, recalled Bridget's haggard appearance and suddenly felt in need of reassurance. "Sam—she is all right, isn't she? She looked—I thought she looked worn out."

Sam frowned and thrust his hands into the pockets of his chinos. "There's some kind of a problem with her blood pressure. She has more tests on Tuesday."

"What? I had no idea."

Sam shrugged. "It was a routine check, she didn't have a clue anything was wrong. She's an elderly *prima gravida*, I guess we should've expected—"

"She's a what?"

"Her age," Sam explained. "She's kind of on the old side for her first child. They told her to take it easy, I wanted to call off the party but ... well, I guess she's

15

still trying to be Superwoman. Maybe you could talk to her? She was in the kitchen just now."

Loretta warmed to him. "Of course. Look, I know it's worrying, but she's always been healthy . . . I'll go and find her now."

"Thanks, Loretta. John, hi, how're you doing?"

He was shaking hands with a latecomer, being introduced to his wife and small daughter; Loretta left them and walked slowly towards the house. One of her colleagues in the English department, a woman of about the same age as Bridget and pregnant with her first child, had spent weeks in hospital the previous summer after high blood pressure was diagnosed. She had eventually given birth to a healthy girl, returning to work so exhausted that Loretta had agreed to take over a couple of her courses. She did not enjoy marking twenty-nine essays on *The Prelude*, or rereading Trollope, but Judith was grateful and the extra money was handy. Loretta now realized she had paid little attention to the details of Judith's condition, seeing her illness as a practical problem which she happened to have the means to solve. It hardly qualified her as an expert on the complications of pregnancy, though she half remembered someone saying Judith's baby was terribly underweight . . .

A furious barking broke out to her right. Loretta turned and saw a puppyish black Labrador making excited sallies towards the barn, stopping just short of the door and nervously backing away. A child was crying, its voice rising and falling in muffled sobs, but she could not see who was in distress or why.

"What's going on?" She appealed to Audrey Summers, who had appeared beside her.

"I don't know." Audrey was tense and alert, standing on tiptoe to see over the heads of the adults milling

16

about in front of the barn. Loretta saw the Labrador's owner struggling with his dog, staggering backwards as it shook off his grasp and darted between the legs of the crowd. He tried to follow, calling the dog's name—"Teddy, Teddy"—and for a few seconds his voice drowned out the cries of the invisible child, now reduced to a series of thin, despairing wails.

Loretta gasped. The crying child was *inside* the barn—inside with the rusty spikes and unguarded machinery she had seen on her first visit, before the house was done up. Dreadful pictures rushed into her head, horror-film images of severed limbs and spouting arteries. Someone began to cry hysterically, and a man's voice shouted over and over again for a key.

"What on earth's going on?" Bridget touched her lightly on the arm, sounding both puzzled and amused. "Sounds like a riot at the very least."

"There's a child—" Loretta's throat was dry. "One of the children's got into the barn, I don't know how." Earlier in the afternoon, from her vantage point on the other side of the lawn, she had seen a heavy padlock hanging from the hasp.

"The window." Audrey nodded in the direction of the farmyard, where a chair was lying on its back below a small, grimy window in the side of the barn.

"OK, everybody, stand back." Sam strode past them, a bunch of keys in his hand. He fumbled for a moment, then lifted the padlock off. The door swung inward at his touch and he took a step forward, then fell back, his hand to his nose.

Stephen Kaplan demanded: "Christ, Sam, what d'you keep in there?" and the area in front of the barn began to clear as people coughed, gagged and retreated. Two boys emerged from the dark doorway, blinking in the brilliant afternoon light, then took to their heels in op-

posite directions, the larger of the two swerving round
Sam and disappearing round the corner into the farmyard. As he went, Loretta caught a glimpse of a familiar
green T-shirt.

"Charlotte!" A woman in red hurried forward, holding out her arms to a small girl whose pale, tear-stained
face was just visible round the door. She scooped her
up, struggling with the child's absurd outfit, a volumi-
nous taffeta creation which was torn in several places
and beribboned with cobwebs.

"Is she hurt?" Audrey started towards the barn, then
stopped and turned back to Loretta and Bridget with an
expression of recognition and dawning horror. The
smell reached them a second later, a sweet, sickening
stench which brought bile into Loretta's throat and doubled Bridget over as though she had been punched in
the stomach.

"It smells funny," the little girl said suddenly, smooth-
ing down her skirt and not looking at her mother. "It
smells funny and the lady won't get up. She's gone a
funny color and she won't get up."

With impeccable timing the Labrador, who had taken
advantage of the confusion to slip inside the barn, chose
this moment to trot out with an object in his mouth. He
paused, wagging his tail good-naturedly, then hurried
past Loretta and Bridget in search of his master.

"Teddy, what have you—"

The dog presented his trophy, falling back on his
haunches and beating his tail on the ground as he
waited for congratulations that did not come. Instead,
Bridget, who had taken a couple of steps towards him
in order to get a better view, clutched at Loretta's arm
and was promptly sick over a mauve hydrangea.

2

"LAWSON, THAT'S AN EASY ONE," SAID THE Inspector, writing it at the top of a new page. "That Nigerian lady who just went out, I had to get her to spell it twice. Even the Americans seem to have funny names—they all friends of yours?"

Loretta shook her head, having recognized the black woman as a postgraduate she had once met leaving Bridget's house in Woodstock Road. As for Americans, she could think of only two: Sam Becker, who hardly qualified as a funny name, and his friend from the computer company.

"Christopher Caesar?"

"Mmm, but that's not how he spells it, not like Julius. Here it is." She flipped back a couple of pages. "C-I-S-A-R, with a squiggle over the *A* but he doesn't insist." There was silence for a moment and Loretta's attention wandered, coming to rest on a garish painting over the stone mantelpiece. It was a female nude in the style of Egon Schiele, not an artist whose work Loretta cared for, and she wondered what it was doing in a room which was otherwise solidly traditional. Not Bridget's choice, she imagined, but that was true of

19

many objects at Thebes Farm. The deep-red walls of the dining room, the polished oval table at which she and the Inspector were sitting, were a far cry from the comfortable chaos she was used to at Bridget's old house; there was no place here for her shabby Habitat sofas and rickety gateleg table. Loretta saw that someone had left a clear plastic beaker on a corner of the gleaming mahogany, where a shaft of late-afternoon sunlight lent it a transient elegance. It was the only indication that there had ever been a house-warming party, that Bridget and Sam's friends had toured the house in twos and threes and filled it with admiring comments.

"Address?"

Loretta reluctantly turned her gaze back to the Inspector, whose name she had already forgotten. "Sorry, I've no idea."

"What?"

She flushed as she realized her mistake. "I thought you meant—" She shook her head, fiddling with her hair to hide her confusion. "I'm sorry, I thought you were still talking about Christopher Cae—Cisar." She stumbled over the name, adjusting the spelling in her head. "Southmoor Road. I live in Southmoor Road." She gave the number.

"Is that the canal side?"

"Yes. You turn right out of Southmoor Place and it's on the left."

"I must've gone past the end of your garden a couple of weeks ago. Funny thing, I've lived in Oxford for years and I'd never been on the canal before. You ever been to that pub at Thrupp? The Jolly Boatman, is that what it's called?"

"There are two," Loretta said tiredly. "The Jolly Boatman's the one you come to first, then there's the Boat." She had left Bridget lying on her bed, hardly paler than she was when the party began but visibly weakened by the prolonged bout of vomiting which followed the discovery of the body. Audrey Summers had volunteered to stay with her while Loretta was interviewed, and Sam had promised to look in whenever he could escape from the bald man in glasses who appeared to be in charge of the police operation, but Loretta was anxious to return to Bridget's bedside. She doubted whether shock could bring on a miscarriage in an otherwise healthy woman, any more than catching sight of a hare could produce a child with a harelip, but Bridget's blood pressure wasn't normal to start with.

"Well, I suppose we'd better get on with it." The Inspector patted her short red hair, sounding almost apologetic, and Loretta realized that the digression about the canal had been intended to make her relax. "This is just preliminary stuff," the woman went on, chatty and reassuring. "Getting everyone's name and address and phone number, and where they were when she was found. Any idea who she is?"

"Me?" Loretta was astounded. "Good God, no. I mean, it never even occurred to me."

"You have a look at her?"

Loretta gave an emphatic shake of her head.

"Very wise. Wish I could say the same about the rest of them, trampling all over the crime scene . . . You'd think they'd have more sense, being dons and all that." A crisp note of disapproval had entered her voice.

Loretta said nothing, aware that the antagonism of the police towards students celebrating the end of finals with showers of champagne in the city streets lasted well beyond the end of the summer term and extended to anyone connected to the university, no matter how elderly or respectable.

"So you were where, when she was found?"

21

"I was on my way to the house, looking for Bridget—Dr. Bennett." Loretta had given up using her own Ph.D. in a city where higher degrees were as common as personal stereos, and Bridget almost never called herself Dr. Bennett, but it was one way of avoiding the Ms.-Mrs.-Miss tangle. She described the sequence of events as she remembered it, ending with the child's deceptively innocent announcement: "The next thing I knew she was saying—"

"This is the little girl, the one in the blue dress? Charlotte Patterson?"

"Yes. Something like—she won't get up, the lady won't get up."

"And you thought—what did you think?"

"I don't know, because that was when the dog—" Loretta pulled a face. "Bridget started throwing up and I was trying to get her into the house, I was scared . . ." She shrugged, embarrassed, not wanting to admit that for a moment she had half expected a revenant to stumble into their midst. "It was a bit like a horror film," she added, attempting to defuse the memory, "you know, one of those Coen Brothers things. I do remember someone coming out of the barn and saying there's a body, so then I . . ."

She paused, unsure whether any of this was relevant, and took silence for assent. "I was sort of holding Bridget, she was crying as well as being sick, and I just dragged her into the house. Audrey was with me, Audrey Summers, and we were halfway up the stairs when someone came and said could she look at the body—she's a GP, not that she could do much . . . I got Bridget onto the bed and went to the bathroom for a towel . . . I was alone with her for ten, maybe fifteen minutes, then Sam came upstairs and said Audrey had gone to get her—that thing for measuring blood pres-

22

sure—from her car. He stayed with Bridget and I came down to make some tea."

"So you can't really be more specific about who did what in the garden from the moment the dog ran out of the barn?"

"No. Sorry. It was very confused."

"Well." The Inspector sighed and put down her pen. "It's not as if there's a shortage of witnesses, quite the opposite." She pulled back the cuff of her silky gray shirt and examined her watch.

Loretta said hopefully: "Is that all?"

"For now. Someone'll be round in the next day or two to take a proper statement. Oh—I haven't got your phone number."

Loretta gave it, adding: "I'm out quite a lot, I use the English-faculty library and the Bodleian, but there's an answering machine." She stood up, as did the Inspector.

"I'll look out for you next time I come past your garden. Go on the canal much, do you?"

"Not this year. I used to have a boat but the wood was rotten and it sort of fell apart." Loretta edged towards the door, not wanting to get involved in more small talk. "Shall I—who do you want to see next?"

"Dudley's got a list—the Incredible Hulk who brought you in." The Inspector smiled, inviting Loretta to share in this small joke at the expense of a junior officer, but she was already thinking about something else.

"There is one thing," she added, fiddling with the door handle. "I assume it's all right for Bridget to stay with me tonight? I've talked to Sam and we both thought it was a good idea to get her away from ... from all this." She gestured vaguely through the window, where a WPC was conferring in a low voice with someone out of vision. "I know you've got a job to do but she's in a state of collapse . . . I gather Dr. Summers has talked to—to someone about interviewing her tomorrow."

The Inspector pursed her lips. "So I've been told. I'll make a note we can get Dr. Bennett on your number. We don't want anyone thinking she's disappeared, do we?" She came round the table, her high heels clicking on the stone floor, and the expression of official disapproval cleared from her face. "You're very wise, actually," she said in her previous confidential tone, "because the press are going to love this one."

"The press? Oh, *God*." This was an aspect of the affair that had not occurred to Loretta, but she realized that a police press officer was probably briefing journalists at this very moment. Her ex-husband, John Tracey, had been a reporter on a south London newspaper in the early days of their marriage, and their evenings were frequently wrecked by his routine calls to the local police, ambulance station and fire brigade. "Anything for us?" he used to ask, assuming a chummy, all-boys-together tone which made Loretta cringe. Five minutes later he would be on the trail of a story, smiling apologetically as he pulled on his raincoat, and she would be lucky to see him again before she went to bed.

"A real country-house murder," the Inspector was saying, leaning back against the table and crossing her slim ankles. "Not to mention the university angle. They all watch *Inspector Morse* these days."

"Do you really have to tell them?" Loretta let go of the door handle and came back into the room.

The Inspector pulled a smart leather bag towards her and removed a packet of Silk Cut. "Do you mind?"

Loretta was about to say she did, then realized that the smoke would at least camouflage the pungent whiff of rotting flesh which wafted through the open window whenever the breeze was in the right direction. Perhaps that was why there had been a feverish handing round of cigarettes in the kitchen when she came downstairs just before the first police car arrived.

"I don't like it either"—the woman lit up and paused to inhale—"but we need their help, especially in a case like this where identification—well, I'm not giving away any secrets if I say identification's our first problem. We give them the story, someone might be on the phone tomorrow morning saying my sister Susan walked out of the house last month after a row with Dad and nobody's seen her since. Anyway, we couldn't keep it quiet if we wanted to. There were over forty people in that garden when she was found, not counting kids."

"You're not suggesting—" Loretta broke off, remembering that Stephen Kaplan occasionally wrote leader-page pieces for the *Daily Mail*; he had ambitions, according to unkind north Oxford gossip, to become a media don like Norman Stone. She had no idea whether his relationship with the paper extended to feeding it sensational stories like this one, but it was no use protesting that Bridget and Sam's guests would never, ever, stoop to such a thing.

"We only give them the basics, of course." The Inspector was roving round the room in search of an ashtray, a column of ash balanced precariously on the end of her cigarette. "Your friend's quite safe, if that's what you're worried about. We're not empowered to tell them where she's staying." She gave up her search, picked up the empty plastic beaker from the end of the table and tapped the ash into it.

"I suppose that's *something*," Loretta said, sounding ungracious even to herself. "Well, if that's all . . ."

The Inspector returned to her seat and flashed Loretta

a friendly smile. "As I said, someone'll be round later in the week for a formal statement. Thanks for your help."

Loretta opened the door to the hall and found her path blocked by a wide uniformed back. "Excuse me." She was close enough to smell the stale sweat which had formed dark-blue half-circles under his arms, but he didn't seem to have heard her. She raised her voice: "*Excuse* me—"

He turned, revealing piggy eyes and a raw-steak complexion.

"Inspector—the Inspector's finished with me."

He picked up a clipboard from the hall table, ran his finger down a list and strode to the open front door without saying a word. "Lawson!"

"No," she protested from behind. "That's me. I'm Loretta Lawson."

He turned, stared at her suspiciously as though it might be a trick, then rechecked his list. "Lawson . . ." He ticked her off. "You know a Dunne?"

"If you want Janet, that's her over there, in the green shorts." Loretta nodded towards a narrow strip of lawn and flowerbed, the only area of the garden which had not been cordoned off with blue-and-white scene-of-crime tape. Eight or nine adults were waiting, unable to leave until they had been interviewed, and their faces swiveled eagerly towards the house as Loretta and the policeman emerged. Their expressions revealed shock, boredom and, in at least one case, irritation; according to Audrey, there had been a noisy scene earlier in the afternoon when Stephen Kaplan, shaking off his wife's restraining arm, had protested at the pace of police inquiries and insisted that he and his family be allowed to go home as he was expecting an important phone call. There was no sign of Jane or the children, but Loretta

26

saw that Stephen was striding towards them, his face thunderous.

"Who's in charge here?"

Loretta drew back into the hall, avoiding the confrontation. Halfway up the stairs she met Sam, who greeted her with relief.

"Loretta—they through with you?"

"So it seems."

"What's going on?" He peered past her, hearing raised voices.

"Just Stephen Kaplan making a fuss—I'd let him get on with it if I were you." She was suddenly weary, the emotional energy which had sustained her through the interview draining away like water into parched ground. She was also very hungry, having eaten nothing all day except a single slice of toast for breakfast.

"OK ..." He didn't seem very sure. "I'd like to get Bridget out of here right now, before the ... before the mortuary van shows up. Could you put some things in a bag—whatever you think she's going to need? Hey, are you OK?"

"I'm tired, that's all." She brushed aside his concern. "Are you coming as well? My lodger moved out last week and there's a double bed in her room."

Sam shook his head, his face suddenly slack and preoccupied. "I have to stay here, keep an eye on those guys ..." He glanced downstairs again and brightened; Loretta turned and saw that Stephen had gone back into the garden, leaving Janet Dunne and the beefy PC in the hall.

"My turn," Janet called up ruefully.

"I'm sorry." Sam spread his hands wide, indicating regret at his inability to intervene.

"Sam?" Loretta touched his arm, anxious to leave.

"Yeah, I'm—" He shook her off, then seemed to re-

27

member who she was. "Sorry," he said again. "I'm sorry, Loretta." He led the way upstairs, the worried look returning as he tapped on the door of his and Bridget's bedroom.

"Honey, it's me."

"Come in."

Bridget's voice was faint and tremulous. Loretta pulled her hair back from her face, massaged the back of her aching neck and followed Sam into the room.

"More wine?" Audrey Summers held up the bottle, reading the label aloud as she waited for Loretta's reply. "*Mor-bi-do*, what's that mean?"

"Soft," said Loretta, looking for her glass. "It's Italian for soft. Now where did I . . ."

"Are you fluent? I'd like to be but I don't have a gift for languages."

"I get by." She spotted her glass on top of the bread bin and passed it to Audrey, who filled it. Behind her a pan of tomato sauce started to bubble on the hob and she turned to lower the heat. "This'll be ready in a couple of minutes. I wonder if Bridget's still asleep?"

"If she is we'll just have to wake her up. She must eat something after all that vomiting. Have you got a tray?"

"In there." Loretta nodded towards an old pine dresser in an alcove to the right of the fireplace. "I'll drain the pasta." She gripped a large stainless-steel pasta boiler by its handles and carried it to the sink.

"Interesting kitchen you've got here, this mixture of old stuff and all that white." Audrey gestured towards the modern bit of the kitchen. "Was it here or did you have it done?"

"I had it done—I wouldn't have been able to afford it otherwise." Loretta divided the pasta between three plates and began spooning tomato sauce on top. She had bought the house almost exactly three years ago when Southmoor Road was still coming up, as the estate agent informed her; many of the houses were occupied by a transient population of genuine Oxford undergraduates and students of obscure private colleges which traded on their connection with the city. It had been Bridget's idea, her excited response to Loretta's glum account of trailing round a dozen unsuitable and hugely expensive maisonettes in London. "Move to Oxford! It's not *that* much cheaper than Islington, but if you buy in the right place ..." Loretta had not treated the suggestion seriously until Bridget sent details of the house in Southmoor Road with the chief attractions picked out in yellow highlighter: the long, pretty garden with a landing stage at the far end, and the fact that it was within walking distance of her own house.

"You've got all that money coming from America," Bridget wheedled on the phone, recklessly inflating the sum for which Loretta's literary agent was likely to sell the rights to her Edith Wharton biography in New York. "What else are you going to do with it? You could put the kitchen here"—by now Loretta had weakened and was standing in the gloomy basement room at the front of the house—"knock an arch through into the dining room, which would give you more light, and then have French windows opening into the garden." Bridget had rushed from room to room, wishing away partitions and unblocking fireplaces with a wave of her hand until they were both convinced that renovating a three-story house (plus attics) was little more than a week's hard work for an enthusiastic owner, an accommodating builder and a couple of strong friends.

"Why don't you start?" Loretta told Audrey, putting a plate of *penne* before her. "There's some grated Parmesan in the fridge. No, wait, I know exactly where it is." She had remembered that the fridge needed cleaning, that its shelves were crammed with dried-up cheese, moldering pots of taramasalata and the remains of a roast chicken which she did not want Audrey to see. She opened the door and reached inside, feeling for the bowl of Parmesan behind a couple of Sainsbury's ready-made curries, then turned at the unexpected sound of Bridget's voice.

"I don't know what that pill was, Audrey, but I feel a bit light-headed." Bridget stood in the doorway, yawning and rubbing her eyes. "Is there anything to eat?"

Bridget had borrowed Loretta's dressing gown, a faded 1930s wrap she had found in the second-hand clothes shop in Walton Street. It fitted Loretta perfectly but the edges did not quite meet over the small bulge of Bridget's stomach, falling open to reveal a glossy blue nightdress with shoestring straps. Loretta's oyster silk, with its border of pastel flowers, looked anemic by comparison.

"Sit down." Loretta hurried forward and pulled out a chair as Bridget swayed slightly in the doorway. "I was going to bring something up but now you're here . . ." She began laying a third place at the table.

"What's this?" Bridget reached for the almost empty wine bottle and appealed to Audrey: "Barbera d'Asti. Loretta always has such good wine. One glass won't hurt, surely?"

"It won't kill you," Audrey admitted—rather tactlessly, Loretta thought, but Bridget appeared not to notice. She bunched the dressing gown in front of her and knelt in front of the wine rack. "OK if I open another one, Loretta?"

They ate in silence, Loretta casting sidelong glances at Bridget to see how she was coping. She had regained some color in her cheeks, and her eyes had lost the dull, unfocused gaze of someone in shock, but the skin around them was pink and swollen. So were her wrists when she reached across the table for the pepper grinder, but Loretta thought this was probably a symptom of her raised blood pressure. Bridget's hair was uncombed and a pale blond tuft stuck up at the back, revealing darker roots below. She was naturally a dark blonde like Loretta, who teased her affectionately about the hours she spent at a hairdressing salon in North Parade, her head wrapped in foil while highlights were put in strand by strand.

"That was excellent, Loretta." Audrey sounded faintly surprised as she pushed away her empty plate. "You must tell me what you put in your tomato sauce."

"There's more if you—" The phone chirruped for the first time in half an hour. Bridget pushed back her chair and made to get up, then looked at Loretta. "Aren't you going to answer it?"

"I turned the answering machine on, there were so many calls." She did not add that each time she picked it up she was afraid that the caller would turn out to be a reporter.

"But it might be *Sam*." The ringing stopped and Bridget looked ludicrously disappointed.

"I don't think so. He called while you were asleep and said not to disturb you. He sent his love and he's going to ring again in the morning."

This was not a strictly truthful account of either of Sam's two calls; it was Loretta who had refused to run upstairs and wake Bridget, pointing out that she needed sleep far more than a conversation which would inevitably remind her of the afternoon's distressing events. She had scarcely got Sam off the phone a second time when Bridget's mother called, startling Loretta with her

31

refusal to believe that her elder daughter was alive, un-injured and resting in the first-floor front bedroom. It had taken several minutes to discover the reason behind Mrs. Bennett's importunate demands for reassurance, but it eventually became clear that the culprit was a thoughtless neighbor who had rushed round to her house in Hitchin with the news that a woman's body had been found at Thebes Farm near Oxford. The neighbor, having caught only the tail end of an item on the television news, encouraged Mrs. Bennett to think that Bridget was the victim, a misapprehension which inflated itself, when Bridget and Sam's phone turned out to be perpetually engaged, into a Technicolor vision of rape, murder and mayhem in the Oxfordshire countryside.

Mrs. Bennett eventually got through to Sam, who explained that the dead woman was a complete stranger, but she insisted on being given Loretta's number to check for herself. Loretta had had to talk to her for nearly half an hour, inwardly cursing the neighbor as either a ghoul or a complete idiot, before she would agree to let Bridget sleep on.

"Did he—I suppose the police are still there?"

"So it seems." Sam's immediate worry, which Loretta had already decided not to mention, was not the police but the press. They had descended on Thebes Farm in cars, vans and even an outside-broadcast unit, waylaying the last of the party guests as they left and hauling a TV camera onto the roof of a car to film over the wall as the body was removed. "The cops are keeping them away from the house but they can't do anything about the phone," he'd said tiredly, adding that he'd watched from an upstairs window as reporters strolled back to their vehicles and punched his number into their car phones.

"Poor old thing," Bridget said fondly, confirming her ignorance of events at Thebes Farm. "I'll ring him first thing, before he goes to work."

"Speaking of which," said Audrey, pushing back her chair and feeling for her handbag at her feet, "I've got surgery at a quarter to nine tomorrow morning."

"You're not *going*?" Bridget seemed astonished, even though Loretta had been trying to read Audrey's watch upside down and now saw it was shortly before eleven o'clock. "I mean, we haven't had a chance to talk."

Audrey stood up. "What is there to talk about? It's probably some ghastly domestic business, like Pauline White." She looked grim as she took her car keys out of her bag. Loretta remembered the event she was referring to, although she had not known Audrey at the time. Bridget had told her the full story: one of Audrey's patients, a single mother in her early twenties, had begun turning up at the surgery with fading bruises on her neck and throat and the occasional black eye. Audrey's attempts to question her produced predictable excuses about bumping into doors and tripping over toys until, one February night, Pauline White's body was found on wasteland behind her home. Her boyfriend, picked up by the police a few days later in Nottingham, admitted strangling her because he thought she was seeing another man. The case became something of a *cause célèbre* in Oxford when a smart barrister, putting up a defense of provocation, got the killer off with a six-year sentence for manslaughter.

"Go to bed," Audrey added, zipping up her bag and swinging it onto her shoulder. "Loretta, can't you find her a good book? You seem to have plenty." She glanced over her shoulder at the dresser, where a couple of hardback novels and several paperbacks sat in untidy piles. "Something nice and relaxing," she said, picking up a biography and studying the blurb on the back. "She's had enough shocks for one day."

"I'm hardly going to offer her *The Silence of the Lambs*," Loretta said tartly.

"But Audrey." Bridget ignored the interruption. "You can't just—you actually saw the body. You talked to the police. So did you, Loretta. They must've said something about . . . well, they must've said *something*."

Loretta began to explain, rather feebly she thought, that the red-haired Inspector had said very little about the murder—that they had discussed boating, and pubs on the canal.

Bridget dismissed her account of the interview with an angry wave of the hand: "You see—still trying to protect me. *Pas devant les*"—she struggled for the right word—"*les enceintes*. I'm pregnant, Loretta, not simple-minded." She turned back to Audrey, who had opened the book and was examining the photographs in the middle. "This woman, no one's said—I don't even know whether she was young or old."

"Mmm?" Audrey lifted her head and her expression darkened. "Bridget, you don't seem to realize, a two-week-old corpse—"

"Two weeks? That's how long she's been dead?"

Audrey closed the book with a snap. "I'm a GP," she said irritably, "not a pathologist. Most of the bodies I deal with are live ones, thank God. I'm only guessing."

"But you said—"

Audrey rolled her eyes upwards. "It was a sort of shorthand. I was hoping to spare you the details. I only had a brief look myself, the smell was so appalling." She hesitated, then began speaking rapidly in medical jargon. "If you must know, I did observe not only postmortem hypostasis but a pronounced degree of marbling—"

"Audrey, I'm not a doctor," Bridget protested. "Not of medicine, anyway."

Audrey gave her a look as if to say "you asked for this" and launched into a grisly account of the features of decomposition: "Post-mortem hypostasis is a condition caused by uncirculated blood draining down to the lowest part of the body. It floods the blood vessels, causing dark blotches which are sometimes mistaken, by the untrained eye, for bruises. It's not uncommon for someone to ring the police and say they've found a badly beaten body when in fact it's just post-mortem hypostasis and the person has actually died of natural causes."

"But she didn't, did she? Die of natural causes."

Audrey said: "Not unless she took all her clothes off and beat herself about the head. I couldn't see any obvious lacerations on the trunk but naturally I didn't move her. The post-mortem will show whether she'd been sexually assaulted—if there's semen present in the vagina it may be possible to use genetic fingerprinting—"

"Oh, for God's sake." Loretta got up and began collecting their dirty plates. "Can't we just drop it? I'm going to have nightmares if I hear much more of this."

Bridget ignored her. "Was she—could you tell if she was killed there? In our barn?"

"That's for the pathologist to establish. He'll examine the body for leaves, grass, insects—anything that doesn't seem to match the place where she was found. Of course, she may have been dragged some distance, or brought there by car . . . That seems most likely."

"It is isolated and we're both at work most days. Even so—"

Audrey tutted. "Leave it to the police. For all we know it may turn out to have been a courting couple looking for somewhere to—"

"A courting couple?" Loretta, who had been listening reluctantly as she loaded the dishwasher, turned to Audrey in disbelief. "What sort of courting leads to . . . to that?" She imagined the dead woman, stripped of clothes and dignity, dumped in a corner of the barn; her killer, a shadowy male figure, sidling round the door with a bundle of blood-stained garments in his arms . . .

"How did he get in there in the first place?" she asked suddenly, the melodramatic imaginary scene giving way to the real memory of Sam struggling with a heavy padlock.

"We only locked it for the party," Bridget said off-handedly.

"And you didn't—you didn't look inside?"

Bridget looked apologetic. "What for? It's Sam who's keen on those old ploughs and harrows or whatever they are. I'd bin them tomorrow." She pulled a face. "Lucky escape, huh?"

"Not really," said Audrey, "you wouldn't have seen anything anyway. There's a hole in the floor, about six feet by three—" She returned the book to the dresser and sketched a rectangle in the air with her hands.

"The sheep bath?" Bridget looked surprised. "You mean she was in the sheep bath?"

"I assumed it had some agricultural purpose. There were a couple of old doors on top of it, and one of those—a rusty thing with spikes. That's why you didn't smell anything, not till those boys pushed them aside." She reached up and adjusted the velvet band which held her long fair hair off her forehead. "I really must go. Monday mornings are always the worst, the surgery's full to bursting . . . When's your next appointment at the John Radcliffe?"

"My—" Bridget looked blank for a moment. "Oh—Tuesday. Tuesday morning."

36

"Let me know how it goes." Audrey came round the table and kissed her lightly on the cheek. "Ring if you're at all worried. Goodnight, Loretta—don't come up, I'll see myself out."

"Want any help with clearing up?" Bridget yawned and stretched as the sound of Audrey's feet receded up the stairs.

"No, leave it. Most of it can go in the dishwasher."

"If you're sure."

"Would you like a book? The new Anita Brookner's over there."

"Not tonight, thanks. That glass of wine's made me sleepy again. Night, Loretta."

They hugged each other, the first physical contact they had had for several weeks, and Loretta was surprised by the familiar angularity of her friend's body. Bridget had always been thin, a slender size 10, and she had not put on much weight during her pregnancy— except, of course, in the obvious place. "Sleep well," murmured Loretta, releasing her.

She tidied the kitchen, her own weariness manifesting itself in heavy limbs and a lack of concentration which allowed a glass to slip from her hand onto the black-and-white tiles, where it split into several large fragments. She collected up the jagged pieces, holding each one carefully between her thumb and forefinger, and was looking for something to wrap them in when the phone rang. She picked it up without thinking and was immediately startled out of her zombielike state by the faint, unearthly echo of a satellite link.

"Loretta? Is that you?"

"Who is this?"

"Geoffrey—Geoffrey Simmons."

"Geoffrey? Where are you calling from?"

"San Francisco. Didn't Bridget tell you I was over here for the summer?"

"Yes—yes, of course." Geoffrey Simmons was a historian, an old flame of Bridget's whom she had unsuccessfully tried to pass on to Loretta. She kept Loretta abreast of his career in a slightly reproachful way, as if to remind her of what she was missing; Loretta now recalled that he was engaged in a research project at Berkeley, collaborating with an American who had written a controversial book on the history of madness.

"Is it true they've found a stiff in Bridget's garden?"

"What?"

"IS IT TRUE—"

"I heard you the first time." Loretta held the phone away from her, protecting herself from Geoffrey's booming voice; she did not know whether she was more astonished by his flippancy or the speed with which he had been informed of events half a world away. The north Oxford grapevine was justly famous, a highly efficient conduit of gossip about academic feuds and amorous liaisons, but she had no idea it extended across continents. "How did you find out?"

"News travels fast," Geoffrey said evasively. "Is she there? I finally got through to what's his name, her husband, his phone's been engaged for hours, and he said to ring you."

"She's just gone to bed."

"Get her to give us a ring tomorrow, all right? You got a bit of paper?"

"No—yes." Loretta found the envelope on which she'd written Bridget's other messages and took down Geoffrey's home and work numbers in case Bridget did not have them with her.

"What a downer, eh?" he said abruptly, switching tack. "How's she taking it?"

"How would you feel if someone discovered a body at your house-warming party?"

"Well, it would depend—"

"*Depend?* What would it depend on?"

"Whether I knew her, for one thing. The corpse, that is."

"Well, she doesn't," Loretta said flatly, then remembered that Bridget had not actually seen the dead woman. "At least—the thing is, Geoffrey, she'd been there a couple of weeks and—"

"All right, no need to go into details," Geoffrey said hurriedly, displaying uncharacteristic squeamishness. His voice faded, was lost in the ether for several seconds, then returned at a volume which blasted her eardrum: ". . . went into City Lights last week and they had the paperback of your book by the till. They're nuts on all that feminist lit-crit stuff over here—you should try and wangle a trip. You won't believe this," he chortled, "but they've actually got a radio program called 'Women Hold Up Half the Sky.' "

"Don't they?"

"Don't they what?"

"Hold up half the sky."

"Come *on*, Loretta."

She smiled to herself. "I'm going to bed, Geoffrey. I'm sure Bridget'll be touched by your concern." The sarcasm was wasted on him, she thought as she put the phone down, but it made her feel better.

Upstairs a lavatory flushed and a moment later Loretta heard the bathroom door open and close quietly. At the far end of the dining room the cat flap rattled angrily, reminding her she had shut the cat out of the house several hours before at Audrey's insistence. Audrey had stiffened at the sight of Bertie and announced she was violently allergic even to short-haired cats, leaving Loretta no choice but to banish him to the garden for the evening.

"All right, Bertie, I'm coming." She went through the arch between the two rooms and bent to release the catch on the Perspex flap, standing back as the animal's sleek head and shoulders pushed through the gap. He had a habit of twisting his head at this point, watching anxiously as the descending flap scraped the length of his wide gray tail.

"Are you hungry? I bet you're hungry." She bent to stroke him and he rubbed against her calves, letting out deep rumbles of appreciation. Loretta returned to the kitchen, the cat trotting expectantly behind her, and removed an open tin of Felix from the fridge. Recoiling from the smell, she scraped chunks of meat and jelly into his dish, dropped the empty can into the bin and put the food on the floor, where he began to eat greedily. She found a day-old newspaper and wrapped up the shards of glass, poured liquid detergent into the soap compartment of the dishwasher and turned the dial to a long, noisy program she used only at night.

"Coming?" she said to the cat, who had emptied his dish and retired to a chair to clean his muzzle. He paused at the sound of her voice and went into a crouch, watching her with unblinking yellow eyes as she went to the door to the stairs.

"Please yourself," she said, reaching for the light switch.

The cat wailed, jumped down from the chair and shot past her, making as much noise as possible with his unsheathed claws on the stair carpet. Loretta smiled, turned out the light and followed him up to bed.

3

"LIFT, *LIFT*. YOU'RE NOT WAVING GOODBYE TO your mum, you know." The dark-haired instructor loomed menacingly over Loretta as she lay on her back in a corner of the weights room. The woman—Karen, Kirsty, some name like that—was dressed from neck to ankle in a shiny red bodysuit which would have shown even a centimeter of excess fat, had there been one to see. She extended an imperious right hand. "Where's your card?"

The three-pound weights Loretta had been clutching in her fists hit the floor with a clang. "Sorry," she said, sitting up and feeling for her attendance card inside the elasticized neckline of her leotard. She had often wondered why it was impossible to buy a leotard with pockets, an oversight she mentioned as she drew out the wrinkled cardboard rectangle and passed it up.

Karen or Kirsty ignored her. "Oh, *well*, you haven't been for two, no, *three* weeks." She sounded scandalized. "I'd better come round with you, see what else you're doing wrong."

The next half-hour took Loretta back to her school-days, to Wednesday afternoons in the gym with Miss

41

Poulson, except that Gillingham Grammar had been equipped with a vaulting horse and climbing bars rather than the latest hi-tech exercise machines. She felt herself regressing emotionally to adolescence, building up a stock of silent resentment as Karen urged her to work harder on her upper thighs or put more effort into her press-ups.

"Twenty-six, twenty-seven—come on, nearly there."

Loretta ignored the exhortation and sank to the floor. Karen's voice was higher and had a less refined accent than Miss Poulson's but it had the same fanatic edge; Loretta rested her cheek gratefully on the soft surface of an exercise mat and inhaled the familiar combination of dust, sweat and foam rubber, trying to summon up a more detailed picture of her old teacher than the middle-aged woman with corrugated hair and a blue Aertex shirt who came to mind. Miss Poulson remained, however, a shadowy figure. Loretta opened her eyes and consoled herself that the gym was almost empty, which meant there were few witnesses to Karen's ruthless exposure of her innate physical laziness.

"Well *done*." Karen beamed as Loretta braced her arms and heaved her torso off the ground three times in rapid succession. "You ought to try Jane's flex'n'stretch class, it starts in twenty minutes, you're much too tense."

Loretta rolled over, dragged herself into a sitting position and examined an abrasion on her right shin, the result of her foot slipping on the rowing machine. "No thanks," she said, picking off frayed skin round the edges of the bruise, "I haven't got time this morning—ouch." She scrambled to her feet and went to the door of the weights room, Karen pursuing her with a stream of unwanted advice.

"You don't want to waste all that effort, you know.

42

You've got to build it up, it's no good coming every other week—"

"I know. Thanks." Loretta cut the lecture short and closed the door quietly but firmly in Karen's face. She came to the gym once or twice a month, usually when she was feeling particularly tired or stressed, and she had no time for the familiar spiel about the benefits of regular exercise. She had joined the previous November, seduced by an advert in the *Oxford Times* offering a free trial class, but she had quickly recognized that her fantasy of thrice-weekly workouts and a body like Madonna was exactly that—a fantasy.

Bridget, who astonished Loretta by volunteering to join with her, had lost interest much sooner. Exercise was boring, she announced after a month in which she had tried just about every class on offer from beginners' aerobics to jazz dance and the ungrammatical flex'n'stretch. Then she met Sam Becker at an early Christmas party and abandoned the gym altogether, telling Loretta with a demure smile that she needed all her energy for the best sex she'd ever had. Loretta returned from a dreary New Year's Eve party at her sister's house in Weybridge to find Bridget in even greater raptures over Sam, their amazing love life and the wonderful time they had spent together over Christmas. Going to the gym seemed tame by comparison, but Loretta suddenly had time on her hands; Bridget hardly seemed to notice that she had cancelled several long-standing engagements, or that their weekly trips to the cinema had been replaced by a perfunctory phone call.

Suddenly in February, her affair with Sam seemed to be over. She turned up in Southmoor Road wearing dark glasses and sniffling into a crumpled handkerchief, saying the break had taken place a week before and she still could not bear to talk about it. Instead she plunged

43

into a hectic round of activity, accepting every party invitation that came along, signing up for French conversation classes at the Alliance Française in Polstead Road and begging Loretta to accompany her to a new dance class at the gym. Then, abruptly as he'd disappeared, Sam came back on the scene. Loretta could hardly believe her ears when, three or four weeks later, Bridget bought her dinner at Browns and announced that Sam had asked her to marry him; this revelation was soon followed by another, a telephone call in which Bridget gasped that she had just done a home pregnancy test and the result was positive. Unable to gauge from Bridget's voice whether this was good news or bad, Loretta asked noncommittal questions which elicited that Bridget did not seem to know. She and Sam had *talked* about having a child, but nothing like as quickly; she had no idea how she was going to cope with getting married, moving house, editing a new edition of *Clarissa* and having a baby ... She hadn't even told him yet, she added—had rung Loretta first to get her own thoughts in order before she broke the news.

Sam's reaction, in the event, was unalloyed delight. He instantly accelerated their house-moving plans, taking Bridget on an exhausting tour of seven or eight addresses in and around Oxford each Saturday and Sunday until they settled on Thebes Farm. Money did not seem to be a problem—Loretta was astonished when Bridget showed her the details of a large detached house with a swimming pool in Rawlinson Road—and they signed a contract without even a hint of a buyer for Bridget's solid but unexceptional semi. It had now been standing empty for several weeks and looked like remaining that way until there was a dramatic improvement in the housing market.

It was nearly half past nine when Loretta emerged

from the gym and ran lightly down the stairs into Park End Street. She felt and looked much better after a hot shower, her hair hanging in damp curls to her shoulders and the grubby jeans she had worn earlier replaced by flowered leggings and a big white shirt. In the deli two doors down she bought fresh white bread, unsalted butter, quince jelly and, as an afterthought, margarine and the least unappetizing brand of muesli she could find. Bridget had been fast asleep when she left—at any rate, there were no sounds of movement in her room when Loretta listened at the door just before eight—but would presumably have woken by now and discovered the complete absence of bread and other essentials. Loretta put her change in her purse, came out of the deli and turned right past the old jam factory, striding towards a busy intersection until she remembered that the newsagent's shop was in the opposite direction, back towards the railway station. The *Guardian*, which she had leafed through before leaving Southmoor Road, had dealt with the discovery of a body in a couple of paragraphs under News in Brief but she doubted whether the tabloids would have shown similar restraint.

She retraced her steps and pushed open the door of the shop, reacting with instant and almost comic dismay to the giant black type of the front pages. "Party Dons in Dead Blonde Probe," she read, and "Nude Blonde: Cops Quiz Partygoers." Underneath the latter, in smaller letters, a sub had inserted the imaginative but inaccurate strapline "Something Nasty in Oxford Woodshed." Loretta drew closer and saw several very similar photos of police vans parked outside Thebes Farm; one enterprising photographer, quicker than the rest, had snapped a picture of a furious Stephen Kaplan getting into his car, hands thrown up to shield his face like a film star pursued by *paparazzi*. Even the *Daily Mail* and the

Daily Express had considered the story worthy of front-page treatment, although it was not the lead item in either paper.

Loretta breathed out heavily, her involuntary "hah" attracting the attention of a middle-aged shop assistant who had previously been immersed in a copy of *Hello!* Oblivious to the woman's mildly curious gaze, Loretta seized a copy of each tabloid, balancing them on her left arm as though to avoid both physical and moral contamination. She completed her collection with one broadsheet, recalling her ex-husband's frequently expressed opinion that page three of the *Daily Telegraph* was to violent crime what page three of the *Sun* was to scantily clad women. By this time the pile of newsprint had become unwieldy and she had to ask for a carrier bag, stuffing the papers inside the flimsy plastic and almost running out of the shop in her haste to reach the privacy of her car in the Worcester Street car park.

The first thing that struck her as she speed-read one paper after another, propping them against the steering wheel, was the sheer inventiveness of the journalists assigned to the story. Their reports contained no new information, other than a line in the *Daily Telegraph* about the post-mortem being conducted that morning by a Home Office pathologist whose name Loretta vaguely recognized. The tabloids got round this problem, as the policewoman had predicted, by exploiting the *Inspector Morse* angle, breaking up the text with mugshots of John Thaw and Kevin Whateley, the actors who played Inspector Morse and Sergeant Lewis. One paper had even roped in its TV columnist to list the "eerie parallels" between the discovery of the body at Thebes Farm and a recent *Morse* episode about a corpse in the potting shed in the fellows' garden of a mythical Oxford college.

Loretta found some of these flights of fancy quite amusing, but her expression darkened when she discovered a reference on an inside page to an eighteen-month-old row between Bridget and another don over course content in the English faculty. The latter, who was famous in Oxford for his scowl and his exclusively male student fan club, had turned a private disagreement into a public slanging match, accusing Bridget in a Sunday newspaper of attempting to impose political correctness on her colleagues. This caricature of Bridget's view outraged her friends and alarmed the warden of her college, whose reactionary views meant that he and Bridget were unlikely to see eye to eye. Loretta was horrified to find the argument revived in print, certain that the article would upset Bridget far more than the wild speculation in other papers about how long the unknown woman in the barn had been dead, and the current market value of what one of them had thoughtfully dubbed "Death Farm."

She collected the papers into an untidy pile on the passenger seat and fastened her safety belt, wondering how long the intense press interest was going to last. It only needed another big story to come along, a threat to "out" a soap-opera star or Princess Diana wearing the same dress two days running, and the reporters laying siege to Thebes Farm would leap into their cars and disappear. In the meantime, they would be riffling through their contacts books in a determined effort to find someone who knew Bridget's temporary address. They might even have discovered it—Loretta pictured Bridget, half-asleep and her hair uncombed, hurrying downstairs to answer the front door and finding herself confronted with half a dozen snapping cameras and a crew from Central Television. They had managed to make Stephen Kaplan, who had no more than a walk-on part in the story, look like the First Murderer; Bridget in her nightie would probably come out of it like Lady Macbeth in the sleepwalking scene. Regretting that she had left Bridget alone while she worked off the previous day's stress at the gym, Loretta twisted the key in the ignition, reversed out of her parking space and drove hurriedly round to the exit.

In Southmoor Road she breathed a sigh of relief: the sole evidence of human activity was a traffic warden idling along the street in the brilliant sunshine, glancing at car windscreens to make sure their residents' parking permits were in place. Loretta, who had renewed hers the previous week, nodded to the warden as she struggled out of her car with her bags and the newspapers, which seemed to have doubled in volume since she had bought them. A woman with a ponytail came out of a house on the other side of the road, wheeling a bike, and waved to Loretta, reinforcing the illusion that it was an ordinary Monday morning. Inside the house she dropped her leotard and plimsolls on the floor, dumped the shopping and the papers on the hall table and returned to collect a pint of milk from the doorstep. Suddenly she stiffened, her hand tightening on the neck of the bottle, as she became aware of voices from the floor below. One was Bridget's, there was no difficulty about that; the other, a man's, was unfamiliar. It did not sound like Sam—Loretta moved quietly towards the stairs, straining to hear, and confirmed her impression that the visitor did not have an American accent. A reporter? The conversation sounded amicable, desultory even, and Loretta found it hard to believe Bridget was having a cozy conversation with someone from the *Sun* or even one of the local papers. A puzzled look on her face, she seized the bag of shopping in her free hand and hurried downstairs.

"Linda Hall—no, you've already got her." Bridget was slouched at the kitchen table, supporting her head with one hand while she drew invisible patterns on the pine surface with the index finger of the other. She sighed heavily as Loretta walked into the room and recited more names in an uncertain voice: "Brian Baker, Janet Dunne—Loretta!" Her face lit up. "I wondered when you'd get back. This is Detective Constable—" She gestured to a man with dark curly hair sitting opposite her. "Sorry, I've forgotten your name."

"DC Sidney." He put down a ballpoint and got up. "Dr. Lawson?" He had a cocky grin which Loretta immediately distrusted. "Nice place you've got here." He extended his hand, forcing her to look for a place to discard her shopping.

"There wasn't—I don't remember seeing a police car." His hand was damp and she drew hers away, glancing surreptitiously at her other wrist as she did so. Five past ten—they'd wasted no time.

"He's CID, Loretta. He's here to take my statement but I'm not much help . . . I mean, we got to the part where I started throwing up over the hydrangeas and that was it." Bridget smiled weakly but she sounded tired and a little despondent. "I slept in," she went on, plucking at the silk wrap she had borrowed the previous evening. "In fact, I was still asleep when, um, when the doorbell rang. We're just trying to put together a list of everyone who RSVP'd in case they've missed anyone. Oh—" Her eyes, which had been flicking from Loretta to the detective and back again, came to rest on the bottle on the corner of the table. "You've got some milk. I was going to make coffee but there wasn't any . . . Well, there was, but it's gone off. You are *hope-*

49

less, Loretta." This attempt at affectionate banter simply underlined her nervousness, and Loretta decided to come to the rescue.

"Is this going to take much longer?" she asked curtly, wondering why Bridget had not insisted on getting dressed rather than allowing the interview to take place when she was at such an obvious disadvantage.

The detective, who had wandered over to the mantelpiece, picked up a china cat, one of a pair, and examined it as though he hadn't heard her question. "This original?"

"It's a copy. Look, I think it would be a good idea if Bridget goes and puts some clothes on while I make coffee."

"No problem, is there, Dr. Lawson?" he asked, putting down the ornament and giving her a frank, open look. He returned to the table, picked up several sheets of paper covered in neat handwriting and counted the names Bridget had given him. "Thirty-eight—must be nearly there. I've got a couple more questions to ask Dr. Bennett—let's see, I should be with you in ten minutes, Dr. Lawson."

"Me?"

"He wants a statement from you as well, Loretta."

She had forgotten. "Oh, all right," she said grumpily. "In that case I might as well go upstairs and get on with some work. You can call me when you've finished." Ignoring the policeman's hopeful glance at the milk, she strode to the fridge and put it in the bottle compartment in the door. "I'll be in my study," she announced, and left the room.

She went upstairs, grumbling silently to herself, and turned into the long double drawing room whose back half she used as her study. The blind was drawn and the answering machine blinked at her from a dark corner, reminding her that she had not checked the machine since the previous evening. Perhaps the police, whose methods she had just been excoriating, had tried to get in touch and sent someone round only when they kept getting a taped message? She crossed the room, pressed the "message play" key and sat down at her desk, rolling her eyes upwards when she heard, interspersed with anxious inquiries from Bridget's friends and colleagues, yet another message from Sam and one from Bridget's mother. She had already counted eight messages for Bridget—none from the police—when, to her surprise, she recognized the voice of her former lover, Joe Lunderius.

"Loretta. You know where I am if you need me." That was all, not even his name, and Loretta was thinking he was the last person she would turn to for help when the tape began to hiss and crackle.

". . . a bit of a long shot," said an unfamiliar voice through the interference, "but I'm trying to get in touch with Dr. Bridget Bennett." He pronounced the three words with a bouncing rhythm, Doc-tor Brid-get Benn-ett. "I don't know if you . . ." Loretta reached across to the machine, turned up the volume, but caught only the closing words: ". . . Denis Goodwin, *Daily Mail*." Her thoughts flew to Stephen Kaplan and she wondered if this was his way of squaring his conscience: providing her number without saying for certain that Bridget would be there. Or maybe this Goodwin person was being circumspect; John Tracey had always gone in for a lot of guff about protecting his sources.

The answering machine began to rewind and Loretta allowed it to finish before pressing a key to store the messages it had just played. Then she stood up and leaned over her computer to raise the blind, letting in a soft mid-morning light which gently illuminated the varnished wood of her desk. She moved her chair into a more comfortable position and switched on the laptop, waiting as it beeped and whirred through its opening procedures; outside, at the bottom of the garden, a narrow boat slid by with a wolflike black dog in the stern. The dog belonged, she was almost certain, to the potter who traveled up and down the canal with a gas-fired kiln on his boat; she had met him waiting to go through a lock the previous summer and bought one of his bowls. The computer fell silent and she keyed in the codes to call up the latest chapter of her book, adjusting the brightness of the screen and scrolling down through the blue letters to the point at which she had broken off on Friday afternoon.

"Emily's radical vision simultaneously awed and terrified Charlotte," she had written, "and this ambivalence manifested itself both in her repudiation of Heathcliff in the posthumous Preface to the 1850 edition of *Wuthering Heights* and in the novel *Shirley*, which she wrote as a tribute to her dead sister. Shirley Keeldar, its eponymous heroine, is Emily as she might have been in more fortunate circumstances—rich and influential instead of poor and unknown. Yet the novel, for all its apparent celebration of Shirley/Emily's androgynous power, nevertheless concludes with—"

It was unusual for Loretta to break off in midsentence but she had been interrupted at this point on Friday by a phone call from a former colleague who wanted her to speak at a weekend conference in Manchester in November. By the time she had turned him down with sufficient expressions of interest and regret to avoid hurting his feelings it was nearly six, barely time to get to the cinema in Magdalen Street for the early-evening screening of *Thelma & Louise*. She had simply saved what she had written, grabbed her bag and rushed out of the house.

"—a conventional happy ending," she typed, picking up her train of thought, "whose effect is to obliterate the heroine; our last view of Shirley, mediated through the eyes of a minor character—"

The phone rang. Loretta let out a little gasp of annoyance and, with her eyes still on the screen, lifted the receiver to her ear.

"Mmm?"

"DC Sidney there?"

"Who?"

"DC Sidney." He repeated it impatiently, as though she was being deliberately obtuse.

"Just a minute. Who's speaking?"

"Thames Valley Police."

"All of them?" He did not reply and Loretta placed the receiver crossly on her desk. She clattered downstairs, making so much noise that Bridget and the detective looked up with startled expressions as she appeared in the doorway.

"Phone," she said tersely, and Bridget pushed back her chair.

"No, it's for—" She indicated the policeman.

"O-kay." He got up and went to the kitchen extension, ignoring her obvious irritation. "DC Sidney—Oh, hello, Sarge."

Loretta shot a wry glance at Bridget, who pulled a face in return, and went back upstairs. At the door of her study she heard a tinny sound coming from her desk and remembered that she had not replaced the receiver. She stretched out a hand towards it, frowned, and on impulse lifted it to her ear. Holding her breath, she heard the Sergeant's voice: ". . . watch what you say till we know for certain, we don't want to alarm her, not yet. Just make an excuse and get back here pronto. Phil, you there?"

"Yes, Sarge. I thought I heard—"

Loretta froze. Then, in slow motion, she lowered the receiver back onto its rest. A few seconds later she heard the double chirrup which told her that the policeman had finished his call, and leaned towards her computer screen in an attitude of deep, though bogus, concentration.

"Dr. Lawson?"

"Yes?" She didn't have to fake a start as the detective appeared in the doorway.

"Something's come up," he said casually. "I'm off now."

"Oh, right."

"Thanks for the co—" He broke off, obviously recalling that both she and Bridget had offered to make coffee without actually doing so. "Don't bother to see me out."

"What about—" She was going to ask about her statement, but he was gone. Seconds later the front door slammed and she got up from her desk, hurried to the other end of the room and saw him getting into an unmarked red car parked in front of her Golf. The engine roared into life, then died as he thrust open the door, half got out and snatched a parking ticket from under one of the windscreen wipers. Loretta jumped back as he threw it contemptuously onto the passenger seat, but he was too intent on making a quick exit to look up and catch her watching him. The car pulled out, too fast for the narrow street, and Loretta shook her head. "Someone's been watching too much *Miami Vice*," she murmured, making light of his abrupt departure and wishing she had not given in to her urge to pick up the phone; eavesdropping was as underhanded as going through a lover's pockets, and the material you turned up as useless. She retraced her steps, trying without much success to focus her thoughts on the forces undermining the authenticity of female characters in fiction, and was for once rather relieved when the phone rang.

"So you're really going to go?" Bridget demanded as she poured milk over the muesli Loretta had brought back from the deli.

"Yes—I told you." Loretta, feeling her cheeks grow red, dipped her knife into the jar for more quince jelly.

"About time," said Bridget, whose spirits had risen noticeably since the detective left. "You've spent far too much time moping after Joe Lunderius."

"I have not."

"God, what do they put in this? It's like soggy cardboard. Here, let me have some of that bread." She hacked off a slice, pulled a tub of margarine towards her and lifted the lid without enthusiasm. "What's he taking you to?"

"*Ariadne auf Naxos* at the Apollo." The call from Christopher Cisar, asking her to go with him to the opera in Oxford on Friday evening, had been utterly unexpected. He had offered the invitation so smoothly, apologizing for the short notice and regretting that their conversation at the party had been overshadowed by the grisly discovery in the barn, that it would have seemed bad manners to refuse.

"Ariadne what?"

"*Ariadne auf Naxos*. Richard Strauss."

Bridget shrugged, admitting her ignorance of opera, and heaped jam on the thin layer of margarine she had spread on her bread. "What do you think all that was about?" she asked, changing the subject. "First they send someone along at twenty past nine in the morning, then they ring up and call him back when he hasn't even finished taking my statement."

"Dunno." Loretta lifted the cafetiere, unwilling to admit, even to Bridget, that she had almost been caught listening in to the detective's conversation. "More coffee?"

"Go on then—half a cup. I did say, you're being very thorough, and he said, Oh, we take hundreds of statements on a case like this. I suppose they're under pressure, especially with all this . . ." She picked up one of the newspapers which Loretta had reluctantly brought downstairs when Bridget suggested they share a late breakfast. "It's Stephen," she exclaimed, looking at it more closely. "I hardly recognized him."

"The best report's in the *Telegraph*," Loretta said hastily as Bridget reached for *Today*. She could not now remember which tabloid had run the piece about the row in the English faculty, but she did not want Bridget to see it.

"Fancy you buying the *Torygraph*," said Bridget, feeling for it near the bottom of the heap. "Right, let's have a look."

"Inside. Page three."

"Got it." Bridget finished her bread and licked jam off her fingers. "Blimey, I'm glad I don't read this stuff every day. Fourteen-year-old girl strangled by stepfather to conceal sex abuse . . . Masked gunmen sought after gangland shooting at south London pub . . . Police seek van driver after stranded woman motorist attacked on the A34. You know, Sam's been on at me to carry a can of what's it called—mace. He's always reading out pieces about sex attacks in the *Oxford Times*."

"Isn't it illegal in this country?"

"Quite possibly, but the police aren't exactly full of good ideas. They gave a talk for freshers this year, this

WPC came along who's been trained to deal with rape victims, and it was all about not walking home alone at night. One of my students got up and said how was she supposed to afford taxis with an eight-hundred-pound overdraft?" She shrugged her shoulders, grimaced and returned to her study of the paper. "Nothing here we don't know already," she said a moment later, throwing it down.

"Except for the post-mortem—it's this morning." For the first time it occurred to Loretta that the two things might be connected, the pathologist's report and DC Sidney's recall to St. Aldates police station. Then she realized she had no idea how long a post-mortem lasted, which made speculation futile.

"Time I got dressed. OK if I have a shower, Loretta? Sam should be here soon."

"You've spoken to him?"

"Yes. I wasn't telling the truth, actually, when I said I was asleep when he—when PC Plod banged on the door. I was a bit embarrassed, opening the door like this." She gestured towards her night clothes. "Anyway, Sam's taken the day off, they keep thinking up new questions and he said it seemed easier not to go in . . . I wonder how long it's going to go on. It couldn't have come at a worse moment, he's so busy at work." Her mood changed abruptly and her face crumpled. "Isn't that callous? When that poor woman . . ." Her hands ranged over her hips, searching unsuccessfully for pockets and a handkerchief.

"Here," said Loretta, pulling off a square of kitchen paper and holding it out. "Use this."

Bridget took it and blew her nose hard. "Sorry," she muttered, dabbing at her eyes. "Either I think about it and get upset, or I try not to and . . . Sam said why don't we have lunch at Browns, take our minds off it—I said yes, but afterwards—"

"Don't you remember when my father died? You took me to that caff in St. Giles and I had a huge fry-up ... I did nothing but eat junk food for about a week. There aren't any rules for situations like this."

"Oh yes, there are," Bridget contradicted. "Imagine what the papers'd make of it, Sam and me sitting in a restaurant the day after ..."

"It's only Browns," Loretta pointed out, guessing that Sam's suggestion had been made, at least in part, because he wanted to have an hour or two alone with his wife. "It's not exactly the Quat' Saisons."

Bridget smiled weakly. "Thanks, Loretta," she said, coming round the table to hug her and kiss her cheek. "You always cheer me up. Listen, can I stay another night? Just till those reporters—Sam said a camera crew turned up this morning, before he was even dressed."

"Of course. There's room for Sam as well if he likes."

"I'll ask him ... Can I borrow some shampoo?"

"Mmm—in the bathroom."

Bridget went upstairs and Loretta poured out a cup of lukewarm coffee. She read her way through the *Guardian*, glancing without much interest at the media section until she came across a news item announcing that her ex-husband, John Tracey, had been nominated for an award for his coverage of events in Romania after the fall of the Ceauşescus. Loretta had not heard from Tracey for several months and she wondered whether she should send him a congratulatory postcard; he had seemed to want to keep her at arm's length since their divorce, and the invitation she had been promised to his wedding to a Cypriot student had never materialized. She speculated on whether this unlikely union had ever taken place, flipping past adverts for assistant producers in BBC radio and researchers at Granada TV, until her attention was caught by a photo spread on the return of the bra on the women's page. Cleavage was back, she read in the accompanying text, and sales of the Gossard Wonderbra were soaring. Frowning at pictures of pouting models in acrobatic poses and plunging necklines, Loretta lifted her hands and cupped her own small breasts, mocking the notion of putting them on display like two half-melons on a plate. She began to consider the possibility of a link between recession and conspicuous sexual display, thinking back to the thirties and Jean Harlow—

"Lo-re-tta!" She swiveled her head in surprise as the muffled shout was followed by a staccato series of raps, both of them coming from the basement area beyond the kitchen windows. Sam Becker was trying the handle of the half-glazed door which provided access to the dustbins; as she got up he saw her face and immediately mimed an apology for startling her. She pointed to the mantelpiece, making a locking movement with her thumb and first finger, and he retreated to the steps, leaning against the railings with his hands in his pockets while she fetched the key.

"Hey, I didn't mean to give you a fright," he said as she let him in. "I tried the bell but nobody came."

"Oh—there's a loose connection, I must get it fixed." Loretta avoided his gaze, more embarrassed than alarmed; she was almost certain Sam had seen her sitting at the table with her hands on her breasts. What must he be thinking: that he had caught her in the early stages of some masturbatory ritual? "Um, why don't you sit down? Bridget's upstairs, she should be down any minute. Can I get you some coffee?"

"No thanks, I've been drinking it with the cops all

morning. Those homicide guys have their own catering truck—"

"Good God, how long are they planning to stay?"

"They won't say." He pulled out a chair and sat down, throwing his head back and stretching his legs under the table in an attitude of exhaustion.

"I mean, what do they expect to find?"

He said offhandedly, shading his eyes with his hands and staring up at the ceiling: "Clothes, I guess—her purse, that kind of stuff."

"But surely you'd have noticed—"

He yawned, buried his face in his hands and then jerked forward into a sitting position. "Sorry, Loretta, I'm bushed. Hi, hon," he exclaimed, his face lighting up as Bridget walked into the kitchen. He got up and enfolded her in his arms, initiating a noisy display of mutual affection which made Loretta turn away and busy herself with filling the kettle.

"Has Loretta told you her news?" Bridget extricated herself and grinned at her friend.

"News?" Sam placed his arm lightly round his wife's shoulders.

"She's going to the opera with Christopher Cisar. On Friday."

"She is?" He sounded surprised. "Sorry, Loretta, it's kind of rude of us to stand here talking about you in the third person."

"Some German thing," Bridget added.

"Ariadne auf Naxos," Loretta said quickly, switching on the kettle even though Sam had refused coffee. She had somehow forgotten he and Christopher were friends, that they might even discuss her between now and Friday. "I don't think it's performed very often," she said in a rush, "I don't even think I've heard it on

60

record, though I did see *Rosenkavalier* in Amsterdam a couple of years ago."

Sam looked at his watch. "You ready, hon?"

"Now? Isn't it a bit early for lunch? My hair's still damp."

"I told Elaine I'd call in at CES first, there are a couple of things I need to do."

"OK." Bridget gave in easily, running her hands lightly over her stomach. She was wearing a dress Loretta had packed for her the day before, not a maternity dress but in the loose style she had favored since her pregnancy was confirmed; she would rather go naked, she had announced with typical hyperbole, than shop in Mothercare.

"Hang on," said Loretta, surprised by the speed of their departure. "What about your messages? I wrote some of them down there"—she pointed to a piece of paper by the phone—"and there's a load more on the answering machine. Your mother rang again this morning."

Bridget immediately looked contrite, but a glance at Sam made up her mind. "I'll have to speak to her later, I think Sam's keen to leave."

"Sorry, Loretta," he confirmed, drawing Bridget towards the stairs, "but I don't have much time. Catch you later, maybe." He steered Bridget out of the kitchen, leaving Loretta to stare after them with a feeling that her hospitality was being abused.

"Wait a minute," she called, taking the stairs two at a time. She caught up with them at the front door, explaining breathlessly that she had a dentist's appointment that afternoon and Bridget would need a key to get back into the house. "There's one in my desk, I'd better give it to you now." She hurried into her study, resenting Sam's unconcealed impatience, and searched for it among the half-used rolls of Sellotape, dried-up felt pens and foreign coins she regularly consigned to the bottom drawer. "Here it is," she said eventually, returning to the hall. "I'll be back about half four."

When they had gone she returned to her study, picked a couple of leaky biros out of the drawer and tossed them in the wastepaper basket. Her computer screen still displayed the incomplete text of her chapter on Charlotte Brontë, but a line had been added underneath, presumably by Bridget. "Great stuff," Loretta read, "when can I see more of it?" Loretta frowned, disliking the idea of anyone, even her best friend, catching a glimpse of her work-in-progress, and deleted the sentence from the screen. After a moment she began to type, stopping occasionally to delete a word or phrase, until she reached a point where she needed to quote from *Shirley*. She was about to get the novel down from a shelf when the phone rang; Loretta ignored it, waiting for the answering machine to cut in, then changed her mind and picked it up.

"Hello," said an unfamiliar female voice, "is Dr. Bennett there?"

"I'm sorry, you've just missed her."

"Hold on, please." Loretta heard her confer with someone, then she said: "This is Professor Cromer's secretary, he's most anxious to speak to her."

"Well, she isn't here and I'm not sure when she'll be back." Loretta bit her lip, thinking it unlikely that Donald Cromer, the warden of Bridget's college, had got his secretary to call because he was worried about her welfare.

"In that case I'd better leave you some numbers. Have you got a pen? Professor Cromer's in New York at the moment, but he's due in Washington this evening and he's very keen to have a word with her."

"All right," Loretta said meekly, and wrote them down. She returned the receiver to its rest, starting when it rang again almost immediately.

"I don't care when she's supposed to go off shift, this is a *murder* inquiry," a man's voice snapped. "If she wants to work regular hours—Hello? Anybody there?"

"Yes," said Loretta, wondering what the police wanted this time.

"That Dr. Bennett?"

"No. She went out—oh, half an hour ago."

"Know where I can reach her?"

"No, sorry." Loretta did not really think the police would march into Browns, interrupting Bridget and Sam's lunch with trivial questions, but she wasn't taking any chances. Anyway, they probably hadn't even arrived at the restaurant yet.

"What about Mr. Becker, any idea where I can get hold of him?"

"They, um, they went out together." In the background Loretta could hear a phone ringing and someone using a manual typewriter slowly and inexpertly.

"Get her to ring St. Aldates police station, will you? Soon as she gets in."

"All right. Who should she ask for?"

"Sergeant Perrot. That's P-E-double-R-O-T. Sergeant Perrot or DC Sidney." The line went dead.

Loretta added the names to the sheet of paper on which she had made a note of Cromer's numbers, writing the single word URGENT in block capitals. She got up, intending to take the paper downstairs and leave it on the kitchen table where Bridget could not possibly miss it, then caught sight of the answering machine. At some point she would have to transcribe the messages from last night and this morning; with an exclamation of annoyance, and some harsh thoughts about Sam

Becker, Loretta balanced herself on the arm of her chair, pressed the "play" key and picked up a pen to summarize a rambling message from the pleasant but scatty librarian of Bridget's college.

4

"THE WHOLE CONVERSATION WAS TERRIBLY polite," Bridget said glumly, playing with the biro she had been using to write out a diary of her movements for the police. "His end of it, that is. Difficult times, the college's reputation, unwelcome press attention—what he was saying, in effect, was would I please keep away from his hallowed bloody portals while he tries to touch some tame millionaire for a new accommodation block. I mean, I can't help it if the papers say where I work, can I? What really pissed me off, Loretta," she went on, changing tack, "is that *you* were paying for the call. Twenty-five minutes to Washington—I dread to think how much it cost."

So did Loretta, who had been trying to reduce the size of her phone bills. Her only consolation was that she had been in bed by the time Bridget got hold of Donald Cromer, so the call would be charged at the cheaper rate. "How did you leave it? He hasn't really banned you from college?"

"Not in so many words." She cocked her head, listening to the spluttering of Loretta's front doorbell. "Oh, God, and I was going to ring Sam before they came.

You ought to do something about that bell, Loretta. Ticking-off number two—you will stay with me, won't you?"

"Course," Loretta said tiredly, getting up. "Don't worry, she seemed quite human when she interviewed me on Sunday. If you explain—"

"I already have. Are you going to let her in?"

"Yes, yes, I'm going."

When she opened the door the red-haired Inspector was facing away from the house, shaking rain off an umbrella, while a man in a leather jacket hung back beyond the railings, avoiding the flying drops.

"Dr.—oh, it's you, Dr. Lawson." The Inspector acknowledged her with a curt nod. "Dr. Bennett's expecting us, I think."

"Yes, come in."

"This is DC Harvey, by the way. I'll leave this here, shall I?" She furled the umbrella and leaned it against a corner of the porch. "I don't want to get your floor wet."

She strode past Loretta, her navy raincoat open over a paler blue suit, and peered into the drawing room. "Where is she?"

"Downstairs. In the kitchen." Loretta followed her, taken aback by the Inspector's brisk, no-nonsense manner. The woman had been quite different on Sunday afternoon, relaxed, sympathetic—it was almost as if she'd assumed a different personality with her semi-official clothes. Perhaps Bridget was right, and the interview was going to be sticky after all.

"Out of the way, puss," the Inspector commanded as Loretta rounded the bend in the stairs. The cat protested volubly as she tried to dislodge him from the bottom stair with her high-heeled shoe, hunching himself into a solid mass and leaving her no choice but to step over him.

Loretta stooped to give him a surreptitious caress as she passed, and the Inspector's leather-jacketed sidekick almost fell over her. She muttered an apology, bumping her head on his chest as she sought to disentangle herself, and arrived in the kitchen uncomfortably aware of the pink glow on her cheeks. She slid past the Inspector, who was shaking hands with Bridget, and propped herself against the sink to demonstrate her role as an observer rather than a participant in the proceedings. The Inspector shot her a questioning look as she sat down, more surprised than hostile, but Loretta pretended to be intent on her examination of a ragged fingernail.

"So," the woman began after a slightly uncomfortable pause. "I'm grateful to you for seeing us so early, Dr. Bennett. As I said on the phone, after your . . . conversation with my colleague, I'm hoping you'll regard this as in the nature of a friendly chat. DC Harvey's got something to show you but first . . ." She picked up Bridget's discarded pen, drawing attention to her slim fingers and scarlet nails—Loretta didn't think she'd been wearing nail polish on Sunday—then dropped it abruptly and looked Bridget full in the face. "Perhaps you don't realize, Dr. Bennett, how your behavior looks to some of my colleagues? We are in the middle of a murder inquiry, a very serious matter indeed, and at this moment there are something like fifty officers . . ." She paused again, as if unsure how to proceed. Her hair looked darker, Loretta thought, in this low, rainy light— more auburn than red. "Some of my colleagues," she went on, leaning back in her chair, "consider your behavior unhelpful if not downright obstructive. No, let me go on."

Loretta and Bridget, who had both begun to protest,

exchanged looks and fell silent. "I said some of my colleagues—the reason I'm here is that I'm prepared to give you the benefit of the doubt. You may not realize, indeed I have the impression your husband and friends"—she turned her head to include Loretta in this latter category—"are trying to protect you from involvement in what they seem to regard as ... as some form of inconvenience. I understand their motives, and their concern for your health"—another glance at Loretta—"but I have to warn you you are being badly advised. Cooperation is what we expect from witnesses in a murder inquiry and we take a dim view of people who don't respond to urgent messages."

"He didn't say it was urgent," Loretta put in. "He said as soon as she got in—"

"Exactly. And when did she—what time did you arrive home—here—yesterday, Dr. Bennett?"

Bridget shrugged. "Half past four—five. Loretta doesn't expect me to clock in and out."

The Inspector pursed her lips. "So you got in at—let's be generous and say five o'clock. Where were you all afternoon, by the way? We tried your college—"

"I had lunch at Browns," Bridget said sullenly. "Sam and I—"

"Presumably that didn't take the whole afternoon? Mr. Becker arrived back at Thebes Farm at just after three, I checked with one of my colleagues."

"Yes, and I didn't feel like coming back here alone ... I knew Loretta was going to the dentist. So I walked up to the Ashmolean."

"The Ashmolean?"

"Yes—why not? There's a picture, Piero di Cosimo, *The Forest Fire*. I often go and look at it."

The Inspector's eyebrows shot up. "How long does it take you to look at one picture?"

"Not *just* one—there's a Ghirlandaio head next to it, and they also have a Giotto. I mean, you don't look at a picture once and think that's it, you see it differently every time—"

Loretta interrupted, thinking Bridget was sounding unnecessarily snobbish: "Does it matter? I thought it was Sunday you were interested in, not yesterday afternoon."

The Inspector let out a "tut" of impatience. "I'm coming to that. What I'm trying to establish at the moment is why Dr. Bennett, who admits coming back here around five, didn't respond to our message. Sergeant Perrot rang again just after eight, which means she had a full three hours—"

"And something like fifteen messages waiting for me," Bridget protested. "Where's that piece of paper, Loretta? I had to ring my mum, my GP—I'm pregnant, you know. I've got an appointment at the John Radcliffe later this morning—"

"I'm aware of that." The Inspector's eyes flashed.

"Bridget—Dr. Bennett has high blood pressure," Loretta said in a conciliatory tone. "She's supposed to rest." She turned to glare indignantly at the male detective, who had turned away with a snort. "What's that supposed to mean?"

"OK, let's cool it. This is exactly what I didn't want . . ." The Inspector lifted her hands in a calming gesture, palms down. She took a few steps towards the arch into the dining room, took a good look at the room and turned back. "All I'm trying to do is impress on Dr. Bennett the importance of giving us her full cooperation. If she's willing—if you'll give me your assurance that our calls will be dealt with promptly in future—"

"Yes, yes," Bridget said impatiently, getting up. "You can skip the lecture, I've got to be at the hospital in forty minutes. Here's your—I've done that thing you wanted." She picked up two sheets of paper from the pine dresser and held them out.

The Inspector glanced at them and frowned. "This is—you moved in on Friday the nineteenth of July and this goes right up till Sunday?" She held the two flimsy sheets side by side. " 'Monday twenty-second of July,' " she went on, picking a day apparently at random. " 'Left house eight forty-five, arrived at college nine thirty approx, lunch with' "—she screwed up her eyes as though she was having difficulty with Bridget's handwriting—" 'with Sally Fi-ser-ova at Pizza Express, college two thirty till five thirty, arrived home six-oh-five approx.' " She raised her head. "It's not exactly comprehensive, is it?"

"I told your—I said I didn't have my diary with me. Anyway, it tells you when the house was empty, which is what I thought you wanted to know."

The Inspector glanced at the second sheet, then folded them briskly together. "All right," she said, "as we haven't got much time ... Harvey." The detective, who had been staring at a wall calendar with a picture of the cathedral in Siena, gave a start, then lifted a flat plastic wallet from his knees and placed it on the table. He unzipped three sides, slid out a sheet of paper and pushed it across the table towards Bridget.

"Oh, that," she said offhandedly. "I've already seen it, it's in the *Guardian* this morning."

"And?" The Inspector waited.

"And what?"

"Do you recognize her? Have you ever seen this woman, or anyone like her?"

"Well—"

"Go on."

"It's hard to tell. It's such a bad drawing."

"I'm not asking you to *review* it, Dr. Bennett. All I want you to do is look at it carefully, artistic considerations aside, and tell me whether—"

The phone rang. Everyone glared at Loretta as though she was personally responsible for the interruption.

After a pause she crossed the room, intensely conscious of the three pairs of eyes following her, and picked it up. "Yes"—she turned to look at the Inspector—"yes, she's here. It's for you." She held out the receiver.

"He's sure?" the woman said after listening in silence for about a minute. A note of suppressed excitement had entered her voice, and she turned her back on them as she fired off a series of rapid questions. "They have? Say it again . . . I'm on my way. Where . . . No, where is he *now*?" She pulled back the sleeve of her raincoat and looked at her watch. "He should be there in what, twenty minutes? OK, I'll be there in ten . . . No, it can wait till I get back." She slammed the receiver down so hard it bounced from its cradle, slithered across the work surface and swung gently by its cord. "Harvey," she snapped, stepping sideways with unconcealed impatience as Loretta bent to rescue the phone. "Sorry, Dr. Lawson, Dr. Bennett, something's come up." She moved towards the door.

"Not *again*," Bridget protested.

"I have apologized." The policewoman looked back into the room, her hand on the doorframe. *"Harvey."* Loretta almost felt sorry for the young DC, who was fumbling with the zip of his document case. He abandoned the attempt to close it, thrust it under his arm and hurried after his boss, ignoring Bridget's reminder that he'd forgotten the drawing of the dead woman.

"Don't worry, it looks like a photocopy." Loretta put

out her hand for the piece of paper as they disappeared upstairs.

"Doc-tor Law-son, Doc-tor Benn-ett. Do you think she was being sarcastic?"

"Mmm? No," said Loretta, who thought she herself had started it on Sunday. She took the drawing and stared at the dead face, at the eyes expressionless as stones. She had read somewhere that Victorian detectives resorted to the supernatural, photographing the irises of murder victims in the hope that the killer's image was somehow imprinted upon them; the occult had failed them, and Jack the Ripper was never caught. Presumably this corpse had decomposed beyond the point where it could be photographed and shown to the public, and there was nothing to be learned from the penciled eyes, not so much as a hint of the dead woman's character. Loretta shuddered, allowing lurid images of putrefaction to rise in her mind for the first time since Sunday evening, and she realized that her slight but instinctive shrinking from the red-haired Inspector was due to an unfair association of the woman's presence with the terrible, overpowering smell from Bridget's garden. She wished she could view the drawing as calmly as her friend, who had pointed it out to her on page two of the *Guardian* with the same expression of mild distaste she had shown for TV pictures of fighting between Serbs and Croats in Yugoslavia on the previous evening's news.

"It's a relief in a way," Bridget said suddenly, moving away and searching for something in her bag. "Not recognizing her, that is. I didn't expect to, of course, but—I suppose it's just superstition," she finished obscurely.

Loretta went on examining the long face and blank eyes, the straggling shoulder-length hair, and wondered

72

if some unknown person was even now gazing at the same picture with a different emotion—horrified recognition. Before she could say anything, the doorbell once again uttered its despairing stutter.

"That'll be my taxi. Sorry, Loretta, I must dash." Bridget seized her jacket from the back of a chair and blew a kiss to Loretta. "If Sam rings, tell him I'll be back about half twelve unless they're running very late."

A minute later Loretta heard her quick, light footsteps on the path, followed by the sound of a car door slamming. She switched on the radio, fiddled with the dial until she recognized a Mozart Mass and turned the volume up a little. Then she pulled out a chair to look at the *Guardian*, which Bridget had picked up in the hall on her way to the kitchen that morning. The latter, who'd been up first in nervous anticipation of the Inspector's visit, thrust the paper towards her when Loretta came downstairs but gave her no chance to read it, launching almost immediately into the account of her late-night conversation with Donald Cromer which was still going on when the two detectives arrived.

"Hi, puss." Loretta reached down as she felt Bertie brush against her calves; the frequent arrivals and departures since Sunday evening had unsettled him and she recognized the anxious rearing of his head as a demand for reassurance. She turned her attention back to the paper, which carried a short and factual report of the murder investigation by the paper's crime correspondent. It was mainly about the post-mortem, which had produced the information that the victim was aged around nineteen and had been killed by a blow to the head with a blunt, heavy instrument. In spite of an intensive search—Loretta remembered all those policemen and women in blue overalls—the murder weapon

73

had not been found, and detectives now believed the woman had been killed elsewhere and placed in the floor of the barn some time after her death. They refused to speculate on the interval between the murder and this event, and they were also being cagey on the question of rape or sexual assault.

"Bertie, *please*." The cat had jumped onto the table and slumped on his side on the newspaper, twitching his tail and obscuring the page Loretta was reading. She rolled him gently away, withdrawing her hand with a sharp intake of breath as he seized it and dug in his claws. "That's enough." She lifted him with both hands, restraining his stocky, squirming body with difficulty until she'd returned him to the floor. He scampered off in the direction of the cat flap, leaving her to reflect that there was nothing in the *Guardian* to explain the abrupt changes of plan in the police investigation, the aborted visits and demands for apparently irrelevant pieces of information. So what if Bridget chose to spend part of Monday afternoon staring at an early sixteenth-century painting? It seemed a harmless enough way to pass the time if you were pregnant, recovering from shock and reluctant to spend the afternoon alone. Loretta got up, stretched and yawned, shaking her head in an attempt to fight off the tiredness which was the result of two nights of restless, disturbed sleep. She remembered that she'd come downstairs without washing and went into the cramped downstairs bathroom, stripping off her T-shirt and splashing cold water on her face and neck to wake herself up. She dried herself vigorously with a towel, went over to the loo and began to unbutton her jeans, lifting her head wearily when she thought she heard the trilling of the phone. It sounded again, impersonal and intrusive against the *Credo in unum Deum* chorus filling the kitchen, and she hurried to answer its summons, naked to the waist and with her jeans gaping open.

"Loretta? Is this a bad moment? This is Janet—Janet Dunne."

"Oh, Janet," she said, relieved. "Hang on while I turn the radio down. That's better. Sorry to sound offhand, there've been so many calls *and* we've had the police round already this morning."

"You as well? Is Bridget there?"

"No, she's gone to the antenatal clinic. What did they want, the police?"

"Oh, that's what I wanted to talk to Bridget about. I may be overreacting but . . . When'll she be back?"

"She said half past twelve. Did they—" She broke off, not knowing Janet well enough to press her.

"That would suit me very well. I've got to drop something off at Somerville later this morning and I gather you're not far."

"Ten minutes' walk if you leave by the back entrance—I'll be here all morning."

"You're sure I'm not interrupting?"

Loretta gave a short laugh. "I've abandoned hope of getting any work done this morning. Do you know where I am?"

She gave Janet instructions on getting to Southmoor Road, warned her about the faulty doorbell and hung up. In the bathroom she pulled her T-shirt over her head, tucked it into her jeans and tied her hair back with the elastic band she discovered in one of her pockets. Then she returned to the kitchen, pulled the *Guardian* towards her and reread the report of the murder. There was nothing, no significant detail she'd missed the first time, and she toyed with the idea of ringing John Tracey and asking him to use his contacts to find out what was going on behind the scenes. She was fairly sure he would know the *Guardian*'s crime correspondent, but she was reluctant to dial his number when they hadn't spoken for so long. Anyway, he was probably out of the country, winning prizes somewhere in Eastern Europe; Loretta stepped back from the table, hugged her chest with her arms and stared out of the kitchen window at the blank basement wall, her stomach contracting as though it contained little cords of anxiety on which someone had just given a sharp tug.

"How long have I known Bridget, who her friends are, when did she meet Sam—that sort of thing." Janet turned her head and glanced out of the window at a passing car, her dark hair a mass of springy curls against the white muslin curtains. She was a vivid, slightly disturbing presence in Loretta's pale drawing room, her coral earrings swinging every time she moved, like animated reflections of the red splashes on her inky-blue dress.

"What did you say?"

"Mmm?" She turned back to Loretta. "Oh, that I didn't mind going over Sunday afternoon again if it was really necessary, but I certainly wasn't going to pass on gossip."

"Gossip? What gossip?"

Janet looked slightly amused. "I didn't mean—all I meant was Bridget and Sam's marriage isn't any of my business. Or theirs, more to the point. But I thought she ought to know the sort of thing they're asking. You know what north Oxford's like, if they talk to enough people they're bound to come up with something."

"Such as?"

Janet shrugged. "Bridget's not exactly *conventional*. All it needs is a word or two, a hint about her lovers—"

"She's never made any secret of that. Anyway, it's all in the past."

"Yes, but ... These are the same people who think a few overexcited kids celebrating in the High Street are a threat to civilization as we know it. It wouldn't take much to persuade them they're dealing with the Whore of Babylon."

"The—" Loretta stared at Janet, astonished. "Whose side are you on?"

Janet sighed. "It's not a matter of sides. In some ways, Bridget's never stopped living in the sixties—she's exactly the kind of person to activate all their prejudices. I assume they've already got a file on her—wasn't she arrested at some demonstration?"

"Only for obstruction. She sat in the road—they didn't actually charge her. And she was fined for possession of cannabis, but that was *years* ago. Before I knew her."

"There you are then."

Loretta gave a snort of contempt. "But that's got nothing to do with ... this business. They brought a picture round this morning and she didn't even know the woman. So what if she's had a few lovers?"

"Loretta, I'm just telling you the kind of questions they're asking and trying to make an intelligent guess about how their minds work. From the way he talked about her, the man who came round this morning, I got the impression she's already put their backs up. She should be careful, that's all."

"Oh, well," Loretta said, relieved, "I know what that's about. They left a message here yesterday and she didn't ring back, though it was as much their fault as hers. She was far more worried about Donald Cromer."

"Donald Cromer? Has he been on to her?"

Loretta pulled a face. "He certainly has. He's more or less banned her from going into college till this is over."

"You see, Loretta, that proves my point. Ever since Cromer became warden she's had to tread very carefully, he's nowhere near as easy-going as Jim Pollock." The latter, an economist who had advised Harold Wilson in the sixties, had been lured to Harvard and replaced by Cromer, who was rumored to be a crony not only of Princess Margaret, whom he regularly invited to dinner, but of Mrs. Thatcher. "Donald's obsessed with scandal, he expects the fellows to behave like Caesar's wife. Do you remember that business at St. Mark's —no, you weren't in Oxford then."

Loretta said nothing and Janet mistook her silence for curiosity. "One of the dons was found murdered in Paris—Hugh Puddephat, does the name mean anything to you? Possibly not, he was a structuralist and that's all a bit passé now, isn't it? Anyway, that's the kind of thing Donald's determined to avoid, especially as one of the other fellows was nearly charged with the murder. He only got off when the master's wife went to the police and admitted they were having an affair . . . Loretta, are you all right?"

"Mmm," she said, getting up and kneeling on the sofa next to Janet. "It gets a bit stuffy in here in the mornings"—she fiddled with the window lock—"especially now that the rain's stopped." The window catch was stiff, needing several attempts before she was able to swivel it round with her thumb, and the window moved only nine inches before jamming in the frame, but Loretta was grateful for the diversion. "That's better," she said, feeling able to face Janet again, and returned to her seat.

Janet looked at her oddly, but said nothing. Instead she uncurled her long legs from the sofa, slipped on her sandals and got up to look at Loretta's bookshelves. "You don't mind?" she asked, glancing over her shoulder. "I'm always interested in other people's books."

"Go ahead," said Loretta and watched as Janet took down a book, read the synopsis on the inside cover and put it back.

"Have you read this?" She turned and held out another, this time a Virago paperback.

"What is it?" Loretta leaned forward to get a better look and recognized a novel by Elizabeth von Arnim. "Mmm, no, I don't think so. In fact, I'm not even sure it's mine. Let's have a look." She held out her hand and took the book from Janet. "I thought so—it's Bridget's." She turned it over and read the blurb aloud in a rapid monotone: " 'First published da-de-da . . . forceful study of the power of men . . . weakness of women when they love . . .' I read another one, *Enchanted April*, and she said this was better. I think it's the one about her marriage to—I've forgotten his name."

She placed the book on the low table in front of her, thinking she should at least offer to return it to Bridget. They had fallen into the habit of lending each other things, clothes as well as books, soon after Loretta moved to Oxford; she had gone to her first formal dinner, in the cavernous dining hall of one of the grandest colleges, where the only illumination came from candles flickering above tarnished silver, wearing a black lace cocktail dress which had originally belonged to Bridget's aunt. She had been quite unprepared for the random, possibly mischievous placement, which had abandoned her to the mercies of a mechanical engineer, a former employee of British Rail who had talked about faults in railway engines throughout the first two

79

courses. The dress had at least given her the confidence to regard her plight with detached amusement.

"Sorry," she said, realizing Janet had spoken. She put up a hand and pushed a few stray hairs back from her forehead, twisting them under the elastic band and wishing she had brushed it out before Janet arrived. "I haven't been sleeping very well . . . What did you say?"

Janet shook her head. "Nothing." She draped herself gracefully on the sofa, glancing at her watch in a slightly surreptitious way which suggested she had had enough of their conversation and was impatient for Bridget to arrive. "Do you think Sam has a record? I suppose he's too young to have been a draft dodger?"

"I should have thought so. I don't know his exact age." Loretta tried to remember when the last American troops left Vietnam—1971?

"Me neither. I don't know much about him at all, do you?"

Loretta said noncommittally: "Well, he hasn't been here long. I know he's got a mother in Boston, though she didn't come to the wedding . . . He seems a perfectly ordinary—"

"A perfectly ordinary what?" Janet prompted when Loretta failed to finish the sentence.

"Oh, I'm not the person to talk to about Sam," Loretta said with feigned lightness, looking down and scratching at a minute paint stain on her jeans. She was unprepared for the rush of emotion unleashed by this trivial conversation, and her ears strained for the sound of Bridget's key in the front door to end it.

"I didn't realize you disliked him so much."

"I don't, I—it's just sour grapes on my part." Loretta dragged at the elastic band, tears springing to her eyes as it brought a knot of torn hair with it. "Bridget's my closest friend, I've known her for, oh, ten years"—she picked savagely at the band, trying to unwind strands of hair from it—"and of course there've been times when we saw less of each other, but it's been such a shock, the way she's retreated into this . . . this *parody* of the nuclear family. She didn't even—it was *Sam* who told me about her blood pressure being too high." She looked up, stung by the recollection of this recent injury which she'd hardly had time to think about, and tossed the elastic band onto the table. "It's as if, all these years, it was all second-best and she really wanted a husband—just like my *sister*. I thought we were different, I thought our generation—" She stopped, horrified by the way in which her feelings had betrayed her into these rash, painful confidences.

"I'm sorry," Janet said after a moment's silence. She shifted on the sofa, sitting up straight and crossing one leg over the other. "Have you—you haven't talked to her about it?"

"Talked to her?" Loretta exclaimed. She felt like two people, one of them struggling unsuccessfully to get the other under control. "That's the problem," she said more quietly. "We don't have conversations like that anymore."

"You don't think—" Janet began cautiously. "Her loyalties must be divided. Perhaps she's afraid to raise it?"

Loretta made an impatient gesture. "I'm sorry, Janet, I'm making a complete fool of myself. Can I get you another drink?"

"No, I'm fine." Janet gestured to the half-full glass of kir on the table. "Aren't you being a little harsh? She's been trying so hard to toe the line this last couple of years, going to Donald's little dinners for industrialists and his mates from right-wing think tanks." Janet made a face to show where her sympathy lay. "Then there

81

was that silly row and Donald, without even asking for her side of the story, accused her of bringing the college into disrepute. She's thirty-six, thirty-seven, and what's she got to look forward to as far as Oxford's concerned? All right, I know she isn't unemployed and sleeping in a cardboard box—I think you have to be an Oxford person yourself to know what it means. Why, anywhere else would be"—she sat back, distancing herself from Loretta's unvoiced disapproval—"second-best. I can't really see her upping sticks and going to work in Reading. That's if there *are* any jobs in Reading."

Loretta shook her head. "Even if it's true, I thought she'd got over it long ago. She said herself it was political—"

"Of course it was, but that doesn't help. Well, I could be wrong, you've known her a lot longer than I have. On the other hand, maybe she put a brave face on for you—"

"For me? Why would she do that?"

"Well, your book for a start."

"My—that was two years ago, and I haven't even got a full-time job." Loretta sometimes joked that she personally was an education cut—forced to go part-time when her college embarked on a money-saving exercise and pruned a quarter of its teaching staff. She had pointed out at the time that the axe was falling disproportionately on female lecturers in all departments, and had even persuaded her union to take up the issue, but the principal replied that it just happened, regrettably, to be the women who did not have tenure. They were, in other words, easier to sack.

"And you review all over the place."

"I need the money." This was partly true, although it hardly made up for the loss of a third of her salary; Loretta had had a succession of lodgers in the past year, the latest departing the previous week, and she would soon have to advertise for another.

Janet leaned forward, picked up her glass and sipped from it. "That's not what people think when they see your byline. To get back to Bridget, I think she was vulnerable and Sam happened to come along at the right time—"

Loretta said: "Some day my prince will come."

"If you want to put it like that. Or you could say he's intelligent, good-looking—"

"Not to mention rich."

"You *can't* mean that."

Stung by this justified rebuke, Loretta cried: "It's all so bloody perfect."

"Of course it is. They've known each other—what? Nine months? You know what it's like, the first few months of an affair. Freud compared it to a temporary psychosis—"

"Oh, *Freud*."

"You're not listening. The operative word is *temporary*. Give her time and she'll get over it."

"What—living in that color-supplement house *and* with a baby?"

"She's not going to give up work, is she? She says she's going back at Christmas and I don't see any reason—"

The phone rang and Loretta let out an audible gasp of relief. "Excuse me," she said, hurrying to the other end of the room.

"Sam," she said a moment later, turning her back on Janet to hide her embarrassment. "Bridget's not back yet, I'm expecting her any minute."

"You saw her this morning? How did she look?"

"All right. Better than yesterday."

"Are you sure?"

Loretta sighed. "She looked fine. Really."

"O-kay." He did not sound entirely convinced. "Listen, Loretta, they think they know who she is."

"Who? Oh, the, um . . ."

"Yeah, and the point is she's *American*."

"American?"

"So now we know why the heat's on us—Bridget and me. These guys"—he sighed—"these guys go for the obvious, they put two and two together and come up with four hundred. She's American, I'm American, there has to be a connection."

"But Oxford's full of Americans."

"Turns out they already suspected—the pathologist spotted some fancy orthodontic work. Now this guy's called in, says he sat next to her on a plane and sure, she did have an American accent."

"This is from the photofit—drawing?"

"Yeah. Why I'm calling, Loretta, is they're setting up a press conference this afternoon and they want me and Bridget at it. I said no way, I want her kept out of this—if I have to get some kind of a medical certificate, OK, I'll do it. Can you ask her to call me as soon as she gets in? I'm staying at my desk, Elaine's going out to get me a sandwich."

"Of course, but—"

"Loretta, I have to go. There's a call coming through on the other line. Talk to you later."

He hung up and Loretta walked the length of the room to where Janet was waiting expectantly for her.

"Apparently they've identified—" Loretta turned her head, at last hearing the sound she'd been waiting for. "Bridget?" She went to the door and saw her friend standing just inside. "God," she said, her tone changing, "you look terrible. Come in and sit down." She took Bridget's arm and guided her into the drawing room, pushing her gently onto the sofa she'd recently vacated. "What is it?" she asked, kneeling beside her and taking her hand, which neither returned Loretta's grip nor attempted to withdraw from it. "What happened?"

Bridget leaned back and closed her eyes. "I'll be all right in a minute."

Janet said: "Shall I get her some water?"

Bridget opened her eyes briefly. "Janet," she said, acknowledging her presence, and closed them again. "No, really. I've had a bad morning, that's all."

"Is it your blood pressure? Has it got worse?"

"Mmm. They wanted me to go in for a few days."

"Into hospital? That's a bit drastic, surely?"

Bridget took a deep breath and heaved herself into a sitting position. "That's what I said," she admitted with the ghost of a smile.

"And did they—what did they say?"

"They said I'm at risk of pre-eclampsia."

Loretta glanced at Janet. "I don't know what that means."

Bridget groped on the floor for her bag, felt inside with her free hand and then gave up. "It used to be called toxemia. I could lose the baby and—apparently it's still the main cause of maternal death."

5

"YOU MEAN THEY OFFERED HER A BED AND she turned it down?" Audrey's voice, at the other end of the telephone line, was incredulous.

"So it seems. Look, I don't know the first thing about—about pre-eclampsia. Is it really as dangerous as she thinks?"

"If it isn't stopped," Audrey said crisply. "If it becomes full eclampsia. Is she there?"

"She's upstairs, talking to Janet—Janet Dunne. Shall I get her?"

"No, let me think. I've got two more home visits which'll take me the best part of an hour, then I've got to try and get a psychiatric bed for a patient . . ." The weariness audible in her voice, Audrey calculated how long these tasks would take and finished: "I could get to you around four. If you have any trouble with the police before then, refer them to me—press conference, indeed!"

"Thanks, Audrey. See you at four."

"What does—Loretta?—what does Sam say about all this?"

Loretta sighed. "He doesn't know. She doesn't want

to worry him, she says he's got enough on his plate with the police—"

"That's the end of my money." Audrey's change ran out and the line went dead.

Loretta moved back to the chopping board, picked up a knife smeared with avocado flesh and used it to ease out the stone. She sliced the avocado halves as thinly as the slippery, aging flesh would permit and arranged them in the center of a large oval plate which she had already decorated with alternate slices of mozzarella and plum tomatoes. There was a full bottle of extra-virgin olive oil in the food cupboard and she twisted off the metal cap, lowering her head for a moment to inhale the tangy scent. She had made an unproductive attempt to question Bridget before coming downstairs, quickly discovering that the consultant's shock tactics—if that was what they were—had backfired. Bridget was in a state of trembling ignorance about the causes of pre-eclampsia, the symptoms to expect if her condition got worse, and the possible existence of alternative forms of treatment to the hospital admission she had already refused.

"Can't we look it up?" she pleaded when Loretta first suggested contacting Audrey. "There's no need to bother her—there's bound to be something about it in *Our Bodies, Ourselves.*"

Loretta had acquired her edition at least a decade ago and thought it was almost certainly out of date but she went obediently to the high shelf in her study where she kept the classic feminist texts she had devoured in her early twenties. *Our Bodies, Ourselves* was usually in the middle, somewhere near *The Dialectic of Sex* and *Sexual Politics*, but on this occasion there was no sign of it. Loretta checked the index of a couple of other health handbooks but found nothing under *P* or *E*.

"Oh, all right," Bridget conceded when Loretta returned empty-handed, "I suppose she'll have to know sometime, seeing she's my GP. As long as"—she lifted a hand to her face and pressed her cheek into the palm—"as long as I don't have to go into hospital. Not yet, anyway." Her eyes were large and frightened, and Loretta suddenly realized what was behind this almost phobic response. Two years ago, when an old friend discovered he was dying of AIDS, Bridget had made regular trips to see him in hospital and returned from each hundred-mile round-trip in a state of quivering indignation about the way in which staff shortages and a lack of basic resources were denying him small comforts in his final days. Loretta did not know whether the situation was as bad in Oxford but she exchanged a look with Janet, shaking her head slightly to convey that this was not the moment to press her. Instead, she diverted the conversation by passing on Sam's message.

"What's the point of that?" Bridget asked when she heard about the press conference. "I mean, what do they expect me to say? I don't know anything, nothing that would interest the scandal rags." She seemed more puzzled than anxious, furrowing her brow as though she'd received a dinner invitation from people she barely knew.

Janet crossed one leg over the other. "I expect they want to ask how it feels, finding a body in your garden."

Loretta frowned and said more confidently than she felt: "It's out of the question, anyway." She thought it unlikely that the police had the power to compel someone to attend a press conference, it wasn't like appearing in court, but it would certainly make things simpler if Bridget was actually in hospital. Feeling out of her depth, slightly panicky even, Loretta had to exert rigid control to prevent herself from blurting out this opinion.

"Sounds like she might have been on holiday," Bridget said suddenly, kicking off her shoes and curling her legs under her on the sofa. It took Loretta a moment to realize that she was talking about the dead woman. "I mean, as she's American. I thought they were supposed to be staying away because of the Gulf War and the recession, but Oxford seems to be full of them."

Janet looked surprised. "Is it? Those open-topped buses don't have many people on them, I wonder sometimes how they stay in business."

"Oh, I'm an expert on those," said Bridget, sounding animated for the first time since her return from the hospital. "One of them stops right under my window at St. Frideswide's, it's the same spiel every time—college founded in 1431, great hall burned down by deranged ex-student in 1582, look over the wall and you can just see the famous clock supported by marble figures of Dante and Virgil ... Actually it isn't Virgil, it's Petrarch, I keep meaning to ring up and mention it to whoever writes the script."

Loretta took this opportunity to slip downstairs, out of earshot, and leave a message for Audrey at the surgery in Woodstock Road. Five minutes later, Loretta heard the single chirrup which indicated someone had picked up the phone, presumably Bridget trying to reach Sam before the press conference. She had finished her call just in time for Audrey to get through from the call box in Wolvercote.

A timer sounded as Loretta shook olive oil and balsamic vinegar in a jar and dribbled the mixture onto the salad, reminding her to remove a Marks and Spencer loaf from the oven. She put the various bits and pieces on the table, wishing she had been able to come up with something a bit more adventurous than an *insalata tricolore* and a bowl of olives, and called up from the bottom of the stairs: "It's ready." She listened for a moment until she heard signs of movement on the floor above, footsteps and Janet's voice getting louder as she and Bridget came into the hall, then returned to the kitchen.

"What did she say?" Bridget appeared first, pale but composed.

"Who?" Loretta was flustered and it took her a moment to remember. "Audrey? She's coming round at four."

"Hmm." Bridget unscrewed the top of the pill bottle she was carrying and shook a capsule onto her palm. "I suppose I'd better take one of these."

"What is it?" Loretta knew Bridget's fondness for quack remedies, ginseng and curious herbal concoctions, and was relieved when she moved closer to see that the typed label on the bottle appeared official.

"Dunno. Something they gave me at the hospital." Bridget put the capsule in her mouth, swallowed and looked down at the three places set at table. "Is there some mineral water?"

Loretta fetched a bottle from the fridge and they sat down to eat. Almost immediately, and to Loretta's relief, Janet began to talk about the book she was writing, a study of Artemisia Gentileschi commissioned by an American publisher who believed there was a market for lavishly illustrated feminist reinterpretations of art history. Janet had just spent a week in Florence, where an exhibition of Gentileschi's paintings, the first major retrospective of her work, was being held at Michelangelo's house, the Casa Buonarroti.

"Judith Decapitating Holofernes," Loretta said instantly, recalling an illustration in a magazine. She was

about to describe the picture, a gory biblical scene of blood-soaked sheets and a severed jugular vein, but stopped abruptly when she realized it would lead them straight back to the subject of murder.

"Yes, she really got her own back on men, didn't she?" Bridget remarked unexpectedly, showing no such qualms. "For being raped, I mean—all those Judiths and Salomes."

Janet sighed and speared a smidgeon of avocado with her fork. "So my editor would like to think."

Bridget refilled her glass with water. "Well, there are rather a lot of them. You look at a picture and it seems familiar, then you realize it's yet another woman with some bloke's head in a basket."

"Don't forget Jael and Sisara. And the flaying of Marsyas, although the attribution isn't absolutely certain. I should say about a third of her subjects involve violent death, certainly as far as this exhibition goes."

Loretta prompted: "But?"

Janet put down her fork and propped her elbows on the table in front of her, resting her chin lightly on her clasped hands. "The problem is that we don't look at male painters in that way—autobiographically. Her father, Orazio Gentileschi, produced at least two versions of the Judith story but we don't assume a personal motive. You have to remember that they were professional painters, they worked to commission, and it wasn't unusual for them to be asked to repeat a successful subject. Heroic women, Judith and Jael and Cleopatra, they were hugely popular throughout the seventeenth century. Baglione painted Judith and so did Caravaggio."

"Who committed a murder himself," Loretta pointed out.

"Yes, but . . ." Janet hesitated, frowning as she thought about how best to express herself. "What I'm

91

suggesting is that it's *how* she painted, not *what* she painted, that matters. The history of art is littered with women artists whose work has traditionally been ignored or dismissed because they *only* painted still life, or in Artemisia's case because of this facile equation between an event we don't fully understand—we don't even know the outcome of Tassi's trial for rape—and the subject of her most famous paintings." Janet paused again, narrowing her eyes and flexing her fingers. She had not seen Bridget's signal to Loretta that the conversation was getting too serious, and before either of them could speak she continued: "The exceptional thing about Artemisia in my view, and I must say it was borne out by seeing the pictures together at the Casa Buonarroti, is her ability to paint women—real women, whether we're talking about the Judiths or an allegorical figure such as the nude in *L'inclinazione*. In the Caravaggio decapitation, for instance, the one in Palazzo Barberini in Rome, Holofernes is in agony but there's something curiously detached about Judith—you wouldn't guess from her face or from the way she's holding her arms that she's in the middle of murdering someone. Caravaggio simply hasn't given her much thought, her reaction to what she's doing or her motivation. Whereas in Artemisia's version, both the Uffizi canvas and the copy in Naples, Judith has a most determined expression and she's bracing her left arm against his cheek—she's definitely *sawing*."

"Please," Bridget exclaimed, suddenly looking queasy again, "let's change the subject."

Janet gave her a startled look and seemed to be about to protest but at that moment they all heard the sound of the doorbell stammering its exhausted message. Loretta frowned and glanced at her watch. "It can't be Audrey yet," she murmured, and appealed to Bridget: "Are you expecting anyone?" Bridget shook her head.

The men waiting on the path, talking in low voices, hardly needed to show their warrant cards for Loretta to guess their occupation. They stood with their legs apart, balancing on the balls of their feet, and the one with dark curly hair turned to her with a cocky, assessing look which made her simultaneously angry and nervous.

"Dr. Lawson?" he asked, sliding his hand out of his pocket just long enough for her to glimpse an official-looking card in his palm. "Sergeant Brandon, Thames Valley Police." He jerked his head sideways at his younger, fresh-faced companion. "DC Yate. Dr. Bennett in?"

"Yes," Loretta admitted, glancing over his shoulder in fear of seeing a squad car which had come to take Bridget away. "But if it's about the press conference—"

"What?" He made it sound as though this was the last thing on his mind. A burst of female laughter drifted up from the kitchen and his eyes narrowed. "Down there, is she?" He leaned over the railings and peered into the basement.

"Yes," Loretta said again, "we're just having lunch." This mild attempt to suggest they had chosen a bad moment had no effect; Brandon advanced until he was so close that Loretta could see the five-o'clock shadow forming on his chin and she had no choice but to fall back. The other detective followed, closing the front door behind him, and suddenly the hall seemed crowded. Loretta retreated further, leading the way down the stairs and trying to explain about pre-eclampsia, but Brandon brushed past her.

"Dr. Bennett?" He strode into the kitchen, with Loretta following and making anxious signs, and gave

Janet the merest glance; he had obviously been well briefed. "Sorry to bother you again, Dr. Bennett, but there's a couple of things." He felt in his pocket and produced two sheets of paper which Loretta, who was just behind him, recognized over his shoulder as photocopies of the handwritten pages Bridget had prepared for the Inspector that morning. Someone had added notes and question marks in blue biro, and ringed one particular day near the beginning.

"Here we are," Brandon was saying, "Thursday the twenty-fifth of July. It says here you left home at ten to nine, a few minutes after Mr. Bennett—Mr. Becker. You come into Oxford in separate cars, is that right?"

Bridget nodded, uncomprehending.

"OK, let's see. You arrived at your—at college around nine thirty, worked for a couple of hours ... You walked round to the Bodleian Library, got there—it doesn't say what time but it would take you, what, ten minutes? Quarter to twelve, say? You worked till about quarter to one, it's all a bit vague, isn't it? Went out for a bite to eat and do some shopping, came back half one. Worked till half past four, nipped back to college to pick up your car and arrived back at Thebes Farm approx five thirty. Mr. Becker arrived half an hour later and you had a friend round for dinner, a Dr. Michie, it says here."

"Yes, he's a friend of Sam's. From the university physics department."

"You don't say what time Dr. Michie arrived, Dr. Bennett, or when he left."

Bridget breathed out noisily, leaving no one in any doubt that she had no patience for such nit-picking. "He came at seven, if you must know. The thing about physicists"—she glanced at Janet as though this might be of more general interest—"the thing about physicists is they like to eat early, I don't know why. I didn't do anything special, there was some fresh pasta in the freezer ... You really want to know all this?"

He nodded.

"Well, I wasn't feeling well and I left them to it after we'd eaten, they had work to discuss. I looked into the dining room about half nine and said good night, and I heard Tony leave around ten. I read for a while and Sam came up after he'd seen *News at Ten.* That do you?"

"Mr. Becker didn't go out at all, then, either during the evening or after you went to bed?"

"Of course he didn't go out. What is all this?"

"Just getting it clear." He lowered his head, stared at the sheet of paper in his hand and then tried a new tack. "It doesn't say where you went for lunch, Dr. Bennett, on Thursday the twenty-fifth. If you could be a bit more specific?" The other detective, standing just inside the doorway, took out a notepad and prepared to write.

"Lunch? This is Thursday two weeks ago we're talking about?" She waited for confirmation and said uncertainly: "I expect I had a sandwich, I did say I'd done it without my diary—"

"Ah, yes, I was coming to that. Can we have a look at it, Dr. Bennett, this diary?"

"My diary—what for?"

"Fill in the gaps a bit, that's all. Things you might've forgotten to mention—you'd be surprised what turns out to be important in a murder inquiry. This sandwich—you make it yourself? Bring it from home?"

"No." Bridget looked comically put out by the suggestion. "I—there's a sandwich bar in Broad Street."

"Sandwich bar in Broad Street." He glanced at his sidekick, making sure he was writing down her answers. "Called?"

She shook her head. "I've no idea. You can't miss it, it's on the opposite side from Blackwell's. Blackwell's main shop that is. Near the—not the art shop, the paperback one." She tailed off, apparently realizing that a shop with no fewer than four branches in the same stretch of street was hardly a useful landmark. "Does it matter?"

"See anyone you know, did you, Dr. Bennett? In the Bodleian?"

Bridget shook her head.

"No one at all? I'd have thought you dons, you'd be bound to know each other."

Bridget smiled. "It's not just members of the university who use it, you know. All sorts of writers and researchers, biographers . . . I don't know what the membership is but it must be thousands and thousands."

"You don't mind if I ask—what were you doing there?"

"I . . ." She hesitated. "Research."

"What sort of research?"

"I was—I had to look something up."

He nodded, waited.

"Polidori's *Vampyre* . . . for a paper I was writing."

"Whose vampire?" He turned and grinned at his colleague. "Spell that, can you, Charlie?"

"Polidori. P-O-L-I-D-O-R-I. It's the first vampire story in English."

"Dracula, eh? Like all those old films?"

"*Dracula*—Bram Stoker's much later, actually."

"Oh." He accepted the correction without interest. "Where'd you actually do this work, Dr. Bennett? Big place, the Bodleian."

"You order the book in the catalog room and then you . . . you collect it and find a place to read."

"Where's that? Where'd you read it?"

"The Upper Reading Room."

"In one of those funny cubbyholes?"

"Yes."

"You remember the number?"

"The number?"

"OK. Just thought you might, staring at it half the day. Staff know you, do they?"

"The staff? I doubt it."

"Not even by sight?"

"They deal with dozens of people every day."

"OK. Thanks, Dr. Bennett . . . Oh, this diary. Where is it, actually?"

"Where? It's—I think I left it at college on Friday. By mistake."

"What's the drill then? All right if we go and pick it up?"

"Pick it up? Good God, no. Donald—Professor Cromer—I'll get it myself if you really think—"

"When?"

"As soon as I—this afternoon."

Loretta said warningly: "Remember Audrey's coming at four."

"Oh." Bridget put a hand up to her hair. "Later maybe, after Audrey's been, my GP."

"OK, Dr. Bennett, we'll let you get back to your lunch. Come on, Charlie, we've disturbed these ladies long enough." He gave a stagey wave and went to the door, turning back to Bridget as his sidekick disappeared up the stairs. "Give us a ring, won't you, when you've got the diary. We'll give you a receipt so it's all nice and official. After you." He stood back to allow Loretta to pass and, when she didn't move, left the room with a slight shrug. Loretta followed him up the stairs to the front door, feeling like an unpaid commissionaire.

97

". . . Donald'll go *berserk* if they turn up at college,"
Bridget was saying when she returned to the kitchen.
Her face was flushed and she moved about restlessly,
trailing one hand along the mantelpiece and looking
down in surprise at the dust on her fingers. "Why do
they—can they *make* me give them my diary? What's
so special about the twenty-fifth?"

"I assume that's when she arrived in England." Janet
poured an inch of water into her glass, drank it in one
gulp and stood up. "Do you have a solicitor, Bridget?"

"A—only the one we used for conveyancing. I'm going to ring Sam." She peered round the room as though
she'd forgotten where the telephone was and Loretta,
who was standing in front of it, held it out to her.

"Talk to him about getting a solicitor," Janet said seriously. "You need someone who's used to dealing with
these people."

Bridget was already dialing. "Elaine? Is Sam there?
When're you expecting him back? Could you? At
Loretta's. Thanks." She replaced the receiver, handed
the phone back to Loretta and said bleakly: "He's gone
to the press conference, apparently. I've left a message."

Janet checked her watch. "I have to go—I've got a
student coming at half past three." She rested an arm
lightly on Bridget's shoulders. "You will do something,
won't you? About getting a solicitor?"

"Mmm." Bridget nodded distractedly and kissed her
cheek. "Thanks for—I'll come up with you," she added,
suddenly changing her mind and moving towards the
door. "They can't just turn up at college without permission, can they?"

"Just a second." Janet turned to Loretta, whom
Bridget seemed to have forgotten. "Goodbye, Loretta.
Thanks for lunch."

"You're welcome," she said automatically and listened with relief as the two women went upstairs, returning to the subject of whether the police could enter college premises without seeking formal permission from someone in authority. The discussion continued on the pavement outside the house and Loretta fell back into a chair, staring into space and rubbing her tired eyes. The kitchen grew dark as unseen clouds passed overhead and she shivered.

"Let's go for a walk." Bridget reappeared, her color still high and her eyes darting round the room as though she was trying to memorize its contents.

Loretta looked up. "A walk? Now?"

"Why not? Audrey won't be here for an hour."

"Shouldn't we—if you've got the key to your room I could go and get your diary." She made the offer unenthusiastically.

Bridget shook her head violently. "*Please*, Loretta—just for half an hour." She turned towards the window as a shaft of brilliant light illuminated the kitchen and said wistfully, if not very accurately: "It's such a lovely day."

Loretta breathed out, throwing back her head and allowing her shoulders to sag. "All right," she said, conceding it was a more attractive way of spending the afternoon than driving into the center of town and looking for somewhere to park near Bridget's college. "Just give me five minutes to clear these things away."

By the time Loretta had loaded the dishwasher, found her sunglasses and persuaded Bridget to borrow a cotton sweater, the sun was no more than a pale disc behind thick clouds. She followed Bridget out of the house, flinching as a gust of wind seized her hair and flung it across her face. Momentarily blinded, she

99

bumped into Bridget, who had stopped without warning at the wrought-iron gate.

"Miss Bennett?"

Loretta pushed her hair back as a dark man in a flashy suit levered himself away from a parked car and strode towards them. His smile faded slightly as he saw Loretta and his eyes flicked back and forth between them as though he was no longer sure which was his quarry. "I've been trying your bell but it doesn't work."

"Who are you?" Loretta insinuated herself between Bridget and the gate. Something in her brain murmured "journalist" and for a moment she thought she'd met him before; then she realized he reminded her of an old NUJ recruiting poster, a film still with a satirical caption which John Tracey used to have pinned on the wall above his desk at the *Sunday Herald*.

"Barry Webb." Discomfited by her scrutiny, he thrust out his hand and muttered the name of a tabloid newspaper. When Loretta ignored it he converted the movement into an introduction, waving forward a woman who had just got out of a car parked on double yellow lines further down the road. "And this . . ." He waited for her to join him by the gate. "*This* is the Contessa Davvero."

Loretta blinked; it was the sort of name she had encountered only in *Hello!*, leafing through back numbers in her sister's loo. The Contessa didn't remotely resemble a reporter or a photographer—she radiated the confidence of a minor celebrity, posing on the pavement like a film star about to be interviewed about her new lover or her new Mercedes. Loretta couldn't imagine why she was here, with this raffish tabloid hack, and she stared in amazement at the Contessa's honey-colored hair, shocking-pink suit and spectacular gold earrings.

"Adviser to royalty and the stars," the reporter said rapidly, like an actor who has belatedly developed doubts about his script, "including the Prin—"

"I *told* you." She slapped his wrist playfully, showing off pink-lacquered nails. "My clients"—her voice was husky, foreign, though Loretta immediately suspected the accent was put on—"my clients must be confidential." She gazed intently at Loretta and raised a slender hand. "Already I am feeling . . ." She closed her eyes, lowering green-painted lids fringed by false lashes. "Yes, is a garden . . . *una capanna.*" Loretta swayed back as the blindingly pink talons came dangerously close to her cheek.

"You mean she's a psychic?" Bridget demanded. "Like a—like Doris Stokes?"

Loretta could not imagine a more inapposite comparison but the reporter was briefing the clairvoyant, sotto voce: "Not *her.* The other one." He turned, checked Bridget's torso for confirmation and was visibly relieved by the sight of the slight bump under her borrowed sweater.

"I've heard everything now. Go on, Loretta."

Webb grasped the top of the gate and pulled it shut, preventing Loretta from responding to the gentle pressure of Bridget's hand in the small of her back.

"*Loretta—*"

"Just five minutes," he wheedled, refusing to let go. "The Contessa's a very busy woman and we've come all the way from London."

"I don't care if you've come from Timbuktu. Would you please let go?"

"You've got the wrong end of the stick," he protested, an inappropriate choice of metaphor for someone involved in a tussle over a garden gate. "It's not an interview we're after. We've invited the Contessa, in view of her amazing track record—"

"Ze case of the buried ballerina," the clairvoyant said in a loud whisper. "Ze Crowdon Crusher."

"The Croydon Crusher," he corrected hurriedly. "Contessa Davvero spent fifteen minutes, just fifteen minutes, at the scene of the crime and described the weapon in *amazing* detail."

"What?" asked Loretta, who had no idea what they were talking about.

"So what's she doing here?" Bridget demanded. "I mean, this isn't where it happened—the scene of the crime or whatever."

"Yes, well, the cops aren't being what you'd call co-operative about that. The Contessa has a feeling about this case, all she wants to do is go somewhere quiet with Miss Bennett and, um, hold her hand—"

"You must be joking," said Bridget, recoiling. "I don't believe in astrology and all that crap. Go on, Loretta." They took advantage of the clairvoyant's voluble and angry response, directed more at the reporter than at Bridget, to slip round the gate.

"Come on, girls. It's not asking much." Webb leaned forward as Bridget passed, lowering her voice so the Contessa wouldn't hear. "If it's money you're after—"

"*Jerk.*" Bridget shook him off and caught up with Loretta.

He called after them, without much conviction: "You're missing a great opportunity."

Loretta turned, holding up her hands in a final gesture of rejection, and was surprised to see the Contessa hurrying towards her as fast as her tight skirt would allow.

"I aff to warn you," she said urgently, grasping Loretta's arm through her thin raincoat. "Is trouble ahead, *big* trouble—"

"Leave her alone," Bridget snapped. "Let go or I'll call the police." She started to walk back towards the house.

"You will be sorry." The woman threw Bridget a savage glance and released Loretta, hissing: "I tell you—be very careful." She clipped away from them on her high heels, walked straight past Loretta's house and stopped beside the reporter's car. He rushed to open the passenger door, waiting obsequiously as she swiveled her legs over the sill like a model at the Motor Show.

Loretta suppressed a shiver as they walked on. "What was all that about?"

Bridget said: "I suppose it sells papers. Hey, you're not getting superstitious in your old age? Come on, forget it."

The reporter's car overtook them near the end of Southmoor Road and Loretta glimpsed the Contessa in the passenger seat, peering into a hand-held mirror. "Sorry?"

"I said, isn't that where your friend lives?" Bridget waved a hand at the house they were passing and named a literary novelist.

"I wouldn't say she's a *friend*. I've met her a couple of times."

"What's her new book like?"

Loretta began a faltering description, unable to dismiss from her mind a vivid imprint of the psychic's distorted features. She had just finished describing the plot when they turned left into Aristotle Lane and crossed the bridge over the canal, lowering their heads as they encountered the full force of the wind. Bridget let out a sound between a gasp and a laugh as a particularly vicious gust took her breath away, slipping her hand into the crook of Loretta's arm and clinging to her as they struggled down onto Port Meadow. When they were safely on lower ground Bridget released her and danced ahead, throwing her arms wide: "Isn't it wonderful? Aren't you glad you came?"

Loretta answered with a smile and stared beyond her to the thin silver ribbon of the river. The fields were flooded with that dramatic light which often accompanies summer rain, coloring the grass a raw green and reducing the lush undergrowth and grazing animals to the flatness of a painted backdrop.

"Loretta."

"Mmm?" She watched a couple of large birds circle above the river, too far away to make out what they were. The previous week she had seen a heron standing in the shallows, solitary and aloof, and she wondered if it was still in the area.

"I've had an idea. Would you mind if I said I'd made a mistake—that I had lunch with you that Thursday?"

Loretta, still thinking about the heron, said: "What Thursday?"

"You know, the one they were so interested in. The police."

She turned her head. "What for?"

"It doesn't make a lot of difference," Bridget said in a rush, "because we did actually have lunch the next day—the Friday, remember? At the Duke of Cambridge? You had kedgeree and we—there was a stupid argument about names, you can't have forgotten."

"No, but why? What's the point?"

"The point—" Bridget was becoming exasperated. "I'd have thought it was *obvious*. I don't want them to see my diary, that's all. If I say we were talking about

104

it after they left and you said, hang on, isn't that the day we had lunch—"

"Wait a minute." Loretta was alert now, her brief interest in wild birds forgotten. "I know it's not very pleasant, the idea of a lot of policemen reading your diary—"

"It's not *that*." Bridget lunged sideways, not looking at Loretta, and pulled the heads off a clump of tall grass. She balled her fist, opened it to toss away the damp foliage and shook her fingers when the damp seeds stuck to them.

"Do you want a tissue?"

"N-no." Bridget rubbed her hands together, then wiped them on Loretta's sweater.

Loretta's fingers closed on the paper handkerchief in her raincoat pocket, tearing it into little pieces. "I'm not sure I—you mean there's something you don't want them to see?"

"*Yes*, Loretta," Bridget said sarcastically, "that's exactly what I mean." She sighed. "I can't explain because . . . well, it involves someone else. All I'm asking you to do is tell a little white lie, say we had lunch on a Thursday instead of a Friday."

"What if . . ." Loretta tried to focus on the purely practical aspects of this proposal. "What if they ask to see *my* diary? I'm sure I wrote it down, the Duke of Cambridge, one o'clock Friday." A year ago she would have assumed Bridget was covering up some sexual intrigue, an assignation with a married man perhaps, but it didn't seem likely, not in the present circumstances . . .

"God, Loretta, all you have to say is you don't keep one. The point is, they already know about *mine*. All you've got to say is we had lunch, went for a walk on Port Meadow—"

"What?" Now Bridget was asking for an alibi for the whole afternoon. She must have spent the time with someone, some man, yet Loretta had never previously doubted her devotion to Sam. Something stirred in her memory, Janet's remark about Bridget's lovers and what the police might come up with if they asked enough people—

"Why don't you just tell me?" she cried. "I won't say anything to—I won't say anything. Then we can work out what to do—"

"Loretta." Bridget's face was white, etched with anxious lines. "Don't you think I'd tell you if—Oh, forget it."

"Bridget—"

"I said *forget it*—forget I ever mentioned it. I'm going back, there's a phone call I have to make. I'll see you at the house." She turned, stumbled briefly on an uneven patch of ground and began walking in the direction they had come.

Loretta watched her go, vaguely aware that the sharp, nervous tugs had started up again in her stomach. "Bridget," she said quietly, then, louder: "Shit. Oh, shit." She swung her right foot and kicked at the soft earth, doubling over in pain when it connected with a concealed stone. Two of her toenails seemed to be broken and there was a jagged scratch on her sandal. Loretta knelt, wiping away mud and blood with the tattered remains of her paper handkerchief. After a moment, when the pain had declined to a dull ache, she stood up, balancing on her good foot and lowering the other gently to the ground. She discovered she could walk, as long as she kept her toes at an angle, and she set off at a hobble, glancing anxiously to the west when a distant roll of thunder signaled the approach of a storm. She increased her pace, not wanting to get caught in the open, and had just reached the bridge when the first drops of rain splashed onto her eyelashes, trickling down her cheeks like cold tears.

6

LORETTA CAME OUT OF THE BATHROOM NEXT morning and paused on the half-landing to stick back an Elastoplast which was flapping loose from her toes. She lifted her head, surprised by the unexpected fragrance of freshly baked bread, and followed it down to the kitchen where someone was moving around, opening cupboards and clinking glasses. She walked into the room and found Sam standing by the table, polishing her cutlery with a cloth like a waiter in a pretentious restaurant.

"Hi," he said, quickly disguising his disappointment when he saw she wasn't Bridget. "I didn't know whether to call you." He lined up a knife beside a place mat, gave a cursory wipe to a dessert spoon and turned back to her with a bright good-morning smile. "How's the foot this morning?"

"Oh, a bit sore." She was suddenly self-conscious, aware that her old Lynx T-shirt just covered the tops of her thighs and she was not wearing any knickers. Sam, by contrast, was wearing an immaculate short-sleeved shirt, a muted tie and neatly pressed trousers, which made her wonder briefly who did his ironing; not

Bridget, unless she really had undergone a dramatic metamorphosis. Loretta felt Sam's cool gaze travel down her bare legs, past the bruise on her shin to the grubby plasters on her foot, and wished she had remembered he was in the house before coming down.

"What can I get you?" he asked into the awkward silence, folding the cloth and hanging it neatly over the back of a chair. "I can offer you French bread, straight out of the oven"—he held up a pink and white bag from the Blanc Patisserie and Loretta caught an even stronger whiff of new bread—"and croissants with or without almond paste. Bridget'll be down in a couple of minutes, she's just taking a shower."

Loretta frowned. "Is she? A croissant, please, plain. Oh, and some grapefruit," she added, noticing he had already peeled the fruit and divided it into segments.

He handed her a bowl and she slid into a chair, keeping her legs tightly together until they were hidden under the table. Sam joined her, eating without speaking so she had a moment to take in the clean linen cloth, the jug of fresh orange juice—a superfluous touch, Loretta thought, after the grapefruit—and the vase of white and yellow freesias. She leaned forward to inhale their thin, mustardy scent and drew back when she felt the beginnings of a sneeze.

"Bless you."

Loretta got up, tore off a length of kitchen paper and blew her nose. "When did you—you've been out?"

"Yeah, the bakery next to Browns opens at seven, seven thirty." He went to the sink, rinsed his bowl under the tap and spooned dark, aromatic coffee grounds into the cafetiere while he waited for the kettle to boil. "This is the first real breakfast I've had since Sunday," he remarked conversationally, then picked up the *Guardian* which was lying on a worktop. "You want to look at the paper?"

She took it unenthusiastically and returned to her seat, her eyes sliding past a story about an alleged atrocity in Croatia and a report citing further evidence that the British economy was slipping into recession.

"They released her name."

"Sorry?"

He plunged down the top of the cafetiere. "Page two—they released her name. Here, let me find it for you." He took the paper back, opened it and read aloud: "Police investigating the death of a woman whose body was found in a barn in Oxfordshire on Sunday said last night they'd identified her as Paula Wolf, 19, from Oak Falls, Ohio."

"Ohio?" A line from a song came into Loretta's mind, something horribly appropriate from an American musical, and she had to prevent herself from humming it aloud: "Why, oh-why, oh-why-oh, did I ever leave Ohio?" She put her hand to her head, acknowledging the deep tiredness which had precipitated this bizarre piece of free association, and was hardly aware of Sam's voice continuing in the background. Her thoughts skipped instantly to her book, to the impossibility of getting any work done until she had had a proper night's sleep, and she began an anxious calculation of the number of chapters she'd written multiplied by five thousand words, the average length of a chapter.

"Loretta?"

Sam was watching her over the paper, brows drawn together, and she realized he had read part of the report aloud and was waiting for her reaction. "Um," she said, grasping at straws, "Wolf, did you say? What was her first name?"

"Paula." He was holding the paper out again, folded

110

open at the inside page, and she exclaimed with genuine interest as she took it from him: "It's you—your picture."

"Yeah, they were snapping away all through the press conference. You want some coffee, Loretta?"

"What? No thanks."

"Juice?"

"Please. Who's the man on your left? Oh, it says here he's the man who recognized her." The caption identified him as Kevin Day, a company director from Essex who had been on the same flight from New York as the dead woman, but his sharp suit and greedy expression had reminded Loretta at first glance of a City shark, gleefully announcing a hostile takeover bid. "He looks very pleased with himself."

Sam snorted as he filled her glass with orange juice. "Can you believe it? The guy was handing out business cards—seemed to think it was some kind of a business opportunity."

"What does he do?"

Another snort. "He sells mobile phones. Moment he saw all those journalists he was in hog heaven."

"Did he sit next to her? I mean, did he *talk* to her?" The flight to London took seven hours and Loretta knew from experience that a neighbor who was determined to make small talk was hard to ignore.

"I got the impression he tried"—he shrugged—"but nothing doing. He said there was a seat between them and he spent most of the night sleeping. When he did wake up she was reading a book, some kind of a blockbuster."

She read quickly through the story and looked up. "So they still don't know why she came to England?"

"Last time I spoke to the cops they were waiting to

hear from her folks—from the cops in Ohio, that is. Maybe she had an English boyfriend."

"Wait a minute." A point had occurred to Loretta and she was no longer listening. "It says here they confirmed her identity through *fingerprints*—they got her name from the airline and then they sent her fingerprints to the States—"

"So?" Sam sipped his coffee standing up.

"Well, surely that means she's got a criminal record? I mean, even under Reagan they didn't fingerprint the entire nation."

"So she's a junkie or something," he said dismissively. "I'm sure we'll find out. I'm kind of surprised the cops haven't called already, I told them I was staying here last night. Listen, Loretta"—he put down his cup and saucer, glanced at his watch—"I don't have much time, but I want to thank you for everything you're doing for Bridget."

"Oh—" She shook her head, unwilling to talk about Bridget after their row on Port Meadow the previous afternoon. "It's me who should be thanking you—for dinner last night, I mean. I haven't been there for ages." Sam had insisted on taking Loretta and Bridget out to eat at the Lebanese restaurant at the bottom of Walton Crescent, where he had impressed her by ordering a bottle of Chateau Musar without wincing at the price. She had enjoyed the meal less than she usually did because of the strained atmosphere between herself and Bridget, but Sam had given no sign that he was aware of the tension or of the longish gaps in the conversation.

"Glad you liked it. Is it OK with you—I wanted to ask if she could stay on here a while? Just till the cops finish up at the house."

She looked at him in surprise, having assumed that

112

Bridget would be going home today. "Yes. Yes, of course."

"Thanks, Loretta." He looked at his watch again, sounding relieved. "Will you excuse me? I'm going to give her another call, I have to leave in five minutes."

He went to the door and Loretta cleared her throat: "Sam?"

"Uh-huh?"

"Did Bridget . . . Oh, it doesn't matter."

"Hey, what is it?" He came back into the room.

"Nothing. This solicitor you mentioned. There's no chance of seeing him today?"

"He's in court. I checked." He reached out and moved the freesias a fraction to one side, standing back to study the effect. "Is that all?"

"Mmm. I'm just . . . you know."

He shook his head. "Tell me."

"Anxious. All these visits from the police. I'm probably worrying too much."

To her surprise, he studied her face for a moment, then sat down. "Loretta, I'm sorry—this is really getting to you, isn't it? I've been so concerned about Bridget I didn't think . . . Listen, hon, everything's going to be all right. I promise."

She shifted in her chair, uncomfortable with this sudden intimacy, and said quickly: "Then why did they come round twice yesterday? I don't like their *attitude*."

He laughed. "You should meet some of the cops we have back home. You ever hear of a guy called Darryl Gates? They're just pissed because they didn't get to her for so long, that's what the lawyer told me on the phone. They reckon to collect most of their evidence in the first forty-eight hours, after that it starts getting"—he narrowed his eyes and moved his hand gently from side to side—"you know, dicey." He leaned across

113

and patted her arm. "Don't *worry*. Listen, I really have to find out what's happened to Bridget—I have a meeting at nine."

"Life goes on?"

"Sure it does." He stood up. "Don't get me wrong, I'm sorry for the woman, but it's not like she's a relative or anything. Hey, you didn't have your croissant." He picked up the Blanc bag and held it out to her. "Go on, eat. You need your strength."

She reached inside, fingers closing on a croissant, and had lifted it to her lips before she smelled the almond paste. She was about to get up and exchange it for a plain one when it occurred to her that her blood sugar was probably low, and she bit into it anyway. The sweet, sticky pastry dissolved on her tongue, her teeth crunched on slivers of almonds, and she began to eat greedily, devouring the whole thing in half a dozen large bites and licking her fingers enthusiastically afterwards. She heard voices on the floor above and got up to make a pot of Earl Grey tea, expecting Bridget and Sam to appear in the kitchen at any moment, but they remained upstairs, conducting an animated discussion in the hall. Loretta warmed the pot, poured boiling water onto the loose tea and carried it to the table, glancing at the home-news pages of the paper while she allowed it to brew for a couple of minutes. She was just pouring an experimental inch into her cup, gazing in approval at the transparent golden liquid, when the cat flap clattered and Bertie trotted into the kitchen. He dropped a small, mangled corpse at her feet and sat down, stretching his front legs and jerking his head round in obedience to a sudden urge to wash his left flank. Then, satisfied that his toilet arrangements were complete, he gazed up at her adoringly and let out a soft yowl.

Loretta screwed up her nose, pushed back her chair

and reached for the roll of kitchen paper. She advanced on the cat stealthily, her hands protected by makeshift paper bandages, and was about to snatch his prey from under his nose when Bridget sauntered into the kitchen.

"Morning, Loretta."

The cat seized the corpse in his mouth and bolted. Loretta groaned, knowing he would probably sneak back later and hide it under a sofa or in a dusty corner of her study. "Honestly, Bridget," she complained, "I'd nearly got it."

"Never mind, he's taken it into the garden. Best place for it."

"He'll bring it back. Half the time I don't know where he's put them till they start to smell."

"Oh, well." Bridget shrugged. With a sudden access of delicacy, she lifted her nightclothes and skirted the minute bloodstains on the floor, dropped into a chair and poured herself a glass of orange juice.

"Mmm, this is what I call breakfast," she said, peering into the Blanc bag and taking out a croissant. Loretta raised her eyebrows, crumpled the unused kitchen paper from her hands into a thick wad and knelt to wipe the floor.

"What, will these tiny hands ne'er be clean?" Bridget intoned for no obvious reason, observing her with interest. "You look like Lady Macbeth in one of those minimalist modern productions. You know, Katherine Hamnett T-shirts and the witches with mobile phones."

"No," said Loretta, thinking she would have read about such a production if it really existed, "I don't." She got up and stuffed the soiled paper into the bin. "You're very cheerful this morning."

"Mmm," Bridget said again, glancing down at her croissant with a secretive smile on her lips. She offered no explanation for her late appearance, but finished her croissant with an abstracted air and lifted a freesia stem to her nose. "Sam doesn't do things by half, does he? Is there any coffee?"

Loretta, who had just filled her cup with tea and discovered it was stewed, reached for the cafetiere and dumped it next to Bridget's plate. "Has Sam gone?"

Bridget didn't answer at once, staring instead at the photograph of her husband on page two of the *Guardian*. "God, what a terrible picture of Sam." She groped for the coffee with her free hand, pouring it carelessly into her cup and allowing it to drip onto the tablecloth. "Yes, he had a meeting. Oh, they've released her name at last." She shook her head, confirming it meant nothing to her, and continued reading. When she had finished she tasted her coffee and immediately pulled a face. "Ugh, it's lukewarm. Is that tea you're making?"

Loretta nodded and Bridget got up, rinsed her cup out and returned to the table. She took up the paper again and flicked through it, folding it open at the letters page. "Oh, good, someone's written in about that piece last week. Did you see it, Loretta? Arguing against tax relief for childcare? Funny piece for the *Guardian* to have."

"No," said Loretta as the kettle boiled and she filled the teapot for a second time. She reached across and switched on the radio, thinking she might catch the nine-o'clock news on Radio Four, but the bulletin had just finished and the announcer was introducing the next program. She turned the dial irritably, searching for Radio Three but unable to remember its frequency. Her ghetto blaster was in a repair shop in Walton Street and the old wireless she had brought down from the attic was a monument to the early days of radio, marking obsolete stations like Hilversum and Daventry.

"Hang on," Bridget protested as a robotic bass line

blasted the kitchen and was quickly displaced by some-one speaking French. "That was Madonna."

"Was it?" Loretta continued her search, pausing over a few bars of country music.

"God, Loretta, don't be so stuffy. Madonna's great, she's so upfront about her sexuality—"

"She's an exhibitionist, and she can't sing."

"What's wrong with being an exhibitionist? At least she's in control, she knows exactly what she's doing."

"In control?" Loretta turned to stare at her. "Only of turning herself into a commodity, which is what women have had to do for centuries. It's true she's doing a better job of it than Marilyn Monroe, but do you really think that's progress?"

Bridget dropped her gaze and turned a page of the paper. "If someone *chooses* to make herself an object—"

"What?" Loretta demanded, turning the radio down. "I can't hear you."

"All I was saying," Bridget said, still in a low voice, "is that power relations aren't that simple. I mean, what you're overlooking is that a woman who chooses to put herself in a—in a certain type of role is actually making a powerful choice—"

"Blimey," said Loretta, "what have you been read-ing? The Marquis de Sade?"

"No." Bridget noisily folded the paper. "Forget it."

"All right." Wondering if she had missed something, Loretta turned the dial back until she heard the familiar breathy voice. "There you are," she said, "you can lis-ten to Madonna and I'll have my tea in the bath. I was going to have one anyway."

Bridget put down the paper and said rather aggres-sively: "What *is* wrong with you this morning? You're not still cross about . . . you know. Yesterday?"

117

"No," said Loretta, not wanting to continue the argument. She poured tea into her cup and held her hand out for Bridget's. "There's milk in the fridge if you want it."

"Loretta—"

"I'm tired, that's all, and I don't want to listen to Madonna. Is that strong enough for you?"

"Mmm, fine." Bridget watched her, visibly weighing up the pros and cons of saying more. She got up and went to the fridge, taking a bottle of milk from the door and adding a fraction to her tea. "Actually, Loretta," she began in a different tone, pressing the foil top back in place, "there's something I wanted to ask you. Could you do me a favor and run me over to the house later this morning? I really need my car—I had to wait twenty-five minutes for a taxi back from the John Radcliffe yesterday. It won't take long, promise."

"This morning?"

"Well, this afternoon if you're busy."

"No, let's get it over." It sounded much more ungracious than she intended and Loretta added: "Sorry, I didn't mean ... Is there any washing you'd like me to do? I'm going to put one on this morning."

"Yes, please," Bridget said hurriedly. "I haven't got much, but it'll save me going home with a bag of dirty washing."

"OK, put it in the machine—you know where it is." She picked up her cup. "Shall we say—what? About half ten?"

"Perfect. Thanks, Loretta."

"Hello, Bertie. Back again?" The cat had reappeared, minus dead rodent, and was rubbing himself against her legs. He followed her out of the room, overtaking her on the stairs and lying in wait to ambush her feet as she turned the corner.

"Careful," she said, trying not to spill her tea, and he bounded away into her study. She saw that the post was lying in an untidy heap by the front door and went to pick it up, her spirits sinking as she recognized two bills: her Visa statement and a renewal notice for her car insurance. She glanced briefly at a postcard from her sister Jenny, on holiday in Normandy with her family, and a couple of letters readdressed to her by the English-department secretary in London. Neither of them looked interesting and she put them on the hall table with the bills, turning over the blue air-mail envelope which had been at the bottom of the pile and raising her eyebrows when she recognized John Tracey's small, obsessively neat handwriting. She slid her finger under the flap and started to ease it open, then changed her mind and carried the letter and her undrunk tea upstairs to the bathroom. Sam's toilet bag, she noticed as she closed the door, was lined up neatly on the floor next to Bridget's, his damp shaving brush sticking out at one end. It seemed that he, too, proposed to stay at least one more night; Loretta sighed as she turned on the taps and wondered when she would have the house to herself again. She poured a generous quantity of oil into the bath, inhaling the steamy jasmine scent which immediately rose from the water, and reached behind her for the loo seat, lowering herself onto it as she tore open the blue envelope and began to read.

"You'll never guess who I heard from this morning," Loretta remarked an hour later as she waited to turn left into Woodstock Road. "John Tracey—I got a letter." The traffic was light and she pulled out, stopping rather abruptly for a couple of teenagers and a dog at a pelican crossing.

"What's he want?"

Loretta glanced at Bridget and laughed. "God, you're suspicious. Actually, to judge by the way his writing gets bigger towards the end, he may have been pissed when he wrote it. It's awfully rambling—there's a long bit about whether the car's all right and whether I'm having it serviced regularly. I mean, you'd think he'd just take the money and forget it." Tracey had persuaded Loretta to buy his three-year-old Golf, which he had owned from new, when her old Panda finally became too expensive to repair. "Then he goes on about the hotel he's staying in, something about the maid not changing his towels often enough and room service refusing to bring him a sandwich after ten o'clock."

"Typical. And you're supposed to be interested in his servant problems?"

"I said it was rambling. Anyway, the point seems to be—it's more of a hint than so many words, but I think he'd like us to get back together."

"He's not pissed, he's bonkers. What about that Greek girl he was going to marry? Is he into polygamy now, or what?"

"I gather that never came to anything. He came back to England on his own and—well, I didn't like to ask. With us being divorced, I mean."

"It's the male menopause, that's what it is. Why'd he write to you, anyway? Couldn't he ring you up?"

"The letter's postmarked Bucharest. He's been traveling all over Eastern Europe—didn't I tell you he's won a prize? He sounded, um, lonely."

Bridget squirmed in the passenger seat. "Christ, whoever designed this seat belt wasn't pregnant. Either you have it down here"—she patted her lap—"and it keeps riding up, or it's round your neck strangling you. Listen,

120

I've got a proposal for you as well—much more interesting than going back to that boring old hack."

"Bridget." Loretta slowed the car and joined the queue for the roundabout at the top of Woodstock Road, wishing she hadn't mentioned the letter. "Anyway," she said lightly, "you're already married."

"That's better. You know I'm going on maternity leave at the end of September? I thought you might like to stand in for me."

"Me?"

"Yes, why not? Wouldn't the money come in handy? This business of having lodgers, you wouldn't be doing it unless you needed the cash."

"It's not so bad, once you get used to it. Anyway, I can't possibly take on another job—I'm in London two days a week for a start. And ..."

"And what?"

"I've never ... I'm not an Oxbridge sort of person."

"Loretta!"

"Well, it's true. I did my first degree at Sussex, if you remember, and then my doctorate at Royal Holloway."

"I know—Egham. Very suburban."

"There you are, that's just what I mean. I *absolutely* wouldn't fit in."

"You might at least listen to what it involves."

Loretta swerved as the driver of a car on her left cut in front of her in his haste to get off the roundabout. "God, how much road do you want?" she called after his retreating back, then said without enthusiasm: "All right, what does it involve?"

"Two sets of lectures, basically. I know how you feel about *Clarissa*, so you can forget that, I'm sure I can talk Andrew Michell into taking it on. And I've switched Emily Dickinson to the spring term, which leaves the Brontës and Gothic."

"The Brontës and . . . the Gothic influence on *Wuthering Heights* is obvious, *Tales of Hoffman* and so on, but I don't see—"

"Oh, Loretta, don't be so literal. The Brontës, full stop. Gothic, full stop. Two different courses. You could teach the Brontës standing on your head. I read a bit of your chapter on *Shirley* when you left your laptop switched on the other day. It's terribly good."

"Thanks, but I really don't think—"

"We want the Kidlington road here." She sat back in her seat, still trying to find a comfortable position, as Loretta negotiated another roundabout. "OK, let's start again. There is something wrong with you this morning."

"With me?"

Bridget turned and made an exaggerated survey of the back seat. "I don't *think* there's anyone else in the car. You are upset about yesterday, aren't you?"

"No . . ."

"If you must know, I rang that inspector woman this morning, while you were having a bath, and told her I'd lost the bloody thing—the diary. So you're off the hook."

"What did she say?"

"What could she say? She was a bit sniffy about it but it's not a criminal offense, losing your diary. Don't start worrying about that. Now—tell me again why you can't teach Gothic?"

Loretta drove along the main road into Kidlington, glancing to her left in search of one of the few landmarks she knew, a vet's surgery where she occasionally took Bertie. "I don't know much about it, that's all. I've read *Frankenstein*, of course, and *The Mysteries of Udolpho*, but not for a long time . . . I'd have to do a huge amount of reading."

Bridget grinned. "I could let you see my paper for *Praeternatura*," she offered. "My ground-breaking exegesis of the role of sexual anxiety in the development of English Gothic."

"Your what?"

"Sounds good, doesn't it? They made me put that because they said the original title was too jokey."

"What was it?"

"*Some Enchanted Evening.* It's all about that night at the Villa Diodati when Mary Shelley got the idea for *Frankenstein.* Remember?"

"Vaguely."

"Course you do, it's all in the Preface. So there they all are: Byron, Shelley, Claire Clairmont—who, incidentally, is the real heroine of that bunch—Mary Shelley, Polidori."

"So that's why you were looking him up in the Bodleian."

"In the—?" Bridget sounded blank for a moment. "Oh yes, in the Bodleian ... Anyway, it's dark, it's raining, they've been reading ghost stories and they're all pissed off. Byron because his wife's left him and he's congenitally gloomy anyway, Polidori because he's jealous of Byron, and Mary—Mary's had all these babies and miscarriages and she's getting fed up with Shelley and his progressive ideas. She was very conservative in her old age, you know. This particular summer, though, she's obsessed with Byron—"

"You've written this for what?"

"*Praeternatura.* They're a bunch of Gothic groupies at the University of Western Wisconsin who publish their own quarterly journal—glossy cover, personal ads from English professors who want house swaps with counts in Transylvania. Only kidding," she added, seeing Loretta's face. "Actually, I've always promised myself I'll go to their annual convention one summer, they go to wonderful places like Romania. Anyway, as I was saying, there's all this frustrated passion, jealousy, intrigue . . ."

"Sounds more like Mills and Boon."

"Loretta."

"Sorry."

". . . with Byron the absolute center, and the result is—Frankenstein's monster."

"You've lost me."

Bridget made an impatient sound. "What I'm saying is, Byron *is* Frankenstein's monster. I know the usual theory is that it's Shelley, but you think about it for a minute. They're both physically deformed—just about *the* most famous thing about Byron is his club foot— and they both have this extraordinary charisma. You know the way from here, Loretta?" They were now on the other side of Kidlington, heading north on the road to Banbury.

"Mmm."

"Slow down then—it's the next right."

Loretta was already braking and she did a fast right turn, just missing a big red Citroën traveling in the opposite direction. The driver hooted furiously as his car sped past the side road.

"Christ, Loretta."

"Sorry. I was thinking about your theory."

"I'd better shut up if that's the effect it's going to have. I wasn't intending to die for it."

"No, go on, we're nearly there."

"OK, if you promise not to fling us in a ditch. Where's Frankenstein the first time he sees the monster? *In bed*. It's practically a seduction scene." She sounded outraged. "There's this powerful mixture of attraction and repulsion, and you can argue—I do, in fact—that Mary's unconscious sexual guilt has transformed the person she loves into a monstrous aberration."

"I'll park round the back, shall I?"

"I should think so. Uh-oh—what are those cars doing here?" Bridget swiveled her head as they passed several empty saloons parked in a line next to the garden wall of Thebes Farm.

"Police?" suggested Loretta, signaling right and driving slowly round into the farmyard on the other side of the house. A little group of people turned to stare incuriously as she parked the car, their blank expressions reminding Loretta of deer at a water hole in a wildlife film; seconds later a ripple of recognition went through them and they surged towards the car, dispelling any doubt as to which was the hunter and which the prey.

"Oh, God," Bridget gasped, "let's get out of here," but a middle-aged man was already pulling open the passenger door, his colleagues pressing in on him from behind so he almost fell into her lap. Loretta flung open her own door and discovered her escape route blocked by an excited reporter who thrust a tabloid newspaper in her face and shouted questions which she was quite unable to hear. To her left Bridget burst into tears and Loretta panicked, jamming her finger on the horn and keeping it there as the startled rat pack fell back from the car. Bridget, with greater presence of mind than Loretta had expected, pulled the passenger door shut and locked it, a maneuver Loretta was unable to imitate because she was afraid to take her finger off the horn.

"Can you close mine?" she shouted above the racket, but at that moment help appeared in the shape of a uniformed policeman who hurried round the corner of the house followed by a man in jeans and a bomber jacket.

"Thank God," cried Loretta, cutting off the noise as

125

the two men ducked under the blue-and-white tape and shooed the reporters out of the yard.

"Must be the first time in history they're actually here when you want them," Bridget observed, wiping her eyes with the back of her hand as she began to get out of the car. Her breathing slightly labored, she faced the two men and demanded: "Who's in charge here?"

The man in the bomber jacket glanced down at her stomach. "Mrs.—Dr. Bennett? Sorry about that. We weren't expecting you."

Bridget frowned. "No reason why you should have been. What are they all doing here, anyway? I thought there might be one or two but nothing like this." She waved towards the journalists who had withdrawn to the road.

"You haven't seen this morning's papers?"

"Only the *Guardian*." Loretta walked round the car to join them. "I'm Loretta Lawson, by the way. Bridget's staying with me."

"Oh, yes." He nodded, looking and sounding distinctly jumpy. "Sergeant Crisp. We're just tying up a few loose ends—"

Bridget said abruptly: "Where's my car?"

"Your car?"

"Yes, a maroon Astra. It was parked over there, where that car is." She indicated an empty police car on the other side of the yard.

"I believe the, er, the forensic team are having a look at it this morning."

"They've taken my car? Without my permission?"

"Mr. Becker said—"

"What? You mean Sam—" Bridget shot a bewildered look at Loretta, who merely shrugged.

"We did speak to Mr. Becker about both cars," the detective was saying diplomatically.

"*Both* cars? You mean you've got his as well?"

"Mr. Becker's car has been examined, yes."

"This is—this is outrageous. I'm going to complain to—" She turned and appealed to Loretta. "Who do I complain to?"

"There is a standard procedure involving the Police Complaints Authority. But I think you'll find—"

"*Jesus.* The garden—what've you done to the garden?" She took a few steps towards the blue-and-white tape, surveying the scene beyond it. "Was it"—she turned back to the Sergeant—"was it really necessary to destroy the garden?"

Loretta went to stand beside her, gazing in astonishment at the trampled turf, the mounds of soil where the herbaceous borders had been uprooted, the trees and shrubs thrown into careless heaps. "God," she breathed, awed by the scale of the destruction. She turned to the detective, who was now looking as though he would like to crawl under one of the mounds of earth and hide. "What's the point—what were you hoping to find?"

He mumbled something about the murder weapon but Bridget ignored him. "Are you coming, Loretta?" she demanded.

"Where?"

"Into the house." Bridget spoke in a loud voice, casting a contemptuous look at the embarrassed policemen. "We'd better find out what else these—these *Nazis* have been up to. See how large the compensation claim's going to be." She lifted the scene-of-crime tape and stepped under it, letting out a little gasp of distress or pain. Loretta trailed after her, preoccupied with her sudden realization that this was the real reason Sam had wanted to delay Bridget's return to Thebes Farm and wishing he had had the sense to confide in her.

"Loretta!" Bridget stuck her head out of the open

front door, and gestured fiercely for her to enter the house.

"Coming." She got as far as the porch, a hollow feeling in her chest which she diagnosed as mild shock, and turned to check that the damage really was as bad as it seemed. From this angle it looked even worse—as though, she thought with a shudder, someone had made a clumsy attempt to clean up after a natural disaster, a hurricane or a tidal wave. A movement on the periphery of her vision made her turn and she saw the uniformed policeman come to an abrupt halt on the path, looking up at the sky as though he was unaware of her presence. It dawned on her that he had been sent to spy on them, that Bridget wasn't even allowed to visit her own house without being kept under discreet surveillance, a suspicion which was confirmed when she turned on her heel and he immediately made to follow. Nudging away the brick which served as a makeshift doorstop with her undamaged foot, Loretta moved smartly into the hall and took intense pleasure in slamming the door in the PC's astonished face.

7

"WELL, THAT'S ONE MYSTERY SOLVED," LO-retta announced, dumping a couple of newspapers on the table in front of Bridget. "Wait a minute," she added as Bridget read a headline and opened her mouth to ex-claim. "First things first. Have you ordered?"

"He's bringing some mineral water. I don't really feel like eating."

"I do." Loretta, who was suddenly ravenous, picked up the menu and went to the bar. She nodded to the bar-man, whom she knew by sight, and ordered ham, eggs and chips, then turned over the menu to look at the list of beers: "And a Corona."

She returned to the table, pleased that she had sug-gested coming here instead of the more crowded Browns, and took off her jacket. The tables were large, easily accommodating six, and as often as not Loretta and Bridget had to share, usually with people who worked in the OUP building round the corner in Walton Street. Today, though, the bar was quiet.

"This"—Bridget held up a paper as Loretta slid onto the seat beside her—"this is unbelievable. I mean, does

129

she look like a bank robber?" She turned to an inside page and indicated a small photograph.

"Hang on, I haven't had a proper look." Loretta leaned sideways to get a better view. "She certainly doesn't. I mean—plaits?"

"And that blouse."

"What she looks like," said Loretta, studying the picture over Bridget's shoulder, "is a member of the Hitler Youth. You know, all those pictures of German womanhood greeting the Führer circa 1936. I mean, it's fifty years out of date." She was silent for a moment, then exclaimed with increasing confidence: "And there's something fishy about it. If they're so sure it's her, why not put it on the front page?"

"They've got Geena Davis on the front page," said Bridget, glancing back for a moment.

"So I noticed—any excuse for a sexy picture. I suppose it *could* be from a school play or something," she went on, thinking aloud about the photograph on page five, "since she only looks about twelve."

"It says here it was taken by the police when they arrested her."

"*No*—I don't believe it. Have you ever heard of someone dressing up like Hansel and Gretel and ramraiding their local Nat West?"

"It says here she chucked a brick through the window."

"Weirder and weirder. I thought banks had reinforced glass these days—you know, the sort where you throw the brick and it comes flying back at you."

"Maybe not in Ohio. I mean, it's hardly Chicago. Maybe she comes from some folksy little town where everyone knows everyone else and they all go to barn dances on Saturday nights."

"Then how come she robs banks?"

"*A* bank."

Loretta tugged gently at the paper. "Let's see, I only skimmed it in the shop."

The waiter placed an open bottle of Corona with a chunk of lime wedged in its rim on the table. He was also carrying a glass which he held up before Loretta in a silent question.

"Yes, please," she said, not wanting to drink straight from the bottle. "And I think my friend ordered some mineral water."

He was immediately contrite. "Sorry. But no food, right?"

"Well . . ."

"Go on. It'll make you feel better."

"All right." Bridget picked up the menu. "I'll have the—the hot chicken salad." As the waiter returned to the bar, she admitted: "I did promise Audrey yesterday—regular meals, afternoon naps. I'm supposed to be the perfect patient."

Loretta reflected that the perfect patient would now be in hospital, tucked up in bed, but she said nothing and tugged at the paper again. "Come on, let's have a look."

Bridget relinquished it. "Murder Girl Was Bank Job Grass," Loretta read, and, in smaller letters, "Dead Blonde's Amazing Secret." The report accompanying these slightly delphic announcements was tagged "World Exclusive" even though Loretta could think of large areas of the globe where the story would arouse as much interest as the color of John Major's underpants. Holding the paper slightly away from her, she began, with some skepticism, to read the breathless tabloidese:

The attractive blonde found murdered near Oxford on Sunday may have been *on the run* from a gang of bank robbers, we can reveal today.

131

The victim, named last night as American Paula Wolf, 20, was a member of a daring gang which included members of her own family, sources have revealed.

In an amazing parallel with the hit film *Thelma & Louise*, in which glamorous actresses Susan Sarandon and Geena Davis (left) go on a crime spree, three members of the gang were women.

Wolf, whose naked body was found by partygoers in the garden of an Oxford don, may (cont. on page five, column three) have fled to England to escape a revenge attack from members of the gang, who call themselves the Copycats.

Her evidence helped put other gang members, including her elder sister, behind bars. Two members of the gang were recently released from prison.

The gang's daring daylight raid shocked inhabitants of the small town of Oak Falls, Ohio, population 6,802. Terrified cashiers and customers dived for cover as the five-strong gang smashed windows at the Flatlands Savings & Loan Bank and stormed inside.

British detectives were tight-lipped about these sensational developments last night. They have no idea how Wolf, who arrived in England on July 25 on a flight from New York's Kennedy airport, got to Oxford or how her body came to be concealed in the garden of the secluded £250,000 house.

A post-mortem carried out on Monday showed that Wolf died of head injuries. Police have still not revealed whether she had been sexually assaulted.

The owner of the murder house, English don Mrs. Bridget Bennett, who is married but uses her maiden name, is expecting her first child in November. She has not been seen at home since Sunday and is believed to be staying at a secret address in Oxford.

Her husband, Mr. Sam Becker, who is also American, appeared without her at a press conference in Oxford yesterday. "My wife and I are deeply shocked," he said. "Whoever did this must be caught before he strikes again."

Loretta lowered the paper. "Doesn't sound like Sam," she observed, "this my-wife-and-I stuff."

Bridget shrugged. "They probably made it up." She had been reading the second paper bought by Loretta on her way to the wine bar and now she remarked: "They're amazing, these psychics—the Contessa, I mean." She pointed at a front-page picture of their glamorous visitor of the previous afternoon, her eyes half closed in what might equally be a state of sexual ecstasy or a trance. "First she says the murderer has a beard, then she hedges her bets and says he may have shaved it off. The only other clue she comes up with is the letter *S*—I mean, how many people have an *S* in their names?"

"Everyone called Smith, for a start. I read somewhere there are 600,000 of them."

"Brilliant. How much do you think she gets paid for all this?"

"Hi, sorry I'm late." Sam appeared at their table, leaning forward to kiss first Bridget and then Loretta on the cheek before unbuttoning his mackintosh and folding it neatly on the far side of the horseshoe-shaped seat. He pulled out a stool and sat down, giving his head a slight shake. "Jesus, what a morning." He breathed out heavily and said by way of explanation: "You wouldn't believe how persistent these guys are, they call every few minutes." He picked up the menu. "Have you ordered?"

"Yes, but I'm still waiting for my mineral water." Bridget waved to attract the barman's attention and made a pouring motion with her hand. His mouth dropped open and he made a pantomime apology before seizing an empty glass and heaping ice into it.

Sam said: "OK, what's good?"

"I'm having ham and eggs"—Loretta pointed to it on the menu—"but I can recommend the kedgeree."

"Niçoise salad, I guess that'll do," he murmured as though she had not spoken. The barman brought Bridget's mineral water and he repeated the order, adding: "And one of those—a Corona." He waited until the barman moved away, then went on: "They all want to know my reaction to this stuff"—he indicated the MURDER GIRL WAS BANK JOB GRASS headline—"and they don't like what I've got to say. Which is, I thought the *National Enquirer* was bad enough—"

"Hold on," Bridget said impatiently, "I want to know about the garden. Have you spoken to Jim?"

"No, I told you, he's doing a job down in Essex. But I left another message with his wife."

"She does realize it's urgent?"

"Hon, don't give me a hard time. I'm doing my best. When they told me they were going to dig I asked them to make sure to cover the roots with earth, it isn't as bad as it looks."

"And the lawn? What about the lawn?"

"OK, so it'll have to be turfed. For Christ's sake, Bridget, if you hadn't gone over there without telling me you wouldn't ever have known. I was trying to *protect* you."

"I'm not a *child*."

"Let's change places," Loretta interjected, anticipating a full-scale row. "Come on, I'll have the stool."

Sam said: "OK." He moved out of her way while she slid out, then flopped on the seat next to Bridget.

"I'm sorry," they said together, and reached for each other's hands. Loretta averted her eyes, shifting her stool and pretending to have spotted something under the table. There was a kissing noise and a moment later she heard Sam say: "Hey, Loretta, I almost forgot. I had a call from your husband."

She forgot her embarrassment and turned to him in astonishment. "My husband?"

"She hasn't got a husband."

"Guy called John Tracey? He called just as I was leaving, that's why I was late."

Loretta stared at him. "He called you?" she asked, unconsciously imitating Sam's speech pattern. "What for?"

"He's a reporter, right? Elaine talked to him and when she said he was your husband I guess I was intrigued. He seems like a nice guy. I told him I was meeting you for lunch and he said could you call him." He glanced at his watch. "Is there a phone in this place? He didn't know what time he'd be leaving the office."

"Leaving?"

"Yeah, he's coming to Oxford."

"To—" Loretta bit her lip, aware that Bridget was watching her intently.

"Niçoise salad?" The arrival of their food was a welcome distraction and she jumped to her feet, calling over her shoulder to the surprised waiter: "I won't be a minute."

She hurried through the swing doors at the far end of the room, pausing in the corridor on the other side where a public telephone faced the door to the gents'.

135

There were half a dozen coins in her purse and she fed them all into the slot, punching in a sequence of figures before she remembered that the *Sunday Herald* had recently moved to Docklands. It took her a moment to summon up the new number but the female voice which answered her call in a slurred monotone was reassuringly familiar.

"John Tracey, please."

"Trying to connect you." There was silence for a few seconds, followed by an internal ringing tone.

"Tracey."

She had forgotten the curt way he answered the phone when he was working. She grimaced and said: "John? It's me—Loretta."

"Hi. How are you?" His voice was warm, unsurprised; it was as if they were picking up a conversation begun two days ago.

"Fine. Sam, Sam Becker that is, he says you're coming to Oxford."

"That's right. The cops have called a press conference at four."

"I wouldn't have thought—it doesn't seem like your sort of story. I thought you only did foreign stuff these days."

"Oh, any excuse to come to Oxford." Loretta moved her weight from one foot to the other, uncertain how to react to this apparent attempt at gallantry, but then he added: "My old stamping ground, you know. There are one or two people I'd like to look up." Tracey had been a mature student at Ruskin, a piece of his history which had temporarily slipped Loretta's mind. "Did you get my letter?"

"What?"

"My letter. Did it arrive?"

"Yes." The doors from the restaurant swung open and

a woman appeared, a striking blonde in a very short skirt who was on her way to the ladies' toilet. Loretta turned her face to the wall and bent her head over the mouthpiece. "I—it arrived this morning."

"This morning? Christ, it would have been quicker to bring it back and post it in Brixton. Listen, how are you fixed for dinner?"

"Dinner? When?"

"Tonight. I'm booked into the Randolph, I always fancied staying there when I was a student."

"The Randolph?" She felt a little surge of relief at the discovery that he did not, as she had feared, expect to stay in Southmoor Road. "I read about your award in the *Guardian*," she said suddenly. "Congratulations."

"I've only been nominated," he said, dismissing it. "About tonight, I know it's short notice. We could make it tomorrow if you're busy."

"No, I . . ." Uncertain of her feelings, she changed the subject again. "Sam said you talked to him about the murder."

"Not so much the murder as the press coverage. You've seen today's papers?"

"Yes, we've just been reading them."

"Yeah, well, the tabloids are supposed to have cleaned up their act because of Calcutt but—"

Loretta had been watching her money dwindle and now the illuminated display was flashing zero. "John, I'm sorry, my money's run out. Ring me when you get to Oxford?"

"OK. *Ciao*, Loretta."

She walked slowly back along the corridor and through the swing doors, realizing they hadn't come to any arrangement about dinner that evening. She was aware before she looked up that Bridget was watching her progress, agog to hear about her conversation with

Tracey, and she was as much relieved as surprised when the barman appeared at her elbow clutching a plate.

"I put it under the lights to keep warm," he explained, sliding her ham and eggs onto the table, and Loretta was able to resume her seat without responding to Bridget's unspoken question. She busied herself with spreading a paper napkin on her skirt and sprinkling salt on her chips, until Bridget could contain herself no longer.

"Well?" she demanded. "How was the great journalist?"

Loretta waited until her mouth was empty. "We couldn't really talk, my money ran out."

"Have you arranged to see him?"

"Hon," Sam said warningly.

"He's going to ring later." Loretta speared a chip and was about to lift it to her mouth when she remembered something. "This press conference," she said to Sam, "are you going?"

"Press conference?" Sam seemed surprised. "This afternoon?"

"So Tracey says. I assumed you knew."

He shook his head, thought for a moment, then shrugged and continued eating. "I guess I'm not invited to this one."

Loretta put down her fork. "But how will we know if anything—if there are any developments?"

Sam gave her a slightly pitying look. "It's a *press* conference, Loretta. All you have to do is turn on the TV news."

She felt her cheeks grow red. "They don't report *everything*," she said defensively. "John used to say—"

He stopped her with an impatient gesture. "If your ex is going to be there, what's the problem? You've got your own deep throat."

Loretta frowned, thinking of the pornographic film, then realized he was talking about the mole who leaked inside information about the Watergate scandal to the *Washington Post*. She smiled ruefully at her mistake, recognizing it as a symptom of sexual anxiety, and told herself she was getting far too worked up about a simple dinner invitation. Sam was looking at her, apparently waiting for a reply to a question she had not heard, and she said: "What did you say?"

"I said, how long were you guys married?"

"Oh, I'd have to work it out."

Bridget said crisply: "Too long. He's bad news as far as Loretta's concerned, John Tracey."

Sam frowned. "What is this, hon? He seemed a nice enough guy on the phone."

Bridget looked at Loretta and mouthed a single word: *"Men."* Loretta responded with a minute shake of her head, dipped a chip into the yolk of one of her eggs and got on with her meal in thoughtful silence.

The banging on the front door was loud and insistent, so loud that whoever it was appeared not to hear Loretta's irritable assurance: "I'm *coming*." She flung open the door and found a sinister figure on the step, a tall man dressed from neck to toe in black leather and carrying what looked like a space helmet under one arm.

"Do you have to make all that noise?" she demanded, her momentary fright receding as she realized he was merely a motorcycle messenger.

"Package for Mr. Tracey," he said impassively and held out a Jiffy bag.

"Mr. Tracey?"

"This is the right address?" He showed her the label on the package.

"Yes, but John Tracey doesn't *live* here."

"Are you going to sign for it or not?"

"Oh, all right." She scribbled her name on his clip-board and he strode off, climbed onto a large motorbike parked a few yards up Southmoor Road and revved the engine with savage force.

"It wasn't my car then?" Bridget, who had been taking a nap in the front bedroom, came downstairs rubbing her eyes.

"No, it was someone dropping off a parcel for John Tracey." Loretta closed the front door and examined the package more carefully, observing that the address label was adorned with a trendy logo and an address in Dean Street.

"God, he's got a cheek. Why couldn't he have it delivered to his hotel?"

"I don't know. It feels"—Loretta turned it over, squeezing the object inside—"it feels like a book. Or a video."

"Open it."

"I can't do that."

"Course you can. It's your house."

Loretta laid the package flat on the hall table as though temptation might get the better of her if she held on to it any longer. "I'll ring the Randolph," she said. "He should have arrived by now."

"What time is it?" Bridget yawned and started down the stairs to the kitchen.

Loretta looked at her watch. "Just gone six."

"Just gone *six*? Where the hell's my car? They *promised* they'd bring it back this afternoon."

Loretta shrugged. "Why not give them a ring after I've phoned the Randolph?"

"All right. Fancy a cup of tea?"

"Yes, please. I'll be down in five minutes." Loretta

went into her study, lifted down the Oxford telephone directory and looked up the number of the Randolph Hotel. She dialed, asked for John Tracey and was told he was out.

"Can I leave a message? Would you ask him to ring Loretta? No, Loretta—that's it. Thanks."

She was halfway down the stairs when the doorbell sounded very faintly and she went back, half expecting to find Tracey on the doorstep. Instead, she opened the door to a young woman who held up a bunch of keys and said breezily: "Mrs. Bennett?"

"No. Are those her car keys?"

"That's right. I've left it back there, in the residents' parking."

Loretta turned as she heard Bridget come up behind her. "Your car's here, I'll have to give you a visitor's parking permit."

"About bloody time," Bridget said ungraciously.

The policewoman was unruffled. "Could one of you sign here, please?"

Loretta stepped back to allow Bridget to pass, and heard the phone chirrup in her study. "Excuse me," she said, and went to answer it.

"Loretta." It was Tracey's voice, low and urgent.

"A package came for you," she said. "By messenger."

"Oh, right." He didn't explain, didn't even seem to be interested. "We need to talk."

"What about dinner?"

"Fine, but something's come up."

"Because I had an idea," she said, aware that her voice suddenly sounded high and unnatural. "You've never seen this house and I thought it might be nice if we ate here. I walked over to the covered market this

141

afternoon, after I spoke to you, and there's this terribly good place where they make their own pasta—"

He said abruptly: "Bridget's staying with you, isn't she?"

"Yes."

"Then I don't think that's a very good idea."

"Come on, John, I know you've never liked her . . ." Loretta lowered her voice as the front door closed and Bridget went past the open door on her way to the kitchen. "Can't you make an effort for one evening? Sam'll be here and I'm sure he won't mind talking to you about the tabloids. It's not like you to pass up the chance of a story."

"You don't understand."

"Yes, I do. We can have dinner on our own any old night, there's no need to rush things. I mean, we've hardly seen each other in the last couple of years—"

"I'm not *talking* about us, Loretta. Loretta?"

"Sorry," said Bridget's voice, "I didn't realize you were still on the phone." There was a click as she put down the kitchen extension.

Tracey groaned: "This is impossible."

"Please, John. I told her I was going to invite you, and I've bought all this food. What am I supposed to say to her?"

He sighed. "All right. I assume her feelings won't be terminally hurt if you and I have a quiet talk before we eat?"

Loretta rolled her eyes upwards. "Course not."

"This package," he said abruptly. "Does it look like a video?"

"That sort of size, yes."

"Do you still have a VCR?"

"Yes."

"Oh, well, that's something. Listen, I have to call the

office and I've got a couple of other calls to make. Shall we say about seven?"

"Fine. See you then."

The line went dead and she put the phone down, belatedly wondering if he knew how to get to Southmoor Road. She decided against ringing back, guessing he would be on the phone to the *Sunday Herald*, and went downstairs to the kitchen.

"Sorry," Bridget said again, pouring tea into two mugs. "I was hoping to catch Sam before he left."

Loretta pointed to the phone. "Go ahead."

"Doesn't matter. Is he coming to supper?"

"Mmm."

Bridget narrowed her eyes. "I hope you know what you're doing."

Loretta reached for the mug without milk, picked it up and sipped her tea.

"Aren't you going to say anything?"

"What can I say? You two have never got on."

"*You* two have never got on is more to the point. You were *miserable* with him, Loretta. Don't you remember?"

"He's coming to supper, not planning our second wedding. Can we skip the lecture? I don't criticize Sam."

"Sam?" She looked startled. "There's no comparison."

Loretta said nothing.

"Why are you looking at me like that?"

"Like what?" Loretta went to the fridge, remarking over her shoulder: "As you say, there's no comparison."

Bridget thought for a moment. "Sarcasm doesn't suit you," she said finally. "You used to be so—direct."

Loretta straightened up and shut the fridge door, a plastic bag in her hand. "Does Sam like black pasta?

143

It's very fresh, they were making it when I went into the shop."

Bridget looked blank. "I doubt if he's had it. What makes it black?"

"Squid ink. I thought I'd made a tuna and lemon sauce. Why don't you get dressed and I'll get on with it?"

"OK. When's the—when's Tracey arriving?"

"Sevenish. I think he wants to watch that video first."

"Video? The one that was biked over? What's it all about?"

"He didn't say."

"Didn't you ask him?"

Loretta emptied the pasta, long black strings of spaghetti coiled together into thick hanks, onto a plate. "No, as a matter of fact. There—doesn't it look great?"

Bridget did not seem very sure. "What's it taste like?"

"Fishy. I thought you were going to get dressed."

Bridget drifted towards the door, then remembered something and turned. "Have you heard any news since we got back?"

"I heard the headlines at five but they didn't mention the press conference, if that's what you mean."

"Oh." Bridget pursed her lips, appeared to be on the verge of saying something but changed her mind and went upstairs. Loretta watched her go and then began assembling her ingredients: a red onion, a head of papery pink garlic, small tins of tuna and chopped tomatoes, a jar of capers and a ripe lemon. Her spirits lifted now she was alone and she began to hum a tune, a Puccini aria, as she coaxed the fat garlic cloves out of their skins, placed them on a wooden board with a handful of capers and started to chop.

8

"YOU ARE SERIOUS? THIS ISN'T SOME KIND OF, I don't know . . ."

"A joke? Does it sound like one?"

"No." Loretta paced up and down the drawing room, arms folded across her chest. For Tracey's visit she had changed into a low-necked black Lycra top which now seemed entirely inappropriate to the occasion and a long narrow skirt which, far from feeling sexy, strained against her calves and hobbled her anxious stride. It was hardly the moment to disappear upstairs and slip into something more comfortable, so she halted at the window with her back to Tracey and said: "It sounds . . . ridiculously far-fetched. I mean, there's no connection, there can't be."

She heard a clink as Tracey finished his drink and disposed of his glass on the coffee table. He was silent for a moment and she could picture his face, irritation fading as his sense of fairness asserted itself and he tried to think of a way to explain.

"What you've got to understand," he said finally, "is how the police work these days—the pressure they're under. The tabloids, they don't make any distinction between a murder and a new soap opera. Each day's another episode and if there isn't a sensational development they make it up, it's a sort of feeding frenzy. Christ, would you like to run a murder inquiry with the *Sun* breathing down your neck? Not to mention having to go on *Crimewatch* and MPs banging on in Parliament about the clear-up rate. Did I ever tell you there was a rumor Mrs. Thatcher was going to go up to Leeds and take over the Yorkshire Ripper inquiry herself if they didn't stop making a mess of it?"

Loretta turned, her eyes wide with interest. "Did she?" Then she remembered the subject of their conversation and filed this juicy tidbit away for another occasion. "Did he explain, this cop you talked to, why on earth Bridget would want to bump off a complete stranger and hide the body in her own garden? Assuming, as I suppose we must, that a pregnant woman suffering from high blood pressure is *capable* of transporting a corpse—"

Tracey gritted his teeth. "Calm down, Loretta, it wasn't like that. All he was doing was marking my cards."

"Sorry?"

"Giving me a steer. Off the record, just to let me know the way they're thinking."

"Blacken someone's name, you mean, without giving them a chance to answer back? I think that's terrible."

"Loretta, you may not like it but there's a relationship between the cops and the press—a symbiosis, to use one of your long words. They tell us things off the record, it gives us an idea where the story's going—what angles we need to have covered. All he said was they're not one hundred percent satisfied that your mate and her husband are in the clear. What is all this about her losing her diary, anyway?"

146

"Keep your voice down," she hissed, playing for time. "They're only one floor down, they'll hear you." She had introduced Tracey to Sam and then left him in earnest conversation with Bridget—something about a problem with the landscape gardeners and whether they should employ another firm—in the kitchen.

Tracey shook his head and felt in his jacket pocket. "This wasn't my idea," he said more quietly, drawing out a packet of Gitanes. "*If* you remember."

"You've started smoking again?"

He put a cigarette in his mouth, struck a match and lit up. "It's a stressful occupation, journalism." He got up, looking for somewhere to discard the spent match, and Loretta watched him prowl the room with the familiar coiled energy of someone used to dodging bullets and having doors closed in his face. She had not yet got over her surprise at his outfit, a cream linen suit which marked a startling break with his long-standing attachment to the fashion of the 1960s, and she felt an unexpected pang of nostalgia for his crumpled old denim and corduroys.

"In my study," she said shortly, seeing he was about to toss the match into the empty grate. "You'll find an ashtray on top of the filing cabinet." He strolled to the other end of the room, glancing from side to side with the professional interest of a reporter, and it occurred to her that his prematurely gray hair had been a blessing in disguise. While other middle-aged men had to live with creeping signs of physical decay, Tracey had done his aging early and had the knack of remaining a slightly more lined version of his youthful self.

"I don't let it get above ten a day," he remarked, picking up the ashtray and dropping the match into it.

Loretta moved towards him, not quite into the study but close enough to speak in a low voice. "Do they know about us?" she said, as near as she dared get to the question she really wanted to ask.

He blew out smoke. "Are they expecting me to report back, is that what you mean? Well, Chief Superintendent, I passed on your suspicions to my ex-wife as requested and she broke down and confessed ... You've accused me of a lot of things, Loretta, but this is the first time you've accused me of being a copper's nark. Don't you remember Roderick Benson?"

"Roderick—yes." Benson was a small-time south London crook, wrongly convicted of murder, whose case Tracey had successfully taken up on his return from Cyprus.

She slumped against the doorframe, lifting her head to look at the hinge impressions, still visible through several coats of paint, which marked the point from which big old wooden doors had once hung. "I don't know what to say," she admitted at last, pushing her hair back from her face. "I mean, she hasn't confided in me. Whatever she was doing that day, though, I'm sure it hasn't anything to do with ... this."

Tracey stubbed out his cigarette and leaned back against the filing cabinet. He said reasonably: "You've got to admit it doesn't look good. There they are, trying to piece together where everyone was on the day the victim arrived in England, and Bridget gives the vaguest possible account of herself *and* claims to have lost her diary. Would *you* write it off as sheer coincidence?"

She made an impatient gesture. "Has Sam told them what he was doing that Thursday?"

Tracey raised his eyebrows, picking up the antagonism in her voice. "Interesting point. His secretary was on holiday that week and he had a temp. She *thinks* he was in his office all day, but she's as thick as two short planks and their offices are on opposite sides of the corridor. However," he added, before she could speak, "this being the age of computers he's got a much better alibi than some dozy girl. Ever heard of an audit trail?"

Loretta shook her head.

"It's basically a security measure." Tracey moved to her desk, lifted the lid of her laptop and switched it on. "It tells you who's used the computer and what for—very useful if you think someone's trying to get into files they're not authorized to see. Industrial espionage and so on. In this case the audit trail has him logging on just before ten and staying on virtually all day. Neat little machine you've got here—what software do you use?"

"Word something? I can't remember. But how does it, the computer, know it was Sam? Couldn't he have left it on, hypothetically I mean, and someone else was actually doing the work?"

Tracey snapped off the blue screen. "No, because they use a repeat authentication process. You have to put your password in at regular intervals, and they use a handshaking system in case someone discovers your password."

"A what?"

"I don't know the technical details, but each time you put in your password it asks you a series of questions—anything from the name of your dog to your wife's star sign. If someone else was standing in for him, he'd have to be very fully briefed—an accomplice, in fact."

"Oh," Loretta said quickly, "I never really thought . . . Presumably it only matters till they find out when she was killed? I mean, as soon as they find someone who saw her alive after Thursday—"

"*If* someone saw her after Thursday. The sightings they've had so far are either vague or unlikely—"

"Sightings? You mean people have come forward?"

"Don't get excited, these things take days to sift through and they mostly come to nothing. She seems to have been a complete stranger in this country, and so far no one's come forward to say she booked into my hotel for two nights. All they've had is people who *think* they may have served her in a shop and the usual bunch of loonies." He swiveled her desk chair round and sat on it with his back to the desk, swinging gently from side to side. "The other question is, how far do you go, chasing red herrings, when someone's behaving suspiciously right under your nose? The cops almost never fit up people they think are innocent," he added conversationally, leaning back and picking up a post-card lying on her desk. He examined the image, an illustration from a fifteenth-century edition of the *Roman de la Rose*, without much interest and turned it over to read the message on the back. Discovering it was blank, he tossed it to one side and added: "Most miscarriages of justice, the famous ones, you'll find cops to this day who think they're guilty. The most they'll admit is that someone in CID may have improved the evidence."

"That's one way of putting it."

"I'm not defending them, Loretta." He swung the chair through ninety degrees to get a better view of her desk and drew a literary journal towards him, tapping the cover with his fingers. "This rag still going?" He scanned the list of contents, casting Loretta an amused glance as he reached her article, "The Importance of Being George: Transsexual Pseudonyms from George Eliot to George Egerton." The journal was printed on flimsy paper, all the impoverished editorial board could afford, and he rustled noisily through it until he reached Loretta's pages. He read for a moment, raising his eyebrows over her theories on literary gender-bending, and dropped it back on her desk. "What worries me," he said, as if he'd only just remembered what they had been discussing, "is *you* being mixed up in all this. I know you're her friend but there are limits."

The door into the other end of the room opened and they heard Bridget's voice: "Loretta?"

She looked at Tracey, appealing for help with her eyes, but he merely shrugged.

"In here," she called, glaring at Tracey, and Bridget advanced into the drawing room until she could see into the study.

"Sorry," she said, seeming to sense that she had arrived at an awkward moment, and attempted to make a joke of the interruption: "It's just that I am eating for two these days and I am rather hungry."

"What time is it?" Loretta looked down at her watch.

"Five past eight. I mean, we can just as well go out, Sam and I—"

"God, no. All I've got to do is cook the pasta."

Tracey said: "Can't it wait till I've had a look at this video? It's all set up." Seeing Bridget's face, he added: "This isn't one of my whims, in fact it affects you as much as it does me."

"What?" Bridget looked unconvinced and Loretta cringed at the speed at which aggression flared between them. She dropped her head into her hand, a gesture Bridget must have seen because a moment later Loretta heard her say: "Oh, all right. Just a minute while I get Sam."

Loretta listened to Bridget's rather heavy step on the stairs and then said urgently to Tracey: "God, John, I wish you'd told me earlier. I didn't know what to say to her."

He looked grim. "Say nothing. Let's have a look at this video and at least we'll have something to talk about over dinner. Hi," he added with false bonhomie as

Bridget returned with Sam. Gesturing towards a sofa, he added: "Sit yourselves down."

Bridget closed the door behind her and joined Sam, giving his hand an anxious squeeze. His face was blank, stony almost, and Loretta guessed he had not welcomed this further delay in eating.

"Let me get some more wine," she suggested, catching sight of her empty glass and thinking she needed another drink to cope with the frigid atmosphere in the room. Tracey lifted his head from the television controls and gave her a cross look but she ignored him and ran downstairs to open another bottle of Chianti.

"Ready?" Tracey demanded as she came back into the room. Loretta nodded, refilled her own glass and left the bottle on the table for the others to help themselves. Curling up on the sofa under the window, well away from Bridget and Sam, she thought of all the things she would rather be doing this evening—marking essays, finishing the mediocre novel she had promised to write about for the *TLS*, even the pile of ironing on top of the washing machine in the downstairs bathroom.

Tracey pressed a button and a blizzard of dots filled the TV screen. It was rapidly replaced by a clock face, white graphics on a black background and a second hand gliding smoothly up to the hour. Loretta heard a familiar theme tune, a series of plangent notes played on an electric guitar, and recognized a montage of film clips as the opening sequence of a current-affairs program on Channel Four: the Pope waving from a balcony, a motorcade speeding along a Washington avenue, the late Ayatollah Khomeini raising his arm in front of an adoring crowd in Tehran. Suddenly the screen went black, and three words appeared in shimmering silver: CRIMINALS FOR CHRIST?

"The Imitators of Christ," a woman's voice began,

classless and authoritative, "are the descendants of a group of deeply religious German immigrants who came to live in America in the 1870s. They settled in fertile farming country in Ohio"—the screen now showed a horse-drawn cart moving across the land at sunset, an animated version of a Hopper painting—"about twenty-five miles from the nearest town. Their descendants stubbornly resist modern inventions like the motor car, the television and the telephone, and their dress has remained largely unchanged for a century. They take their name from a famous devotional work from the fifteenth century, *The Imitation of Christ*, and try to follow the precepts laid down by its author, the German monk Thomas à Kempis." Shots of horses being unhitched from the wagon and led into a stableyard, women in long dresses and modestly covered heads emerging from clapboard houses to greet their menfolk.

"Yet try as they might," the commentary continued, "the elders of this isolated, inward-looking community have not been able to insulate themselves entirely from the outside world. In the last five years, a new militancy has grown up among younger members of the sect, who accuse their parents and grandparents of having become complacent—in their words, spiritually flabby."

On screen, a group of young people gathered in the dusk, holding aloft flaming torches as they filed along a path towards a large barn. "In accordance with the wave of religious fundamentalism sweeping America, they have adopted a stricter—some would say fanatical—moral code, demanding that the community take a more active part in carrying out the teachings of Christ as outlined by Thomas à Kempis and by the Bible. To this end, they have embarked on a series of increasingly violent actions which have split this small community and which now threaten its very existence. In tonight's

153

Open Eye, we look at the young Americans who have become *Criminals for Christ*."

There was a reprise of the theme tune and Bridget said in a slightly sarcastic voice: "This is all very interesting but I'm not sure—"

"Shhh," Tracey said rudely and, to Loretta's surprise, Bridget fell silent.

The commentary resumed: "The actions began four years ago with a peaceful picket of a bookstore in a nearby town selling material which the young people considered an affront to the teaching of Christ. They attempted to persuade customers not to buy magazines featuring Madonna, for example, and they also denounced the work of self-professed atheists like Gore Vidal." A disembodied hand began tossing magazines and novels into the center of the screen, flames playing about their edges. "Soon the young idealists, frustrated by the indifferent response to their efforts, resorted to direct action. They invaded the bookstore, took down any book or magazine they considered offensive, and made a large bonfire in the main street." The magazines were now burning merrily but the image faded and was replaced by what looked like a shopfront. The camera zoomed in to the words lettered in decorative glass on the window and Loretta let out a cry of recognition.

"Shhh!" the others exclaimed in unison as the commentary continued: "Encouraged by the publicity given to the public book-burning, the young people turned their attention to another target: the two local banks. Imitating Christ's expulsion of the money-lenders from the Temple, they launched a violent attack which earned them their nickname—"

"The Copycats," Loretta and Bridget cried together, drowning out the commentary.

154

Tracey leaned forward and freeze-framed the screen, as smug as Loretta had ever seen him.

"The newsdesk secretary remembered seeing the film," he explained modestly, sitting back on his heels. "By the time I got in she'd already rung up Channel Four and got the name of the company who made it."

Sam leaned forward, picked up the wine and filled his glass. "This is the first time you've seen it, right? So you don't know—I guess we're all wondering the same thing, whether she's in it."

Tracey shook his head. "I talked to the bloke who produced the film and he doesn't remember her. He said only one of them was there, one of the kids who were arrested, that is, and he kept well out of their way. Either that, or the elders warned him to lie low. They were very cagey about what happened to the others, apparently, and at least one of them was still in prison."

"So that bit was true," said Loretta, thinking back to that morning's lurid headline. "But the rest—"

"Yes," said Bridget in a belligerent voice, addressing Tracey, who was crouching on the floor by the television, waiting to restart the film. "How come they got it so wrong? There's quite a difference between a bank robber and a religious loony who goes around chucking bricks through windows to protest about what's it called? Usury?"

Tracey lowered himself onto the floor, sitting with his legs apart and feeling for his cigarettes. "They used a stringer in the States, they don't have their own guy in New York anymore. The most likely thing is that the cops were sitting on the story and she got a second-hand version from someone who wasn't officially on the case. Either that or she sent over a garbled version and it was tickled up in the office. All that stuff's re-written by the subs, you know."

Bridget said: "Another illusion shattered."

Tracey gave her a contemptuous look and Loretta, cross with them both, turned to Sam and said in a loud voice: "We still don't know, of course, what she was doing in Oxford, unless there's something about it later in the film. I suppose they *might* have followers over here but I haven't heard of them. Not that it's my subject," she added, "Christian sects."

"Oh." Tracey sounded disappointed. "That's precisely what I was about to ask you." He flicked ash into the empty grate and addressed Bridget and Sam. "How about you two? You know of any cults with American connections round here? I remember when I was at Ruskin they used to come round in twos wanting to know if you were saved—Jesus freaks, we called them."

Loretta frowned. "Sure you're not thinking of the Festival of Light? Cliff Richard and Dana? My best friend at school had a Cliff Richard phase and she went to those dreadful concerts."

"Mormons," Tracey said reminiscently, drawing on his cigarette, "we used to get them as well. You could always recognize them by their short hair."

"It doesn't go on so much these days," Bridget said thoughtfully, forgetting her hostility to Tracey. "Though one of my students did get mixed up with those people who drive around in a bus. You remember," she said, appealing to Loretta, "it was parked next to the Taylorian in St. Giles and two of them stopped us outside Boots. What are they called?"

Loretta remembered two rather aggressive young men in military fatigues who had tried to thrust religious pamphlets into her hands. "The Sons of God," she said. "Are they American?"

"Sounds worth a look," Tracey began but Sam interrupted: "I don't see the connection here. These guys you're talking about, they're born-agains, right? These people"—he gestured toward the flickering TV screen—"these people sound more like the sects you get in places like Montana. They don't exactly go out begging people to join. It's, like, members only."

Tracey shrugged and stubbed out his cigarette. "OK, but if there's been a split . . . I mean, the whole *point* about the film is the kids have got pissed off. I know it's a long shot, but has anyone got a better idea?" There was silence and he added: "So how do I go about getting in touch with these Sons of God?"

Loretta said, not very hopefully: "The telephone directory?"

Bridget frowned at her. "How about looking in *Vade Mecum*? I'm sure it lists religious groups, Christian societies, that sort of thing."

"Where do I get a copy?"

Bridget shrugged. "W. H. Smith's? Unless Loretta's got one?"

Loretta glanced towards her study. "I did, but I don't know where I would have put it. Haven't you seen it?" she asked, seeing Sam's incomprehension. "It's a student guide to Oxford, I usually get it for the list of restaurants. You know, if you want to know the best West Indian restaurant in Cowley Road, that sort of thing." The reference to food jogged her memory and she looked at her watch. "Shouldn't we eat? After all, we know she—" She hesitated, realizing they had tacitly adopted this distancing mechanism when referring to the dead woman and feeling uncomfortable with it. "We know the—the victim isn't in it and we can always watch the rest later."

"Thank *God*," said Bridget, following Loretta's lead. She reached for her almost empty glass of Aqua Libra and nudged Sam, who was sitting beside her with a far-away look on his face. "Come on," she said, "food. Junior's getting restive."

Loretta, who had never expected to hear arch remarks of this sort from Bridget, felt Tracey's gaze upon her as she stood up and deliberately avoided his eye. "Bring your glasses," she instructed, picking up the bottle and moving to the door.

Downstairs in the kitchen she went to the hob, turned up the flame under the pasta cooker to bring it to a rolling boil and returned the tuna sauce to the neighboring ring. She lifted the lid and was favorably impressed by the color and aroma of the contents, which she stirred gently with a wooden spoon. A noise from the dining room made her turn and she was just in time to see the gray cat, poised on the edge of the table with a slice of prosciutto dangling from his mouth.

"Bertie!" He growled as she rushed towards him, leaping from the table with an awkward motion which upset a bowl of fresh figs and sent them crashing to the floor. Loretta watched his tail vanish under the descending cat flap, leaving behind the spilt fruit and a ragged slice of meat which was all that remained of her lovingly prepared first course.

"Four basic course modules of two terms each—Shakespeare, The Novel, Major Poets, and Use of English. Is that agreed?" Bernard Shilling, head of the English department, removed his glasses and surveyed his staff. There was no verbal response from the lecturers slumped around the rectangular table in their usual postures of indifference, resentment and despair; Bernard looked down at his notes, creating an interval of silence which was quickly broken by murmurs of discontent and the noisy repositioning of chairs.

"Major Poets," Digby Richards whispered, nudging

Loretta in the ribs as a preamble to one of his bad jokes. "I told you it was political."

"Digby? Did you want to say something?" Shilling pounced on the one member of staff he disliked as much as Loretta.

"These Major Poets, Bernard," Digby responded innocently, exaggerating his South African accent. "I was wondering if you could give us an indication of who they might be."

Bernard's bushy eyebrows shot up. "I'm sure we have the expertise to draw up a list, when the time comes. In consultation with the sponsor, of course."

"Of course."

Bernard felt in his waistcoat pocket and took out an elaborately engraved fob watch. He frowned, shook it and held it to his ear, unwilling to admit that it had stopped working and he had no idea what time it was. It was a curious fact, much discussed in the department, that his relentless drive towards what he called "modernization" had been accompanied by a sartorial regression to dandyism which expressed itself in tweeds, brogues and side whiskers—a subconscious admission, Digby said, that the driving force behind all the jargon was a complete capitulation to Victorian values.

Bernard put on his glasses, glanced furtively at the pink Swatch watch worn by the woman on his right and shuffled his papers. "If that's all, I'd like to move on to the subsidiary modules which, on the face of it, present more of a problem. I've examined all the teaching currently done in the department and I have to say that in an ideal world I would find some of it hard to justify— very hard indeed," he finished, removing the glasses again and glaring at Loretta and Digby. "The days are gone," he continued, "when educational institutions could afford to construct a curriculum based haphazardly on the research interests and career ambitions of individual members of staff ... Indeed I would go as far as to say that what has gone on in certain university departments in recent decades amounts to a fraud on the young people entrusted to them and on the taxpayer." He stopped, daring the glum faces round the table to mount a challenge.

"In the modern world," he intoned, "with fierce competition for limited resources, I consider it no bad thing that we should all be asked to justify ourselves, to explain why Subject A should be taught rather than Subject B when Subject A is esoteric and of no obvious relevance. To that end, I have drawn up a questionnaire for each of you"—he reached for a pile of A4 sheets on the desk behind him—"which Mrs. Whittaker has kindly photocopied and I shall now pass round. You'll see that you are asked to provide a brief description of the courses you currently teach, the number of students who've opted for each course in the last three years, a breakdown of the class of degree obtained by those students, and an explanation of the relevance of the subject in the light of current educational parameters."

There was silence for a moment as the questionnaire was handed from person to person and the nine lecturers—the entire staff of the English department except for two lucky individuals who happened to be on holiday—absorbed its contents. It resembled a flow chart, Loretta thought, with boxes to be ticked and key words underlined; she picked up a pen and, heedless of the consequences, scribbled the title of her course on Edith Wharton, Henry James and the American novel followed by the words "useful background reading—Merchant-Ivory films."

"Not now, Loretta," Bernard said testily as she began filling in a second box. "I'm assuming some of you will have to check with Mrs. Whittaker if your own records aren't up to date. Yes, Michael?" He turned to deal with a query from the other side of the table and Loretta threw down her pen, recalling the rumor which had flashed round the department at the end of the summer term to the effect that departing third-years were going to be asked to evaluate the performance of their lecturers on a scale of one to five. It was Bernard's attempt to show his enthusiasm for the government's new, consumerist approach to education, Digby told her at the time, but she had refused to believe him. Now it seemed all too likely that the rumor was true, and that she was at the mercy of kids like the pouting blonde twins who had unaccountably signed up for her Virginia Woolf seminars. Loretta remembered her mortgage and had to stifle a moment's panic, telling herself she wasn't out of a job yet, but Bridget's suggestion that she stand in for her at St. Frideswide's during the autumn term suddenly seemed like a lifeline.

"Bernard," a voice said tentatively, and she looked up to see Chloë Calder sitting back in her chair, holding the questionnaire away from her so she could read it over the top of her half-moon glasses. Chloë was in her fifties, clever but unworldly, and Loretta listened with dismay as she proceeded to spring the trap Bernard had set for opponents of his commercially sponsored two-year degree course. "Bernard," she said again in her hesitant upper-middle-class voice, "Chaucer *has* no industrial or professional application. That is, one might argue, one of his chief virtues."

Loretta and Digby exchanged anguished looks as Bernard squared his shoulders and entered the fray. "May I remind you, Dr. Calder, that one of the purposes of this exercise is to increase student numbers by making ourselves as attractive as possible to potential sponsors? If the two-year accelerated degree course is to work, we have to persuade industry that we at Fitzroy College do not have an outmoded, ivory-tower mentality . . . One of the worries most frequently expressed by the companies I've been talking to is whether their management trainees would retain a commitment—" The door opened and Mrs. Whittaker, the department secretary, insinuated herself into the room. Bernard said testily: "Yes, Margaret, what is it?"

The secretary, mortified at having occasioned his anger, turned to glare at Loretta. "Phone call for Dr. Lawson—I did say she's in a meeting but the caller insists it's urgent."

Bernard tutted. "This is the vacation, Loretta, you're only being asked to sacrifice *one* afternoon to discuss the future of this department. All right, Mrs. Whittaker, you may go. Loretta, could you be as quick as possible?"

Loretta pushed back her chair and left the room, closing the door as Bernard launched into an account of a meeting he'd recently had with senior management at Marks and Spencer.

"Who is it?" she called after the secretary's disapproving back, following her into the department office.

"A Dr. Bennett."

Loretta seized the phone. "Bridget? What's happened?"

There was a snuffling noise at the other end and Bridget said in a small voice: "I'm at the police station, St. Aldates, they sent a car for me. *Please*, Loretta, you've got to help me."

"Where's Sam? Your solicitor—is he with you?"

"*No.* I can't talk, I'm not alone. Loretta, can you come?"

Mrs. Whittaker was watching her and Loretta point-

162

edly turned her back. "They haven't—they haven't said anything about charging you?"

"No." Her voice got even smaller. "But I'm scared . . . they're listening, Loretta."

Loretta made up her mind. "OK, the next train's at twenty past four, I might just make it. What about the solicitor? Have you called him?"

Bridget whispered: "No, because of Sam. I don't want him to find out . . ."

"All right, I'm on my way." She added the only advice she could think of: "Say *nothing*, nothing at all. They haven't changed the law yet and you have a right to silence. I have to go now or I'll miss my train."

She put the phone down and strode to the open door, turning at the last minute to address Mrs. Whittaker. "I have to go back to Oxford, could you tell Bernard—" She felt for her bag, remembered she had left it hanging over the back of her chair in the seminar room and added: "Never mind, I'll tell him myself."

She hurried out of the room and along the corridor, sliding into the meeting as quietly as possible and circling the table until she came to her chair.

Bernard glared. "Sit down, Loretta, we're just about to—"

"Sorry." She grabbed her bag and swung it onto her shoulder. "I have to go back to Oxford."

"Oxford?"

"I do live there," she snapped, hardly registering a sympathetic wink from Digby Richards as she backed out of the room. In the corridor she broke into a run, narrowly avoiding a collision with a dark-haired woman as she hurled herself through the swing doors at the far end. Out in the street she spotted a cab bowling along in the wrong direction and waved frantically just the same.

163

"Paddington Station," she cried, throwing herself inside and falling back against the worn upholstery as the driver performed a violent U-turn. The taxi sped towards Euston Road and Loretta checked her watch in the hope that she would arrive at the station in time to phone Tracey at his hotel. It did not look very hopeful and she slumped sideways against the window as the taxi stopped at a red light, staring out with a fluttering anxiety which seemed to place an invisible barrier between herself and the outside world. A young couple strolled past, arms entwined in the summer sunshine, and as she watched the boy bent to snatch a kiss with a careless grace which reminded her of a Doisneau photograph.

The light changed to green and the cab lurched forward, leaving the lovers behind. Loretta swiveled her head to catch a glimpse of them through the rear window but they were gone, into a shop or a side turning. An abandoned newspaper skittered across the pavement, blowing against the ankles of a middle-aged man who kicked it aside with hardly a break in his stride. Loretta sagged against the backseat, resting her chin on her outstretched arm, and only then remembered that her questionnaire was still lying on the table in Bernard's office, her childish attempt at sarcasm visible to anyone curious enough to pick it up.

9

THE CONCOURSE AT OXFORD STATION WAS teeming with people, the automatic doors from Platform One blocked by a party of teenagers whose luggage, flung down in a sprawling heap, constituted an obstacle course of bulging holdalls and trailing straps. Loretta picked her way through it, skirted the small group of people clustered below the TV monitor displaying departure and arrival times and made her way to the phones. Most of them took cards, not cash, and the few pay phones were in use, with half a dozen people waiting impatiently to use them. Loretta screwed up her face, debating whether to join the queue or go to the newsagent's at the far end of the cavernous station building and buy a phone card. A hand seized her arm and she twisted away, incomprehension replacing alarm as she exclaimed: "John! What are you doing here?"

"Looking for you." He took her arm again, gently but firmly, and started to lead her away from the polyglot babble of voices explaining why they were late, issuing instructions to their secretaries and cooing into their loved ones' answering machines.

She hung back, protesting: "I don't understand, I was going to call you."

"If you're worried about Bridget, she's all right. I gave her a lift to your place."

"You did?" It took Loretta a moment to adjust to this new situation, in which the rescue mission she had nervously rehearsed on the hour-long journey from Paddington was no longer needed. Relief flooded through her and she began eagerly: "Does that mean—"

Tracey stopped her. "Not here. Let's find somewhere to talk. There's a snack bar place at the other end, it doesn't look much but at least we can get a cup of tea." He propelled her through the crowds, his expression grim, and relaxed his grip only when she made it clear she was not going to bolt out of the building. As they joined the short queue in the snack bar he looked about him and said: "What happened to the old station?"

"What? Oh, they pulled it down."

Tracey inspected the few bits of food remaining in the glass display cabinets, a couple of plastic-wrapped sandwiches and some lurid pizza portions. "Two teas," he said doubtfully to the woman at the till, "One black. And a packet of biscuits."

"What sort?"

Tracey shook his head. "Doesn't matter. I missed lunch," he explained to Loretta, feeling in his trouser pocket and drawing out a couple of pound coins.

"I'll grab a table," she said as a train drew into the station and there was a stirring among the blue Formica tables. She zigzagged through the seating area, threw her bag down on a seat and cleared the table of a random assortment of empty cups, hamburger containers and a half-eaten chocolate brownie. She looked for a bin, couldn't see one, and had no choice but to heap the rubbish on one side of the small table.

166

"Christ," said Tracey, joining her, "what a dump! But we can't talk at your place and I didn't think you'd want to go back to the Randolph." He sat down, tried to move his chair nearer to the table and discovered it was fixed to the floor. An expression of disgust crossed his face and he eased the lid from one of the Styrofoam cups he had brought with him, tossing it to one side and tearing open the packet of biscuits. "Brontë?" he queried, reading the manufacturer's name on the cellophane wrapper. "I didn't know they made biscuits. Want one?"

Loretta shook her head. "Has Bridget—did she ask you to come?"

The biscuits were friable and he wiped crumbs from his mouth before answering. "Not exactly. I'd arranged to see this DS who's dealing with the press and when I got to the station she was just coming out of the main door. White as a sheet and looking like she might keel over any minute, so I got her into the car and took her back to your place. Has she seen a doctor lately? I don't know much about pregnant women but for a moment there I thought we were looking at a miscarriage ... I tried to get a message to you, save you rushing back, but that old bat who answers the phone—" He paused for her to fill in the blank in his memory.

"Mrs. Whittaker."

"That's the one. She informed me in her usual dulcet tones you were no longer in the building so I went back to the nick, then set off to meet you. I'd forgotten about that bloody awful one-way system." He remembered something and his forehead creased anxiously. "By the way, those notices in the car park, the ones that say twenty minutes only on station business. They don't wheel-clamp you or anything? I don't mind the odd ticket but I haven't got time to hang around getting the car unclamped."

Loretta shrugged, unaware that there was such a notice; she rarely drove to the station and almost never parked there. Tracey shook his head and finished his second biscuit, washing it down with tea and taking out his cigarettes. He saw her face and added: "Sorry, Loretta, but it's so smoky in here another one won't make any difference."

She looked away, her gaze coming to rest on a youth of eighteen or nineteen at a nearby table. He was gaunt and unnaturally pale, his pallor emphasized by an all-black outfit of jeans and leather jacket, and his hunched posture reminded her of the boy in a government anti-heroin poster. Across the table Tracey inhaled deeply and she turned back, observing his half-closed eyes and the almost sensual look of pleasure which came over his face as smoke filled his lungs. She shifted uncomfortably, disturbed by this unsought exposure to other people's addictions, and reached across to touch his arm. "But you said—they have at least let her go."

Tracey didn't answer at once but peered round for an ashtray, eventually tapping a trembling column of ash into an empty hamburger box. "They're building a case," he said in a flat voice, not looking at her. "They're not there yet but what they have got . . ." He paused, examining the glowing tip of his cigarette as though it was an object of rare interest. "They didn't bring her in just for the fun of it," he began again. "They've got a witness who was in the Bodleian that day and he says she was there for an hour at most."

"What?"

Tracey ground out his cigarette and produced a spiral notebook, turning back through pages covered in a mixture of longhand and his own eccentric shorthand until he found what he wanted. "Marc Testard," he read in an Anglicized French accent, "he saw her arrive in the Upper Reading Room about quarter to twelve. He says she was there about an hour and hurried off looking upset."

"Never heard of him," said Loretta. "And I don't see how—they can't have interviewed every single person who was in the Bodleian that day. How would they know who was there, for a start?"

"Routine detective work," Tracey said, "the boring stuff you don't usually read about. First they checked she really did request a book, something about vampires?" Loretta nodded. "Actually she asked for it earlier in the week and it was waiting for her. So they have a look and it's only what, fifty or so pages? *And* big print. I mean, unless she's a *very* slow reader . . ." He paused. "So then they go through all the request forms, everyone who asked to look at a book in the Upper Reading Room that morning—"

"Which must run into hundreds."

He nodded. "I wrote it down somewhere if you really want to know." She shook her head. "OK, so once they've got a list they divide it up by subject, assuming arts people are a better bet than, I don't know, zoologists. This Testard bloke, he's a postgrad in the English faculty so they sent a DC round to his flat and asked, do you know Bridget Bennett, and he said—"

"Shit."

"He didn't, actually. He said he knew Bridget by sight and he remembered her arriving because it was just after he got there himself. He waved but she wasn't looking in his direction and it's hardly the sort of place you call out."

This was perfectly true, Loretta admitted to herself, thinking of the slightly menacing hush of an academic library. Tracey watched her for a moment, then added: "You also ought to know they have no sightings of her, the victim I'm talking about now, after that Thursday. No hotels with a missing guest, no friends who thought she'd gone off for a few days in the Lake District."

"The Lake District?"

"I meant, for example."

"But she's not exactly your average tourist, is she? Do they know what she was doing here, by the way?"

"No, but her brother's arriving tomorrow. There's been some difficulty talking to the family, they won't use the phone so they're having to send messages back and forth through the local cops ... Anyway, they've apparently overcome their objection to modern technology long enough to send this guy over and he gets in to Heathrow first thing tomorrow morning."

Loretta turned her head away, not knowing what to say. The thin boy was gone, his place taken by a very old man whose name and address were inked in enormous capitals on the side of a shabby suitcase. "WALTER WEEDON," she read, and the name and number of a house in Staverton Road, north Oxford.

Tracey said, still in the same matter-of-fact voice: "What was she up to, Loretta? Has she told you?"

She looked down. "I knew she wasn't in the library all day," she said in a low voice, "but I'm sure it hasn't got anything to do with ... I mean, I feel very awkward about this." She picked up a flimsy stick of white plastic, a rather inadequate substitute for a teaspoon, and pressed it down on the surface of the table until it snapped. "I'm pretty sure she was with a man, I don't know who."

"Jesus, Loretta, she's how many months pregnant?"

Loretta swung her head listlessly from side to side, examining every mark and scratch on the Formica surface. "I know. But it's Sam she seems to be worried about, as far as I can make out. Not the police." She lifted her head, suddenly hopeful. "You don't think she

170

told them the truth this afternoon? When she realized how serious it was?"

Tracey snorted. "You didn't see her come out—ashen's not the word. Remember that old movie, the one where Diana Dors is in the condemned cell? Well, she made Diana Dors look like a champion hurdler by comparison. At least we don't have the death penalty these days." He felt for his cigarettes again, lit one, and was sitting back to enjoy it when he saw her expression. "Come on, Loretta," he said roughly, "it can't be that much of a shock. I told you last night—"

Loretta made an impatient gesture. "You're just trying to scare me."

Tracey began to lose his temper. "Of *course* I'm trying to bloody scare you," he snapped, accidentally blowing into his cigarette and sending sparks into the air. He waved them away and leaned forward: "Answer me two questions, OK? One, did she do it? Two, if she didn't what the fuck *was* she doing that Thursday that she's being so secretive about?"

Loretta squirmed in her seat, aware that the violence of his language was attracting attention. "Of course she didn't do it," she hissed. "Who do you think we're talking about, Myra Hindley?"

Tracey said more calmly: "She's pregnant, Loretta, it's a well-known fact pregnant women do funny things. Their hormones—"

"Oh, yes," she interrupted, throwing her head back, "eating asparagus at five in the morning and beating complete strangers to death. It's in all the textbooks."

Tracey regarded her quizzically. "So you're an expert all of a sudden? What's happened, your biological clock begun to tick after all?"

Loretta shrugged. "You know my feelings about chil-

171

dren. Other people's are fine but I've never had an urge to pass my genes on."

Tracey checked his watch and leaned forward. "I said I'd call the newsdesk before six," he announced shortly, grinding his second cigarette into the ashtray. "If I were you, Loretta"—he held up his hand, preempting the protest rising to her lips—"if I were you I'd have it out with her pronto. Tell her if she doesn't want to become the Oxford One—"

"One what?"

"Sorry, bad joke."

"You can say that again."

He looked her straight in the eye. "I'm doing my best, Loretta. Do you think I'd have volunteered for this story if I'd known it was going to be like this?"

She remembered his letter, and felt her cheeks grow red. "Sorry," she said, "you're absolutely right. I'll go home at once and talk to her. Where will you be this evening?"

"The Randolph. Give me a call?"

"OK."

"Loretta?"

She looked at him, seeing for the first time how unhappy he was: he looked tired, he needed a shave and his suit looked as though he'd slept in it.

Tracey said: "Nothing. Speak to you later."

Loretta walked blindly away and immediately collided with a hard object which turned out to be Walter Weedon's suitcase. The old man began struggling to his feet as she bent to apologize and their heads almost collided, coming so close that Loretta glimpsed his badly fitting false teeth and the stale tobacco flakes trapped in the wispy hairs above his upper lip.

"Sorry," she said, flinching. The old man fell back in his seat, goggling up at her, and the accusation in his rheumy eyes stayed with her as she hurried across the concourse, through the main doors and into the open air.

The West Indian taxi driver who drove Loretta home was inclined to chat, having recognized her from a previous trip between the railway station and Southmoor Road. His niece, he reminded her, had just taken her A levels and was waiting for her results; she was worried about her history paper, and he asked Loretta's advice on what the girl should do if she did not get the grades she needed for a place at Liverpool University. Loretta explained the clearing system in a rather distracted way, preoccupied with the question of what she was going to say to Bridget, and had already counted out the fare and a small tip when the car drew up outside her house.

"Thanks," the driver called, waving through the open passenger window as he drove off, and she hurried up the path to the front door. Her key slid easily into the lock but the door grounded on an obstacle which turned out, on closer inspection, to be the free newspaper which arrived every week in spite of Loretta's pleas to the delivery girl. She curved her hand round the bottom of the door and worked it free, flattening out the crumpled front page and discovering that most of it was given over to a sensational account of the murder at Thebes Farm. Whoever laid it out was a bit behind with his or her cultural references, dredging up a still from *Bonnie and Clyde* to illustrate the now discredited bank robbery angle; the paper had gone to press too early, Loretta guessed, to print the step-by-step rebuttal issued by the police at the previous afternoon's press conference.

She stuck out her heel as she read and pushed the door shut, calling out: "Bridget, I'm home." Seconds passed without a reply and she became aware of a stillness and silence which suggested the house was empty—no faint footsteps on another floor, not even a radio playing.

"Oh, *God*," she moaned, going to the bottom of the stairs and repeating the name more loudly. The only response was from the cat, who stretched and yawned as he slunk down from the first floor with every appearance of having passed the afternoon asleep on Loretta's bed. She brushed his head absently with her fingertips, left him rolling on the floorboards and went into her study. The message light was blinking and, drawing a piece of blank paper towards her, she leaned across and pressed the "play" button.

"Good afternoon," said a woman's voice—breezy, professional, not someone Loretta knew. "This is a message for Bridget Bennett from Belinda Green at Barrington Properties. I'd be grateful if she could ring me back as soon as she gets in. It's about her house in Woodstock Road, I showed a gentleman round this morning and he's just phoned me with an offer. The time is quarter past four on Thursday afternoon, August the fifteenth."

The machine bleeped and a second voice spoke into the room, this time in a South African accent which Loretta had no difficulty in recognizing as Digby's.

"Well, Loretta, aren't you the clever one, sneaking off like that and missing Bernard's little surprise. This guy turned up after you left, a potential sponsor no less, and gave us a lecture on what industry expects from us. We were all having such a good time it ran over, so Bernard's fixed another meeting next week." Loretta frowned, remembering she had to go to Paris for four days and foreseeing trouble from Bernard. Digby went on: "I tore up your questionnaire, by the way, just in case you had second thoughts and decided you want to

174

keep your job. There's a spare one in your pigeon-hole—you can't say I don't look after you. You also left your *Guardian* and I've finished the crossword—four down is 'uninhibited.' Easy really. Bye."

Another bleep, and Loretta pulled a face as she heard Sam leave another of his solicitous messages for Bridget: "Hon, just checking you're OK, I thought you were planning on taking it easy this afternoon." He gave a nervous laugh and added: "Maybe you're sleeping—I don't want to be a pain in the butt but you do know what the doctors said. Call me anyway, soon as you wake up."

Loretta put her hand out towards the machine, thinking the messages had finished, but it bleeped again and a mellow female voice said: "Hi, this is Professor Dolores del Negro calling from the Women's Studies Group at Berkeley, University of California. I'd like to talk with Dr. Loretta Lawson and get her response to an idea I have about her coming over here and giving some lectures . . . I *loved* her book on Edith Wharton. I got her number from Geoffrey Simmons and I hope she won't mind me calling her at home. She can reach me at the following number—" Here she rattled off ten figures so fast that Loretta missed the last two, followed by a detailed account of her movements over the course of the day: she would be in a meeting all morning but hoped to hear from Loretta in the afternoon, West Coast time.

Loretta looked at her watch, considered the time difference and worked out there was no point in calling Professor del Negro before 10:00 P.M. She hardly heard the tape rewind, standing by her desk in a dream as she savored the prospect of telling Bernard Shilling to stuff his sponsors and his accelerated degree course, ignoring for the moment the fact that there had been no hint on the tape of how long she was being invited to Berkeley for, or how the trip might be financed. The woman had mentioned lectures, in the plural, which might mean a whole term ... Loretta, whose idea of San Francisco was an amalgam of images from *Tales of the City*, pictured herself strolling along a tree-lined street of clapboard houses populated by cheerful transsexuals and gay nuns on roller skates. This fantasy was so agreeable that the ringing of the phone failed to puncture it, and she was still in a daydream when she lifted the receiver.

"Hello?" The caller was female, a stranger who asked very politely to speak to Bridget Bennett.

"Bridget?" Loretta replied, coming back to earth. "She's not here. To tell you the truth"—she gave a short laugh—"I haven't a clue where she is."

"Not to worry. Is that Loretta? I think we did meet once, my name's Jane Kaplan. I was just ringing to let her know—she left a message for Stephen and I just wanted to let her know he's out of the country till next week, at a conference in Budapest. I've got a number, if it's urgent, but he isn't going straight there—"

"I shouldn't worry," said Loretta, unable to think of any urgent reason why Bridget should want to speak to Stephen Kaplan. "But I'll certainly tell her you rang."

"Thanks. How is she, by the way?"

"Oh," said Loretta, hardly knowing how to answer. "Bearing up. You know."

"Yes, well ... Give her my regards."

Jane Kaplan rang off and Loretta bent over her desk to add her name below the message from Barrington Properties.

"Loretta?"

She turned. Bridget was standing just inside the room, swaying slightly and blinking in the early-evening sunlight which streamed in through the study window.

"Loretta?" she said again, slightly hoarse. "Sorry, I didn't hear you—I took two of those tablets and I feel a bit woozy."

The swaying became more pronounced and Loretta hurried forward to support her. "For God's sake sit down," she said and led Bridget, unresisting, to a sofa in the other half of the room. She had just made her comfortable when there was a faint double *ping* from the hall and Loretta lifted her head. Not the police *again*? She glanced out of the window and saw no sign of a patrol car, though that didn't prove anything. Knuckles rapped on the door, suggesting the caller was becoming impatient, and Loretta left Bridget and went to answer it.

A woman in jeans and a red shirt was standing on the doorstep. She smiled when she saw Loretta and said: "Your bell doesn't seem to be working. Sorry I'm a bit early."

"Early?" Loretta stared at her, trying to think what Marilyn Ramsell, a teacher she had met through the local Labor Party, was doing on her doorstep.

Marilyn gave her a puzzled look. "It is tonight, isn't it?"

Loretta put a hand up to her face as realization dawned. "Oh, God," she admitted, "it completely slipped my mind." Two months ago, at a meeting of the Oxford branch of Charter 88, she had reluctantly agreed to speak at the August meeting on the implications for women of a written constitution in Britain. Marilyn had volunteered to help her, and they had discussed it briefly on the phone about a week later.

"I can't do it on my own," Marilyn said, visibly alarmed. "I mean, we agreed you'd take care of all the legal stuff, a bill of rights and so on."

Loretta interrupted her, anxious to avoid a scene.

"You'd better come in," she said, stepping back. "Look, you go on down to the kitchen and I'll be with you in a minute, there's something I have to take care of first. Yes, down the stairs—make yourself a cup of tea or something."

In the drawing room Bridget had stretched out on the sofa, one hand cradling her stomach. "Who is it?" she asked.

"Don't worry, nothing I can't deal with. Listen, Bridget"—she knelt beside her, brushing Bridget's hair back from her sticky forehead with her right hand—"I have to go out for a while. Will you be all right? I'll come home as soon as I can."

"Where are you going?"

Loretta shook her head. "You won't believe this. I promised to speak at a Charter 88 meeting, I don't see any way of getting out of it. Is Sam staying here tonight?"

"I'm not sure, he's going to ring. He had to go over to the house, something to do with the police." She shifted uncomfortably on the sofa. "I think I'll go back to bed, I'm so sleepy."

"OK, I'll come up with you. Put your legs on the floor, that's it. We'll get you back to bed and I'll bring you—what? Tea?"

"Yes please."

"Can you wait for food till I get back? I can pick up a Chinese takeaway."

"Chinese sounds great."

Entering the kitchen a few minutes later, Loretta was astonished to find the table covered in lined A4 paper. The kettle stood cold and empty, and there was no sign that Marilyn had availed herself of Loretta's offer to make tea.

"I made a few notes," she said modestly, gesturing

178

towards her research, and began to read out some of the headings: "Active citizenship, what it means for women; an elected second chamber; reform of the monarchy; whether we should include reproductive rights; reform of the judiciary—that's your bit."

Loretta winced, turning away so Marilyn couldn't see her face. She was hungry, desperately anxious about Bridget, and the prospect of spending the best part of the evening in the dreary Women's Institute building in Middle Way filled her with dismay. Seizing an apple from the fruit bowl and biting into it, she said indistinctly: "I'll just make some tea, I've got someone staying." She filled the kettle and switched it on; then, not wanting to waste a minute, she ran upstairs to her study, where she began pulling books from the shelves, tossing them aside one by one as she conducted a frantic and largely unsuccessful search for inspiration for her speech.

LORETTA PADDED DOWNSTAIRS INTO THE kitchen next morning, her head aching and her eyes screwed up against the brilliant white light reflected at her by the cupboard doors. She pulled open a drawer and pushed aside antihistamines, seasickness pills and a tube of Savlon, stared in surprise at a packet of hypoallergenic condoms which she couldn't remember buying, and finally located a strip of paracetamol tablets at the back. Swallowing the pills with the dregs of a carton of orange juice made her feel slightly sick, so she pulled out a chair and sat down, breathing in a curious amalgam of stale Chinese food and fresh coffee which made her feel worse. Foil containers covered the table, most of them nearly full and resembling an illustration in a cheap, garishly photographed cookery book. Next to her elbow slices of beef and green pepper curled up through congealed black-bean sauce; another tray, in which bean sprouts and an unidentifiable white vegetable cohabited in a glutinous mess, was virtually untouched.

"Yuk," she said, wrinkling her nose, and began stuffing foil cartons into the white plastic bag supplied by the takeaway. When it was full she lifted the lid of the swing bin and dropped it inside, hoping the various sticky liquids would not leak. It was only when she returned to the table to remove her empty plate that she noticed a note in Bridget's spiky handwriting, written on the back of an envelope and lying next to the warm coffee pot.

Loretta,
Sorry about last night. I meant to get up when you came in but I must have dropped off to sleep, those tablets are really powerful. Sorry about the food, I've left a tenner in the envelope to cover it. Also, I've borrowed your green jacket, I didn't think you'd mind. The inquest's at 10:30

Loretta glanced at her wrist but she was not wearing her watch.

and I'm meeting Sam at the coroner's court. J. Tracey's going to be there as well, he called last night just after you went out. So did your mother—didn't sound important but she said could you ring her back. No other messages—see you later.

Much love,
Bridget

Loretta peered into the envelope, saw a single ten-pound note, and lay back in her chair. She felt awful, a combination of too much to drink and indigestion, the result of eating immediately before going to bed and consuming a bottle of red wine as she did so. The meeting had dragged on till just before ten and she stopped at the Chinese in Walton Street on the way home, realizing belatedly as she walked through the door that she did not know whether to order food for Sam. The pay phone in the takeaway was out of order so she had no choice but to buy enough for three, making a complete guess at what Bridget and Sam might like. This was a mistake, for she arrived to find the house in darkness; only the presence of the cat, stretched out against the spare-room door when she tiptoed upstairs, suggested that Bridget was inside and fast asleep. She opened the door quietly, restraining the cat with her other hand, and heard Bridget's even breathing; too tired to consider whether she was acting from consideration or cowardice, she left her to sleep and tiptoed back down the stairs to the kitchen, where an absurdly large Chinese feast awaited her.

Loretta yawned and put her hand up to cover her mouth, then moved zombielike to answer the phone.

"Mmm?" she yawned.

"Dr. Bennett?"

"No, sorry."

"Is she there? Or would I get her at St. Frideswide's? I *think* we have the number in our files."

"No, not at college. Can I take a message?" She reached for the envelope with Bridget's note on the back and prepared to write.

"This is Belinda Green at Barrington Properties, I rang yesterday about her house. The thing is, we've had an offer—"

"Oh, yes." Loretta pictured herself taking down the message the previous afternoon, when she arrived back from London, and gave a guilty start as she realized she had not passed it on. "I'll remind her as soon as she gets in," she said, concealing her memory lapse.

"The thing is, it's rather urgent. Professor Lal, that's the gentleman who's made the offer, he's anxious to know whether it's acceptable before he goes back to Newcastle. It is *Friday* . . ."

"Yes, I know."

"And the other thing is, we've been picking up Dr. Bennett's post and sending it to Thebes Farm, but I didn't know if it was all right to go on doing that in the circumstances."

"Oh, I'm sure it's all right," Loretta assured her. Any letters posted today probably wouldn't arrive until Monday, and she was hoping Bridget would return home over the weekend.

"If you're sure."

"Absolutely. And I'll get her to ring you the moment she gets in."

This seemed to satisfy the estate agent, who put the phone down. Loretta yawned again, picked up the kettle and held it under the cold tap. She had not consciously thought about what day it was until Belinda Green jogged her memory: now she remembered that she was going to the opera that evening with Christopher Cisar.

"Oh, God." Loretta turned off the tap and leaned against the sink, dismayed by the prospect of being trapped in a theater seat for three hours. Joe Lunderius had mocked her for what he called her "greatest hits" approach to opera, and it was true that she preferred listening to a tape of highlights from Mozart or Rossini to sitting through a live, unabridged performance. In her present hungover state, it even seemed possible that she might fall asleep; Loretta put down the kettle and put a hand up to her face, imagining she could feel tiny lines forming around her eyes. Her hair, too, was visibly suffering, hanging limply about her face as it did when she was coming down with a cold. For a moment she toyed with the idea of using this as an excuse to cry off and her hand went to the phone, dropping away when she realized she would have to look up the CES number in the phone book. The company's offices were on Osney

Island, Bridget talked about them often enough, but Loretta remembered the directory was upstairs and gave up.

She pushed herself away from the sink with a little grunt of irritation, saw the *Guardian* lying on a chair and leaned forward to pick it up. It was open at an inside page and her eye was caught by a small headline in News in Brief. "Oxford Murder: Police in New Appeal," she read, followed by a couple of paragraphs which reported that detectives leading the inquiry into the murder at Thebes Farm were still trying to establish the victim's movements after getting off the plane at Heathrow. "Someone, somewhere, must have seen this young woman," a spokeswoman was reported to have said, and the story went on to repeat details of the date, time and number of her flight to England and what she was believed to have been wearing. A final, one-paragraph sentence made Loretta's eyebrows shoot up: the police had, it seemed, spent the previous day digging up the drains at Thebes Farm in a final, fruitless attempt to locate the murder weapon.

Loretta put the paper down, shocked by the police's single-minded concentration on Bridget and Sam's house. The place must now be in an even worse mess, and she wondered whether there was any obligation on the police to tidy up afterwards. The phone sounded again and she picked it up, hoping it wasn't her mother demanding to know why Loretta had not yet returned her call of the previous evening.

"Loretta?" Not her mother but John Tracey, brusque and businesslike against a noisy, echoing background. "Listen, love, I'm calling from the coroner's court and I can't talk long. We're on our way back to your place and I wanted to make sure you were in. I don't suppose you have a fax machine?"

"A fax machine?"

"Or a modem? OK, in that case you'll just have to—" He broke off and his voice grew faint, just loud enough for her to make out that he was arguing with someone who also wanted to use the phone. "Sorry, love. Listen, if the library rings before I arrive, can you just take down anything they've got? They know what I'm after. See you in about ten minutes."

"Wait," Loretta protested, "what's all this about?" but Tracey had already gone. She remained where she was for a moment, surprised by the brevity of the inquest, until a glance down at her bare wrist reminded her of her state of undress. Ten minutes, Tracey had said, and even allowing for traffic delays she had barely time to wash her face and get dressed before he arrived. Her headache cranked itself up a notch and she cast an anguished glance around the kitchen before hurrying into the dining room and throwing open the French windows to clear the sickly smell of food. Then she ran upstairs, pulling her T-shirt over her head as she went and narrowly missing the cat, who had stationed himself watchfully on the next-to-top step. A moment later she was in the shower, holding her head back from the stream of water to keep her hair dry and rekindling an old resentment against John Tracey for using her as an unpaid secretary.

"Slow down, I'm taking this down by hand. The what of November did you say? Twenty-second. And this is 1988? Hold on." Tracey took the receiver from his ear and turned to glare at Bridget and Loretta. "Can you two keep your voices down? I can't hear a thing she's saying." He waited until they'd fallen silent and swiveled back to his notebook, which was on the worktop next to the phone. "OK, go on," he said, pen poised.

185

"Aged thirty-two and she was from where? Andover. She did?" He whistled. "Picked the wrong one there, didn't he? No, I didn't mean—" He held the phone away from him for a few seconds, muttering "Blimey" in a barely audible voice, then returned the receiver to his mouth. "What is this," he said, "the Canary Wharf branch of SCUM?" Loretta's eyes widened, picturing the slow-moving elderly men who had run the *Sunday Herald* library in the old days and wondering if they had all retired rather than move to Docklands.

"OK, OK," said Tracey, backtracking fast. "I take all your points and if we could just get back to the story. You're sure that's the lot? Could you do me one more favor and fax it over to the Randolph? The Randolph Hotel in Oxford. I don't know their fax number but if you ring the main switchboard ... Yeah, hang on." He turned to the cover of his notebook and read out the number. "Make sure you mark it urgent to me, because there are other hacks staying there and I don't want it falling into the wrong hands. All right. Yes, all right. I'll be on this number for a while if you—" The connection had obviously been cut at this point for Tracey banged the receiver back into its rest and said sarcastically: "Thanks, Sheila." His annoyance had disappeared, however, by the time he turned back to Loretta with the tense, eager expression she knew to mean he was on the trail of a hot story.

"There's going to be one hell of a row," he said, his eyes gleaming. "Four attacks on women in, let's see, two and a half years—since the autumn of eighty-eight. All on the same stretch of road, and the cops haven't said a *word*."

"But what's it got to do with"—Loretta waved her hand, feeling a superstitious reluctance to use the word "murder" in Bridget's presence—"with, you know, Thebes Farm?"

"Hah," Tracey exclaimed with deep satisfaction. "I'm coming to that. You should've been at the inquest."

"It was extraordinary, Loretta," Bridget confirmed, looking as elated, in her own way, as Tracey. "I mean, I was half expecting—" She stopped, glancing nervously at him.

"What happened?" Loretta demanded.

Tracey said: "Shall I?" and Bridget nodded.

"OK, the first thing is, the brother's supposed to show up and he doesn't."

Loretta raised her eyebrows, thoroughly confused.

"So the cops are hopping mad—two of them were at Heathrow to meet his plane this morning and he wasn't on it. There's no message, nothing, and it's the middle of the night in Ohio. These people, the Copycats, they aren't on the phone so they have to wake up the local cops and get them to go out there at first light. Anyway, he's just explained all this through gritted teeth, Superintendent Dibden, when the coroner says, 'In that case can we turn to the day she arrived in Britain—what progress have you made tracing her movements?' Etcetera etcetera. And he says—what he says is they have new evidence which links her disappearance with a series of attacks on women on the A34."

"The A34? But the coach from Heathrow to Oxford goes on the M25 and the M40. Even if she hired a car it's a long way round. And presumably the first thing they did was check with Avis?"

"Ah, well," said Tracey, making the most of telling the story. "It turns out they've got a witness—two, in fact. Someone rang on Tuesday, as soon as her description was in the papers, to say he'd seen her getting into a van at some roundabout just north of Newbury, but they didn't believe him for the reasons you've just been saying . . . Until yesterday evening, that is, when this woman got in touch. You know that tunnel you go through when you're leaving the airport? Goes up to the M4? *She* says she saw her, the Wolf girl, hanging about there trying to get a lift, so she stopped and asked her where she was going. She said she was hitching to Oxford; this woman tried to tell her how dangerous it was but she wouldn't listen. In the end she, the driver, told her to hop in and she'd take her as far as Newbury. She'd hired a car to go to Bristol, apparently, so she had to go along the M4. She was going to come off the motorway and drop her at the bus station but there was a lot of traffic and by the time she got to Newbury she was running late. The roundabout's a few miles north of town so the girl said, just drop me here. Unfortunately, it looks like she got straight into the van belonging to this bloke who—" Tracey drew his hand flat across his throat in a vivid but inaccurate illustration of his meaning.

"God," said Loretta, putting herself in the woman driver's place, "she must feel terrible."

Tracey was eager to finish his story. "The key thing is the van," he went on, "because it seems to have been used in all the attacks. *Including* the one last Friday night—"

Bridget said: "It was in the *Telegraph*, remember? A woman who was attacked when her car broke down."

Loretta nodded.

"The point being," Tracey continued inexorably, "that the police have known about the attacks for a while but they didn't issue a warning." He held up his hands, palms upwards. "I mean, it's one thing to say you don't want to encourage copycat attacks, but if you go down that road you have to accept that you're putting women at risk—women who might otherwise not use that stretch of road alone," he finished confusingly. He began feeling in his pockets and Loretta said quickly: "Sorry, I offered you coffee. Could you switch the kettle on again, John?"

"Mmm? Oh yes, right." Her attempt at diverting him from his search for cigarettes was successful, for he leaned across, pressed the switch at the back of the kettle and picked up his notebook. "All right if I use your phone? Don't worry about the bill, I'll get them to send you a check to cover it." Before she could speak he'd picked up the phone and dialed three figures. "Hello? It's a Geneva number—the name's Stannion. S-T-A-N-N-I-O-N, Denise. Route de . . ." He hesitated, then spelt out a street name. "Route de L-O-E-X." He waited a moment, drumming his fingers impatiently on the worktop, then began to write. "Do you happen to know the code for Geneva?" He added more figures, jiggled the rest and dialed again. "It's an organization called Women Against Rape, I haven't got their address—"

He looked questioningly at Loretta, who shook her head slightly and said: "Somewhere around King's Cross, but I'm not sure."

"That'll be it." He took down another number and prepared to dial again.

"What's this Geneva number?" Loretta said in a low voice to Bridget; she was pretty sure Tracey would forget his promise and leave her to foot the bill.

"Answering machine, damn." He stayed by the phone, clicking his tongue several times as a variety of expressions flitted across his face.

"She's the one—the woman who gave her the lift," Bridget whispered. "She works in Geneva, and apparently she didn't see an English paper till last night."

"Is Tony around?" Tracey was saying, his back to

them again. "Yes, please." He waited a moment, then said: "Tony? You know these international unions based in Geneva—do you happen to know the name of the post office lot? Or the number? No, don't worry, it's not an industrial story at all, I just need to speak to someone there. Why do you ask?" Loretta, who was aware of the intense professional rivalry which existed between journalists on the *Sunday Herald*, permitted herself a little smile as Tracey said warily: "Denise Stannion, as a matter of fact. You do? What's she like? The press office"—his tone changed—"well, that helps. All right if I mention your name? Listen, if I have any trouble getting hold of her I'll ring you back. Thanks"—writing again—"I owe you a pint."

Bridget said quietly: "Marvelous, isn't it? The British journalist at work."

"Mmm." The kettle boiled and Loretta, who hadn't had so much as a cup of tea for breakfast, got up to make coffee. "John," she said, tapping him lightly on the shoulder as he waited for the Geneva number to ring.

"Hello?" He was off again. "*Parlez-vous anglais?* Thank God for that. The press office, please. Hello, is Denise Stannion there? Oh." He looked at his watch. "What's the time difference? And she'll be back at one thirty, Swiss time? Yes, please. Would you ask her to ring John Tracey? Here's my number." To Loretta's relief he gave the number of the Randolph Hotel, then rang off. "Damn," he said, as though it was a matter of huge personal inconvenience, "I forgot they're an hour ahead. Still, bloody early to be having your lunch."

"This woman," said Loretta, "what do you want to speak to her for?"

Tracey gave her a pitying look. "How long's it take to drive from Heathrow Airport to Newbury? An hour at least, ninety minutes in heavy traffic, and they must have talked about something. I don't know what this Stannion woman told the cops but I assume the girl said why she was here—to take part in an ice-dancing display or whatever."

"Ice dancing?" Loretta looked up from plunging the lid of the cafetiere.

Tracey shook his head. "It's the one-way system, I've gone past the ice rink so many times I've got it on the brain."

Loretta took three mugs out of the dishwasher and Bridget said: "How come you were able to get all the details of these attacks so fast? If you're saying nobody knew they were connected ..."

Tracey looked up from studying his notebook. "That's one of the advantages of the new computer system. All you have to do is put in a name or a word and it prints out every reference ... I rang from the coroner's court and got them to do a search for anything mentioning the A34—excluding roadworks, of course." He tapped his notebook. "And here it all is. Thanks, Loretta." He took the mug of milky coffee she was holding out to him, sipped from it and put it down beside him on the worktop. "I've got to go, they're faxing that stuff over to the hotel and I don't want to clog up your phone." He leaned towards Loretta, kissed her cheek and waved to Bridget. "Don't bother to come up. Talk to you later."

Loretta sat down with her coffee, staring after him. "I'd forgotten what it's like, journalism," she said, and turned at a slight movement from Bridget. Her head was cocked, listening, and when the front door slammed she let out a heartfelt sigh of relief. "God, Loretta," she said, slumping forward over the table, "I can't tell you what a relief ... I never thought," she said, raising her head slightly, "I never thought there'd come a day when I was glad to hear there's a rapist on the loose but after yesterday . . . I was half expecting to walk into the courtroom and they'd arrest me." She laughed loudly and almost hysterically. "I've never been so frightened. I had to hang on to Sam or my legs would've given way."

"Does he know? Not *again*," she exclaimed as the phone sounded, thinking the interruption could not have come at a more inopportune moment. The female caller asked for Bridget and identified herself as the estate agent who had phoned yesterday. "For you," said Loretta, handing the phone over.

"You have?" Bridget said, her face lighting up. "How much?" Her manner became businesslike, and Loretta could see from her expression that she was doing a series of mental calculations. "Well, it's a lot less than I'd hoped. I know, but the mortgage . . . You don't think he'll go up five thousand? Oh, I see, a cash buyer. Can I think about this? I'll have to talk to my husband, anyway, and my solicitor. No, that's fine, give me half an hour and I'll call you back." She put the phone down and turned apologetically to Loretta. "Some chap called Professor Lal has made an offer on the house, it's a bit low but he's a cash buyer and he wants an answer by the end of this afternoon. Sorry."

Loretta sighed. "I'll be upstairs," she said, picking up her coffee as Bridget began dialing another number.

"Loretta—"

She paused by the door but Bridget shook her head helplessly and spoke into the phone. Loretta shrugged, went back for the *Guardian* and carried it and her coffee up to the ground floor.

Loretta pushed open the door to the ladies' lavatory at the back of the restaurant and glanced furtively to her left. The open doors of the cubicles confirmed she had the place to herself and she went to a washbasin, balanced her evening bag on the edge and examined her reflection in the mirror. She had drunk two glasses of wine at the theater, one before the performance started and another during the interval, and the alcohol had brought a slight flush to her cheeks. Her hair, tied back with a black ribbon, had worked loose and hung in spiral curls, softening the outline of her face. Her lipstick had all but disappeared and she hastily rubbed off the last traces, reaching in her bag for the gold tube and re-applying it with hesitant strokes. The color was new, a deeper red than she usually wore, and the face which looked out of the mirror seemed for an instant to belong to someone else, someone sexier and more self-assured than she had felt for several months.

Loretta tilted her head, getting used to this new version of herself. She would be thirty-eight in three days' time, a fact her mother had pointed out in a frosty phone call just before Loretta left the house to meet Christopher Cisar. She took a step back from the mirror, thinking that her face, if she didn't look too closely at the fine lines below her eyes, could easily be that of a much younger woman. Even her crushed silk dress, which had felt ridiculously out of place in the crowded foyer of the Apollo Theatre, looked soft and seductive now she was no longer surrounded by posters announcing forthcoming appearances by Bobby Davro and the Chippendales.

The door from the restaurant to the lavatories slid open and Loretta hurried into one of the cubicles, not wanting to be caught posing narcissistically in front of the mirrors. When she emerged, a woman with long dark hair was leaning over one of the washbasins in an attitude of concentration, retouching her lips as Loretta

193

had a moment before. Their eyes met in the mirror and they both laughed spontaneously, sharing a silent joke about a ritual first encountered at school discos.

"You'd think it'd be easy after all these years," the woman said, blotting her lips on a tissue.

Loretta rinsed her hands at the other washbasin. "It seems rather frivolous but I wish I could get the hang of a lip pencil." The dark woman grinned and slid open the door to the restaurant, leaving Loretta to dry her hands.

Christopher Cisar gave her a puzzled look as she slid back into her chair. "You meet a friend back there? You were gone so long I almost sent a waitress after you."

Loretta smiled apologetically. "How's the wine?" she asked, still relieved by her discovery that he was not the teetotal health freak she had originally taken him for.

"Fine." Christopher still looked slightly suspicious. "You sure you're OK?"

"Mmm." Loretta tasted the wine, a Californian white which had arrived while she was away from the table.

"In that case"—Christopher leaned back in his chair—"why don't you tell me what got you so steamed up at the opera?"

Loretta lifted her head. "What?"

"You were fine till somewhere near the end, then you began shifting around in your seat."

"Did I?"

"M-hmm."

"Well, it did get rather silly. When Zerbin—Zerbinella—"

"Zerbinetta."

"Yes, when Zerbinetta started handing out advice to Ariadne. I mean, my German's not *that* good but I got the gist. We're such helpless little creatures, as soon as the next man comes along we throw ourselves into his

194

arms, we just *can't* help it . . . The librettist, what's his name?"

"Hugo von Hoffmannsthal."

"Yeah, well, maybe it's something about the Germans—like Wedekind and Lulu. When he has her say her ideal lover is a sexual maniac or words to that effect. It's exactly what I'm writing about at the moment, the way writers produce all these banal theories about female sexuality and put them in women's mouths."

He grinned. "I get the point. So what do you think Ariadne ought to do? When she wakes up and discovers Theseus has dumped her in the night?"

"Ariadne? There's not much she *can* do, is there, stuck in a legend? All I'm saying is, there's no need to overdo it."

"Isn't that kind of defeatist? I guess she and Zerbinetta could set up some kind of cooperative—grow vegetables or something till the coastguard happens along."

"Of course," said Loretta, thinking aloud, "she *is* pregnant, which is a slightly limiting factor."

"Who is?"

"Ariadne. Doesn't anyone mention it in the opera? Maybe they don't."

"Not as I recall."

"Interesting. Because the point is that not only has she betrayed her father, helping Theseus to kill the Minotaur and get out of the maze, she's actually pregnant by him—"

Loretta felt a light touch on her left arm and turned to see a thin-lipped, nervous woman smiling at her. "Harriet!" she exclaimed without enthusiasm. "Where are you sitting? I didn't see you." She peered over her

195

shoulder, looking for Harriet's husband, and saw him wave at her from a table in the far corner.

Harriet's eyes darted to Christopher and back to Loretta. "I tried to catch you when you went to the loo but you were miles away. How *is* Bridget? We only got back from France last night and I haven't had a chance to ring."

"Quite well, in the circumstances. They're keeping an eye on her blood pressure, it's higher than it should be, but mentally she's . . . pretty well." Loretta thought, but did not say, that delirious was a more apt description; the unexpected sale of her house, coming immediately after she had been let off the hook by the bizarre new development in the murder investigation, had sent Bridget into a state bordering on euphoria. She had insisted on giving Loretta a lift to George Street, talking all the way about her plans for the next few weeks and stopping the car to give her a big hug when they got to the Apollo Theatre.

"Do you know Christopher Cisar?" Loretta asked, remembering her manners. "Christopher—Harriet Hunt. Harriet's a friend of Bridget, in fact I don't think we've met since—"

"Since she moved from Woodstock Road," Harriet confirmed. "You know she actually invited us—I mean we would have been *there*, at the party, if we hadn't been in France. I was absolutely *amazed* when I read about it, Frank brought a copy of the *Daily Express* back from Avignon, it was the only English paper he could get, and there it was on the front page. And then on the news tonight, before we came out, they said it was something to do with a rapist on the A34?" She paused, waiting for Loretta to pick up this cue.

She said reluctantly: "I wasn't at the inquest so I've only heard secondhand. The connection seems to be a van, the one that was used in these attacks on the road to Newbury. Someone saw her getting into it, apparently. My"—she glanced at Christopher—"a friend of mine who's a journalist says they're interviewing the other women who've been attacked, trying to establish the make and so on."

Harriet screwed up her eyes. "But I had no idea about these attacks on the A34, I drive that way every month to see my mother and you'd think ... Well, we should have been *warned*."

"Excuse me." The waitress came up behind her with two plates, an onion tart for Christopher and *quenelles de brochet* for Loretta, giving Harriet little choice but to move aside.

"I suppose it'll be in *The Times* tomorrow," she said regretfully. "Listen, Loretta, why don't you join us for a drink if we're still here when you finish? We've only just finished our main course." She nodded to Christopher and went back to her husband.

"Eat slowly," Loretta urged, sotto voce, when Harriet was out of earshot. "Her husband's the most terrible bore, he's a fellow at St. Anthony's. Bridget feels sorry for her, I can't think why else she'd go on seeing them."

"She's watching us," Christopher said warningly.

Loretta pulled a face and picked up her fork. "Oh, well. Listen, there's something I wanted to ask you about computers."

"Computers?"

"Isn't that your—I thought it was your field."

"It is. But I couldn't help noticing how your eyes glazed over at the party when I started to tell you about the engine-simulator program."

She blushed. "What?"

"Come on, you were almost comatose." He grinned, then said: "OK, what do you want to know?"

197

"Well," she said diffidently, just wanting to get something clear in her own mind, "someone was telling me about a thing called an audit trail. Apparently it's a sort of log, you must have one at CES, and I just wondered if there was any way—" She froze, her fork halfway to her lips, as the street door opened and two men walked into the restaurant. A woman slid out from behind the bar to greet them and Loretta could see a conversation going on about tables, the woman looking doubtful and glancing at her watch. For a moment she thought she was safe, that they would turn and leave without noticing her, but then the woman turned and pointed uncertainly to the party of four who had just finished coffee at the next table. Both men swiveled their heads in obedience to her gesture and Loretta tensed, guessing what was about to follow.

"Loretta." John Tracey stalked to her table and glared down at her, a thunderous expression on his face.

"Hello, John." She put down her fork, controlling her own anger and assuring herself that she owed him no apologies. "How's the story going?"

"The story?" He looked blank for a moment, then said cruelly: "I thought you'd lost interest now your mate's in the clear." His companion, a tall bearded man who had followed Tracey to Loretta's table, coughed politely behind him. Tracey turned. "I don't think you've met my *ex-wife*, have you, Mark? Mark Dawson, *Independent on Sunday.*"

"This is Christopher Cisar," said Loretta crisply. "Now, if you'll excuse us, our food's getting cold."

"Oh, yes," Tracey said bitterly, "we don't want to break up the party. Come on, let's go somewhere where the company's a bit more congenial." He wheeled round and collided with a waitress, who was, fortunately for both of them, empty-handed.

198

Mark Dawson called after him: "John? What's the problem?" but Tracey was already wrenching open the door to the street. Dawson held up his hands in mute apology and hurried after him, disappearing into the warm night.

Loretta leaned back and closed her eyes. "I *can* explain."

Christopher said: "Why should you? It's none of my business if the guy still carries a torch for you." He picked up his knife and fork and resumed eating.

"Is that all? Don't you want to know the whole story?"

"Nope. This tart is terrific. Are you going to let that mousse go cold?"

Loretta gazed at him for a moment, looked down at her untasted *quenelles* and picked up her own fork.

11

THE ROOM WAS DARK AND LORETTA'S EYE-
lids fluttered open to an illusion of unfamiliarity, of objects lost in shadow or eerily illuminated by the glacial
light of the moon. A gleam in one corner, just within
her field of vision, was the dressing-table mirror, perfectly angled to reflect its cold beam; she gazed for a
moment at the ceiling, searching for the hair-thin crack
which branched from the rose, then let out a small, involuntary sound of pleasure as Christopher's hands
parted her thighs. She glanced down at his head, over-
whelmed by sensations she had not known for months
as his tongue caressed and teased her, and her disappointment when he suddenly pulled away was acute.

"Did you hear that?" He sat on the end of the bed,
listening intently, but Loretta was too disappointed to
take in what he was saying. Instead she reached forward
without speaking and tried to draw him back, before the
exciting sensations subsided entirely.

"No, listen." He pushed her gently away, got up and
went to the window, where he pulled a curtain across at
waist level while he stared down at the garden. Loretta
propped herself on one elbow, heard a distant sound be-

tween a shout and a cry and said crossly: "It's only kids. Come back to bed." She fell back, frustrated and embarrassed in about equal proportions, and was astonished when Christopher padded across the room and began retrieving discarded clothes from the floor and a chair.

"What are you *doing*?"

"I'm going down. Looks like you've got visitors in your garden."

Loretta sat bolt upright. "In the garden? Impossible—they'd have had to come through the house."

"All the more reason to go look." He tucked in his shirt, zipped his fly and returned to the bed, his hand closing on her wrist as she reached for the lamp. "No lights. Let's find out what's happening first." He kissed her on the lips, parting them with his tongue to reassure her that he was going reluctantly, and went to the door. The brass knob turned soundlessly, and Loretta saw his dark form slip from the room.

"Hang *on*." She scrambled off the bed, not wanting to be cast in the role of helpless female, and promptly tripped over a shoe. "Christopher," she called, on hands and knees, "wait for *me*." She lunged for the chair in the corner, pushed herself upright and seized an old T-shirt from the heap of clothes. *"Christopher."*

"Shhh," he called warningly from the floor below. She pulled on the T-shirt and felt her way after him, whispering in a nervous, urgent voice: "Shouldn't we—what about the police?" He did not reply and she glanced back at the pale shape of the phone on her bedside table, wondering how long the emergency services would take to answer if she dialed 999. She didn't want to be left holding the receiver while Christopher grappled with a burglar two floors below, and she had recently heard a radio program alleging that sick and

201

frightened people were frequently left waiting twenty minutes or more. She hurried onto the landing, throwing a worried look at the closed door to the other bedroom where Bridget was, as far as she knew, tucked up and fast asleep. Relieved that they hadn't already disturbed her, Loretta felt for the banister and began tiptoeing down the stairs in her bare feet.

Her progress became easier at the half-landing, which was illuminated by the cold light of a street lamp shining through the fanlight above the front door. She took the remaining stairs two at a time, grasping the newel post and swinging round onto the basement steps without a pause. She was unprepared for the dark tunnel after the bend and her shoulder brushed the wall, knocking a picture askew, as she hurried down to the kitchen. Here the street lamp came to her aid again, streaming through the uncurtained basement windows and reflecting coldly off the white cupboards.

"Christopher?" She spoke in a loud whisper. "Where are you?"

"In here." His voice came from the dining room. "Where's the key?"

"What key?"

"To these doors."

"Oh—I'll get it. What can you see?"

"Zilch, because of the steps, but somebody's out there all right."

She lifted the key from its hiding place on the mantelpiece and tiptoed to the French windows, registering a slight nervous shock when her hand brushed Christopher's bare forearm. She slid the key silently into the lock and turned it, reaching for the handle only to find that he had got there before her.

"I'll go first."

"It's *my* house," she whispered.

202

"For Christ's sake—this may be a *burglar* we're arguing about." He yanked the doors open, stepped out onto the paved area and ran lightly up the steps. Loretta saw him silhouetted against the limpid night sky for a few seconds, then he strode forward and said in a loud voice: "OK, who's there?"

Loretta crept out behind him, unsure whether she most dreaded hearing a stranger's voice or—and this was her other reason for not calling the police—that of John Tracey in a drunken rage. Instead she stopped dead on the bottom step, hardly aware of the cold paving stones under her feet, and listened in astonishment to a woman's voice saying the same thing over and over again.

"You *bastard*," it howled and sometimes, by way of variation, "you fucking, *fucking* bastard." Loretta unfroze and ran up the steps, fearing that Christopher was being attacked, and saw him struggling with a figure in a billowing white dress who appeared intent on throwing herself into the oily water of the canal.

"Loretta," he appealed, turning his head, "can you help here? I can't do anything for this goddam dress—"

Loretta ran the length of the garden, slipping and sliding on the wet grass, and skidded to a halt on the edge of the small landing stage. The intruder broke free from Christopher, screamed one final obscenity and collapsed on the water's edge, transforming herself at once into an exhausted ballerina. Pale skirts settled around her and she bowed her head in a gesture of despair reminiscent of Giselle—although, as one corner of Loretta's brain admitted, she knew little about ballet and was probably thinking of an imperfectly remembered photograph. The recumbent figure began to shake with sobs and Loretta exchanged a glance with Christopher, saw that he was as much at a loss as herself, and bent to touch the stranger's bare arm.

"Are you all right? Are you hurt?"

The fragile beauty lifted her head, revealing an unexpectedly plump décolletage. "Of *course* I'm not all right. Someone's just tried to fucking *rape* me."

Loretta jerked back. "Rape you? Who did?"

The girl—close up, she looked no more than sixteen—smoothed her lustrous dark hair, sniffed vigorously and dabbed at her eyes, leaving trails of mascara on each cheek. A faint splash, like an oar in water, alerted Loretta and she went to the water's edge, straining to make out any sign of movement between the tree-hung banks.

"See anything?" Christopher joined her, resting a hand briefly on her shoulder.

"N-no. I thought I heard something but . . ." Loretta was trying to work out how far the girl's assailant might have traveled by now—how soon he could leave the boat without being stranded, like his victim, in a garden without access to the road. Presumably he would get off at Aristotle Lane, by the bridge, and disappear along Polstead Road. "I *am* going to call the police," she told Christopher in a low voice, thinking there was at least a chance of apprehending the would-be rapist, and was astonished when the girl let out an angry wail. "Christ," she exclaimed, "are you trying to make things *worse*? You can't call the *police*."

Loretta glanced at Christopher for reassurance. His eyes narrowed and he tapped his right nostril, a gesture she did not immediately comprehend. "But you said someone tried to rape you," she began, turning back to the girl, "and the obvious thing . . . I mean, they may be able to *catch* him." She stopped in confusion as Christopher's meaning—nose candy, cocaine—dawned on her.

"Only Adam bloody Hall," the girl said, leaping to her feet. "I'll deal with *him* tomorrow." She gazed down at the quivering layers of silk chiffon and began to make violent but ineffective brushing motions. "*Shit*, there's grass stains all over my dress, that's thirteen hundred quid up the spout."

Loretta gasped. "Thirteen hundred pounds?" She had seen similar dresses in a shop window in Oxford, ball gowns with velvet bodices and flounced skirts, but had no idea that they cost so much—or that anyone could afford them in the middle of a recession.

"Mummy bought it for my twenty-first," the girl continued, scratching at the fragile fabric with her fingernails. "She'll be *furious* when she finds out." She gave the material one final swipe, as though showing it who was boss, and turned crossly to Loretta. "Are we going to stand here all night? I mean, Adam's gone off with my bag and stuff and I have *no idea* how I'm supposed to get home." She jerked her head towards the house. "This your place?"

Loretta nodded.

"Right then. If you take me to a phone I'll call a cab."

Loretta started across the grass, the whisper of silk behind her indicating that the girl was following. "Where do you live?" she called over her shoulder, wondering how easy it would be to get a taxi at one, perhaps even two o'clock in the morning.

"Dorset."

"*Dorset?*" Loretta repeated, stopping in her tracks.

"I'm in Oxford for the *weekend*," she added, bumping into Loretta and pushing her none too gently towards the back of the house. "Charles, he's bloody Adam's best friend, they used to live on the same staircase at St. John's . . . Charles's parents are away so he invited us all to a party. Oh, shit," she added, as though it was only a minor hindrance, "I don't know the address."

Loretta turned on the light in the dining room. "You're staying there and you don't know the address?"

The girl snapped: "It's a big house on the river. Charles picked me up at the station so I didn't really take in where we were going. God, I could *kill* Adam."

She followed Loretta into the kitchen, gazing about her without interest as Christopher locked the French windows. "How many bedrooms do you have?" she asked abruptly. "Since it looks as though I'll have to stay the night."

Loretta's eyes opened wide. "Two, actually, and they're both occupied. I suppose I could make you up a bed in my study. You haven't told us your name, by the way."

The girl's eyes narrowed. "Why should I?"

Loretta said sarcastically: "Just a whim on my part. I like to know who people are before I offer them a bed."

"Caroline," her guest announced ungraciously.

Loretta gestured that she expected more.

"Caroline . . . Wilson."

The surname was obviously an invention but Loretta was too tired to make anything of it. "I'm Loretta Lawson," she said briskly, "And this is Christopher Cisar."

Caroline glanced out of the window, peering up at the street. "Where are we? I mean, what road is this?"

"Southmoor Road."

"Where's that?"

This time Loretta rolled her eyes upwards. "Jericho. Don't you know Oxford?"

"Yes, but not this bit. I lived in college for the first

two years and last year I shared a house in Osney. Can I have a glass of water?"

"Help yourself, you'll find a clean glass in the dishwasher. I'm going up to see about this bed."

In the drawing room she pulled cushions off the sofa, carried them into her study and made a makeshift bed on the floor.

"Loretta? Need any help?" Christopher stood in the doorway.

She straightened up. "You could get a sheet and the spare duvet from the airing cupboard. In the bathroom."

A moment later he was back with a bundle of bedding. "Will this do?"

"Mmm. Think I should put a pea under her mattress to see if she's really a princess?" Before he could answer she slid past him and went to the top of the stairs. "Caroline, come up and I'll show you where you're sleeping."

The girl appeared, yawning, viewed the sleeping arrangements without enthusiasm and asked Loretta for directions to the bathroom. She left the room in a swirl of chiffon, offering not a word of thanks, and they heard a door slam on the half-landing.

"I was wrong," said Loretta, taking Christopher's arm "she's actually Prince Charming. Come on, let's go back to bed." She shivered and Christopher put his arms around her.

"Cold?"

"A bit." She allowed her head to fall against his chest.

"Tired?"

"Mmm."

He put a hand under her chin and lifted her face to his. "But not *too* tired?"

"Certainly not." They laughed, exchanged an increas-

207

ingly passionate kiss and stumbled upstairs to Loretta's bedroom.

Loretta lay in the bath next morning, idly attempting to turn on the hot tap with the toes of her right foot. Her feet were long and bony, the first two toes flexible enough to pick up a sheet of paper from the floor, but the tap dripped and she had turned it off with such force that it now refused to budge. Instead she pointed her toes and made circles in the air, humming a line from *Ariadne auf Naxos* and not really minding that the water was growing cold. Celibacy was overrated, she thought, pleasantly reminded of the night's exertions by the mild soreness of her inner thighs. She sat up and reached for the soap, thinking she had been in the bath long enough; Christopher had gone off to play squash with a colleague at nine, she didn't have to worry about him, but she still needed to find a set of clothes to fit Caroline Wilson and discuss how she was going to get back to her friend's parents' house. Perhaps she would be able to find it in daylight, although Loretta didn't really want to waste a sunny morning driving her round the various streets which backed onto the river.

She slid under the water to rinse off the soap, holding her head clear, and climbed out of the bath. A blue bath sheet hung on the towel horse and she dried herself vigorously, belatedly noticing a faint pong which suggested the towel had been used once too often. She tossed it into a corner and pulled on the clothes she'd brought down from her bedroom: fake Pucci leggings and a thin cotton top. A pair of earrings lay on the lid of the laundry basket and she threaded them through the lobes of her ears, let down her hair and ran her fingers through it. Then she scooped up the damp bath sheet, unlocked the bathroom door and sauntered down the stairs to the ground floor.

The door to her study was firmly shut. Loretta raised her free hand to knock, hesitated, and decided to put off the encounter until she had drunk a cup of coffee. Her post was lying on the hall table and she glanced through it, putting to one side a couple of early birthday cards and tearing open a Jiffy bag with an address label announcing it had been sent by the *Literary Review*. It contained the first volume of Antonia White's diaries, which Loretta had agreed to review for the magazine, and she opened the book and read a postcard from Lola, the deputy editor, as she went downstairs. The door to the downstairs bathroom was ajar and she elbowed it open, hurling the dirty towel inside as she passed.

"Hello?" she called on entering the kitchen, just in case Bridget or Caroline were already up. There was no reply but someone had been in the room recently: newspapers littered the kitchen table and a half-full pot of coffee stood on the draining board. Loretta felt the side of the cafetiere, found it was still hot and poured herself a mug of coffee, leaning back against the sink with her arms folded and her thoughts drifting agreeably. She had arranged to meet Christopher tomorrow night, at the Phoenix cinema, and Bridget was supposed to be returning home today, as soon as her cleaner had finished clearing up the mess, muddy footprints and turned-out cupboards, left by the police. Looking forward to an evening alone, Loretta lifted her mug and tasted her coffee, which was tepid and stale. She was about to throw it away when an upside-down headline caught her eye: WHY WEREN'T WE TOLD?

It triggered an old memory, John Tracey delivering a lecture on newspaper style over breakfast at their flat in south London and explaining in boring detail his objection to questions in headlines. His training as a journalist had been sporadic and on the job, handed down by an elderly chief sub in the weekly newspaper office in Chiswick where he had been office junior, and consisted of a series of inflexible injunctions which interested Loretta not one jot. It had pained him, on arriving at the *Sunday Herald*, to discover that house style required him to use single rather than double quotation marks, and when he wrote at home their living room was littered with sheets of paper angrily torn from the typewriter when he realized his mistake. The memory of Tracey bent over his old Remington at their dining table prompted another image, wholly imaginary this time but no less vivid, in which Loretta saw him hunched miserably over his Tandy at the Randolph Hotel, struggling to meet a deadline while she pottered about her kitchen and indulged in some mildly erotic fantasies. His illusory presence rapidly became so dejected and accusing that it was almost a relief to lean forward and seize the newspaper which had prompted this melancholy train of thought, even though a picture below the headline confirmed Loretta's assumption that it referred to the Thebes Farm murder. A middle-aged man glared at her from the paper as he got into a parked car, as if she had called out his name; Loretta dumped her coffee, pulled out a chair and began to read:

Angry women's groups and student representatives rounded on police in Oxford last night, demanding: WHY WEREN'T WE TOLD?

They were reacting to the shock revelation at yesterday's inquest on a murdered 21-year-old that a sex beast has been preying on local women for three years—and no warnings were ever given.

SEX BEAST

Police believe that the man, who drives a blue van, killed for the first time three weeks ago after earlier attacks on at least four women. All the attacks have taken place on the A34 trunk road—the main route from Oxford to Newbury, Southampton and the southwest.

The body of the dead woman, an American tourist, was discovered in a barn at the isolated home of an Oxford don on Sunday afternoon. The cause of death was a severe head injury and police now believe she was picked up by her attacker while hitchhiking.

The inquest on Paula Wolf, from Oak Falls, Ohio, was adjourned after the detective leading the murder investigation, Superintendent Eddie Dibden (left), told the court he had reason to link her death with the other attacks (turn to column two, page five).

There was uproar as he admitted that another incident took place a week ago, 15 days after a witness saw Miss Wolf getting into a van at the junction between the A34 and the M4. The victim, aged 24, was beaten about the head and left for dead after her car broke down near Didcot.

Jane Hilton, a 24-year-old postgraduate at women-only Somerville College, said at a hastily arranged meeting in the city last night: "A car is the one place a woman on her own feels safe. Now it appears we can't even drive without putting ourselves at risk—and the police have said nothing."

ESCAPE

Another woman, who wanted to remain anonymous, said she believed she had a lucky escape nine months ago, when a man approached her as she changed a wheel on the hard shoulder south of Abingdon after a tire blew out. When he saw her 12-year-old daughter in the passenger seat, the man ran back to his own vehicle and drove off.

The woman, a 36-year-old nurse, claimed she reported the incident to the police but they showed no interest because she was unable to give them the registration number of the other driver.

Last night Supt. Dibden tried to defuse the row. "Our decision not to publicly link the attacks was taken after careful consideration and to avoid the possibility of copycat crimes," he said in a statement. "Many women have heeded our warnings about the dangers of hitchhiking and, regrettably, we are now dealing with a new type of opportunist crime in which offenders actively seek female victims in a vulnerable position after their vehicles have broken down.

"My officers have been involved in a painstaking attempt to amass evidence which might lead to an arrest and two considerations were uppermost in our minds. We did not wish to unduly alarm women about a type of crime which is thankfully still rare, and we were anxious not to stimulate further attacks by this man or anybody else.

"We naturally regret the distress that this decision may have caused but I would like to say on behalf of all my officers, whom I know to be a dedicated and hard working bunch of men, that the criticism we now face is ill-informed and shows that, in the current adverse climate, the police simply cannot win."

Labor MP Avril Duncan denounced Supt. Dibden's remarks as a "smoke-screen" and said she would raise the matter in Parliament after the summer recess. A spokeswoman for a London-based group, Women Against Sexual Terrorism (WASTE), added:

"When are the police going to stop defending themselves and start defending women?"

Drivers' organizations, including the AA and RAC, said they are looking into the possibility of offering cheap car phones to their members so that stranded women would not have to leave their cars—

"Hi, Loretta." Bridget walked into the room, looking relaxed and rested and carrying one of the bags in which Loretta had packed her clothes on Sunday evening. "I didn't hear you get out of the bath. Are my clean things still on top of the washing machine?" She nodded in the direction of the downstairs bathroom.

"Mmm. I was just reading this." Loretta held up the paper.

Bridget blinked, as though it was an effort to transfer her thoughts from packing, then sat down opposite Loretta. "They really have cocked up, haven't they?" she said with some satisfaction. "To think they spent all that time persecuting me about that stupid diary when they knew perfectly well ... Give it here a minute." She reached across, took the paper from Loretta's hand and read in a mock-pompous voice: " 'The criticism we now face is ill-informed and shows that, in the current adverse climate, the police simply cannot win.' Bloody cheek," she said, throwing the paper down. "I don't know how he's got the nerve. Funny, I was just wondering the other day whether I should get a car phone now that we live out in the country. I mean, say the car did break down on the way home?"

"Don't they cost a fortune?"

"Oh, the call rate's ridiculous but you'd only use it in an emergency. Want some coffee?"

"It's cold, I was just going to make some more."

Bridget pushed back her chair, gesturing to Loretta to

stay in her seat. "I feel like a new woman this morning. Where d'you think the papers came from? You were out of coffee so I went to that little shop in Walton Street, they didn't have much of a selection but it's better than nothing." She turned on the cold tap and held the kettle under it, adding rather archly: "Your other guest didn't complain, at any rate."

Loretta's eyes widened and she steeled herself for a barrage of questions about herself and Christopher. "Gosh," she said carelessly, "you must've been up for hours. He'd arranged to play squash at nine, that's why he went off so early. Why are you looking at me like that?"

"He?" Bridget turned off the tap, a startled look on her face. "I'm talking about a sulky young woman who borrowed ten quid off me for a taxi. Hang on," she added, a new note entering her voice, "you don't mean . . . you and Christopher? Well, *well*." She shook coffee grounds into the cafetiere, showering them onto the worktop below, and returned to the table with an eager grin on her face. "Come on," she said, sitting down and folding her arms, "I want to hear *all* about it."

Loretta ignored her. "Did she—Caroline whatever-her-name-is. Did she say where she was going?"

Bridget shook her head, not much interested.

"I don't suppose she left an address?"

"No. What is this, Loretta? Isn't she a friend of yours?"

Loretta closed her eyes in an attempt to remember where Caroline said she lived. She remembered leading the way into the house, Caroline just behind her and Christopher bringing up the rear . . .

"Dorset," she said in a puzzled voice, realizing that she could not recall, or Caroline had not told her, the name of the town or village. Ten pounds was hardly enough to get her all that way, especially after paying a taxi fare to the station. Another thought occurred to her and she got up and looked round for her bag. "Sorry, Bridget," she added, locating it, "I'll pay you back. Ten pounds, did you say?"

"Don't worry about *that*. Who is she?"

Loretta took two five-pound notes from her purse. "Some girl who jumped off a boat in the middle of the night and landed in my garden. I suppose it counts as date rape, not that he managed it, of course, since she escaped."

"Date rape? In a *boat*?" Bridget made it sound as though she did not know what young people were coming to.

"Christopher thought they'd been doing cocaine, she was very anxious I shouldn't call the police."

"Quite right, they'd probably have arrested her at once if the way they treated me is anything to go by. No, I don't want it," she insisted, pushing Loretta's money away. "I've been here all week and all I've given you is that measly tenner for the Chinese takeaway. You know," she added, changing the subject as Loretta gave in and put the money away, "it's been a real eye-opener, seeing their methods at first hand, the police. I mean, you always wonder why people confess to things they haven't done, the Birmingham Six and that man in the Carl Bridgewater case, but when you're actually in that little room and they ask you the same thing over and over again—"

Loretta exclaimed: "Surely she didn't go off in that dress? I was going to lend her a skirt or something."

"What dress? You're babbling, Loretta. She had on a perfectly ordinary pair of jeans when I met her."

"Jeans?" Loretta stared at Bridget for a moment, then turned to look at the half-open door into the bathroom.

215

Hurrying across the kitchen, she kicked the soiled bath sheet out of her way and said incredulously: "She's taken my jeans."

"What?"

"She's stolen my jeans," Loretta repeated, coming back. "And my black T-shirt. They were with your stuff on the washing machine and now they're gone." She wheeled round and ran upstairs, leaving Bridget to gape after her.

In Loretta's study the blind was still down and the floor strewn with bedding. Loretta clambered across the sofa cushions, her bare feet sinking into the duvet, and snatched the white dress from its resting place on her desk. It weighed less than she expected and she crushed it against her body, shaking the skirt until its many petticoats flared out and then settled against her legs. The boned bodice stood out from her chest and she thought that, elegant though it was, she would happily exchange it for her old Levi's. She threw it over one arm, carried it downstairs to the kitchen and held it up in front of Bridget.

"She was wearing *that*?" the latter demanded. "In a boat?"

"Mmm. Thirteen hundred pounds, she said it cost."

Bridget whistled. "Some of my students have to live on that for six months."

"What shall I do with it? It's not exactly me." Loretta wiggled her hips and the chiffon swayed.

"The Oxfam shop? Pity about the grass stains on the skirt." Bridget's hand hovered over the cafetiere, ready to plunge the top down, and she said: "The coffee's made, if you've finished playing at *Come Dancing*."

Loretta arranged the dress on her Lloyd Loom chair and took down two clean mugs.

"You still haven't told me about you and Christopher," Bridget said, and Loretta felt her cheeks grow warm as she took a bottle of milk from the fridge. "It must have gone *spectacularly* well if you actually let him stay the night."

"There's nothing much to tell," Loretta lied, lining up the mugs on the table and avoiding Bridget's eye.

"Come *on*. Where did you go to eat? I didn't hear you come in so I assume you didn't come straight back here after the opera and drag him upstairs."

"Of course *not*." Loretta poured out the coffee. "We went to North Parade, as a matter of fact, which turned out to be a bit of a mistake. Guess who walked in?"

Bridget narrowed her eyes. "Nelson Mandela? Prince Edward? How should I know?"

"John Tracey."

"Uh-oh."

"He was with some bloke from the *Independent*. He was absolutely furious, he just turned round and stormed out."

"How did you explain that to Christopher?"

"I didn't, he was very calm about the whole thing."

"He can afford to be, he's bigger than your dearly beloved. It's a bit awkward, though."

"Is it?"

"Well, yes. Presumably we won't get any more inside information." Bridget picked up the *Sun* and pointed to its front page. "I haven't read every single word of every paper," she went on, "but they're so excited about the rapist angle that there's nothing about that woman, Denise something, the one Tracey was trying to get hold of yesterday."

"If he did, I'm sure it'll be in the paper tomorrow."

Bridget looked doubtful. "It's not the same, though, is it? And we still don't know how she ended up in my garden. I mean, did he just drive around with the body in his van till he saw our house? We get the *Independent on Sunday*, not the *Sunday Herald*; I suppose one of us'll have to go out in the morning."

"You're still planning to go home, then?"

"Mmm." Bridget sipped her coffee and added a little more milk. "I'll give Sam a ring in a minute, see how Mrs. Crossley is getting on with the clearing-up. Her daughter was going to help her, the married one from Kidlington, so it shouldn't take all day. What are you doing?" She smiled slyly. "Seeing Christopher?"

"No." Loretta shook her head. "I'm going to Paris on Monday, I've got a few things to sort out before I go—"

"Paris? On your birthday? What for?"

Loretta looked sheepish. "You know—the *Fem Sap* editorial collective meeting, it's always in August. I'm going to stay on for another day as I haven't had a holiday this year—go to the Louvre, that sort of thing."

"You are *good*, Loretta, the way you never miss a meeting. I saw your piece in the last one, about pseudonyms, I thought it was very clever. By the way"—she leaned forward, studying her mug of coffee as though there was something unusually interesting about it— "have you thought any more about what I was saying? About standing in while I'm on maternity leave?"

"Yes, actually." Loretta remembered Bernard Shilling's plans for her own department, and her need to make contacts elsewhere. "If you really think the English faculty will agree to it ..."

Bridget lifted her head and grinned. "*Course* they will. I'll wave your Edith Wharton book about, show them a few of your articles. I'll get on to it on Monday, make a few phone calls, it'll be all fixed up by the time you get back." A cloud crossed her face, and Loretta wondered whether it was because she realized this was a rash promise. "When *do* you get back, by the way?"

"Thursday."

"OK, give me a ring. I'll even print my *Frankenstein* paper out for you." She threw back her head and laughed, her momentary doubt apparently dispelled. "It'll be just like old times," she added, and Loretta did not point out that she and Bridget had never actually worked together.

The phone sounded and Loretta got up to answer it. "Yes," she said, turning to look at Bridget, "she's here and we're both well. Do you want to speak to her?"

She passed the phone across, mouthing, "Sam," and sat down to look at the *Guardian* Weekend section. The cover consisted of a grainy black-and-white image of a burly man being led, handcuffed, from a dock and the coverlines promised a feature, inside, about a mass murderer who had killed and eaten his victims in Finland. Loretta hurriedly turned the pages past the gruesome details, also ignoring a profile of a South American novelist by an English publisher she had once met and disliked at a party, and arrived at Colin Spencer's cookery column. She read with interest a recipe for spinach roulade, wondering whether to make it for supper that evening, and got up to find a piece of paper on which to make a shopping list.

"Listen," Bridget said unexpectedly, putting the phone down, "Sam says they arrived late, something about Mrs. Crossley's daughter having to give her husband a lift somewhere first, so why don't I take you out to lunch? A birthday treat, as you're not going to be here on Monday."

"I was going to go to Sainsbury's at Heyford Hill, but I suppose I could do it later."

"Course you can—they're open till six or something. Why don't we go to the Feathers in Woodstock and sit outside? I'll just finish packing, it won't take me a minute. All right?"

Loretta smiled, touched by Bridget's enthusiasm. "All right. I might even drop in at the Oxfam shop in Summertown on the way back." She got up, went to the Lloyd Loom chair and gave the white dress a last twirl before putting it away in a large plastic bag.

12

THERE HAD BEEN, LORETTA LEARNED FROM
the *Sunday Herald* the following morning, dramatic developments in what was now being described as the
A34 murder inquiry. The story, under John Tracey's
byline, took up most of the front page; she walked
slowly from the hall to her study, reading that the van
used in the attacks was now believed to be darkish blue
in color, probably an A- or B-reg Ford Transit. Alan
Stocks, the 29-year-old motor mechanic who had seen
Paula Wolf getting into it, recalled "distinctive" letter-
ing on the side of the van; he, along with two of the
surviving victims, had agreed to answer questions under
hypnosis and the police were said to be "very excited"
about the results, although they were being cagey about
the precise details. All they would say was that they
now had evidence that the Transit was being used to
carry "hazardous loads," a quote which prompted the
insertion, at this point in the story, of a photograph of
the rear doors of a lorry with its number plate blacked
out and bearing a HAZCHEM sign, the standard indicator
of the presence of toxic chemicals.

The story continued on page two, where Tracey had

not been able to resist crowing over his success in obtaining an "exclusive" interview with Denise Stannion, who had spent Friday evening being "debriefed" by two Thames Valley detectives in Geneva. Loretta spread the paper out on her desk, surprised to learn that Tracey had flown to Switzerland the previous day. "Denise Stannion," she read, swinging gently from side to side in her desk chair, "lives in a second-floor flat in Onex, an exclusive suburb of Geneva. Thirty-two-year-old Mrs. Stannion, who is British and works at the headquarters of an international trade union in the city, chain-smoked as she described her first sight of Paula Wolf, the young American who was soon to fall victim to the A34 killer."

Loretta wrinkled her nose, disliking the style of the piece and thinking it bore all the hallmarks of having been written against a deadline. Tracey would have been smoking just as furiously as Denise Stannion, his consumption was heaviest when he was under pressure, and she pictured the two of them straining to see each other through a miasma of blue cigarette smoke. She read on:

"She was at the side of the road just before the underpass," Mrs. Stannion told me, "where the road goes up to the M4. She was trying to wave down cars and my first thought was that she was in danger of being run over. I pulled in, wound down the window and asked what on earth she was doing. She asked me if I was going anywhere near Oxford and I said no, but there was a bus from the central bus station. She looked disappointed and started moving away from the car, so I called after her that it was dangerous to hitchhike on her own."

Mrs. Stannion's hand shook as she stubbed out one

cigarette and lit another. "She ran behind the car and tried to flag down a lorry, which missed her by inches, it was almost as if she didn't care what happened to her. I got out and ran after her, the traffic was swerving to avoid my car and I was afraid there'd be a crash. I grabbed her arm, shouted that I could take her most of the way and she got in the car."

Mrs. Stannion says her passenger was quiet and docile, readily admitting she had just missed a coach to Oxford and in any case couldn't really afford the £7 single fare. Mrs. Stannion describes Ms. Wolf as "silent, morose almost" and was surprised when she took out a thick paperback book and began to read.

"I couldn't see what it was until I asked her to look at the map on the backseat to see how close we were to the Newbury exit on the M4. Then she closed it and I saw it was the Bible. I'm not religious myself, but she was American and I've heard about all those TV evangelists in America, so I assumed she was born-again."

This was confirmed when Mrs. Stannion asked Ms. Wolf why she was going to Oxford and she replied enigmatically: "To do God's will." Mrs. Stannion says that trying to engage her in further conversation was like "getting blood out of a stone" and Ms. Wolf soon returned to studying her Bible.

"The traffic was much heavier than I expected and I realized I was going to be late for a TUC meeting in Bristol," Mrs. Stannion told me, close to tears. "I had intended to take her into Newbury, it's two or three miles south of the M4, but when I saw how late it was I asked her if she'd mind me dropping her at the roundabout. Naturally, if I'd had any idea that other women had been attacked on that road I'd

223

never have left her there." Mrs. Stannion arrived at her meeting half an hour late, returned to Geneva two days later and knew nothing of Ms. Wolf's death until she read about it in an English paper on Thursday evening.

The rest of the story was made up of bits and pieces, including the fact that Superintendent Dibden was "exasperated" about the nonappearance of Ms. Wolf's brother at Heathrow on Friday morning. The reason for his failure to get on the flight was "a dispute within the strict religious sect of which he is a member"; Tracey explained that the Imitators of Christ opposed air travel except in the most dire emergency and had overruled Karl Wolf's unilateral decision to come to England and make a formal identification of his sister. The matter would now be decided at a two-day "prayer vigil" involving the whole community over the weekend, and Tracey hinted that this behavior was testing Superintendent Dibden's patience to the limit. Detectives from the Thames Valley force were ready to fly to Ohio, he said, if "communication difficulties" continued. A final paragraph declared abruptly that a bundle of bloodstained clothing found in a foxhole near Thebes Farm during a police search on Thursday was still being examined by forensic scientists, but a connection with the A34 murder had been ruled out. There was a researcher's byline in minute type at the bottom of the story and Loretta guessed it had been cobbled together in the office from various faxes sent by Tracey and last-minute calls to police headquarters in Kidlington.

Just how busy Tracey had been was revealed by a line in bold, awkwardly positioned after the name of the researcher. "Murder, Morals and the Media," it proclaimed, and urged readers to turn to a feature on page seven. This splitting-up of single stories across several pages, which Loretta disliked, was a result of the *Herald*'s transition from broadsheet to tabloid, coinciding with its physical removal from Holborn to Docklands. She merely glanced at Tracey's feature, an analysis of press reaction to the murder illustrated by a rag-out of tabloid headlines and a mugshot of Superintendent Dibden; it was written in a calmer, more ironic style, and described the way in which news stories were now "processed" to resemble popular fiction by tabloid journalists, sparing their readers the task of thinking for themselves. There was nothing in it that Loretta disagreed with, she could have written much of the article herself, but she found it hard to reconcile Tracey's magisterial rebuke to the popular press with his own obsessive pursuit of what he described as "sexy" stories—a term which referred not to their content but to the almost sexual buzz he seemed to get out of chasing them.

Anyway, Loretta thought, turning the sadly shrunken pages of the *Sunday Herald*, Tracey was now technically a tabloid hack himself. She began reading an article by a member of the shadow cabinet, a nostalgic piece about the heyday of black-and-white films, then lifted her head, suddenly aware that the house was completely silent. Even Bertie had not come home, presumably because the warm weather had lured him into a longer than usual exploration of the canal bank. She shrugged off a little *frisson* of anxiety and reached for the phone, intending to ring Bridget and talk about Tracey's article, then put the receiver back and withdrew her hand; it was Bridget and Sam's first full day together since the discovery of the body a week ago—a week ago *today*—and she felt shy about interrupting them.

Instead she folded the newspaper, tossed it onto the

floor and reached into the top drawer of her desk, where the agenda of the *Fem Sap* editorial meeting had been lying unopened for nearly two weeks. She had had advance warning, in phone calls from Paris and Munich, that the magazine was facing yet another financial crisis and she had put off reading the details as long as she could. Now she tore the envelope open and pulled out a thick wad of paper, the top sheet a prickly statement from the treasurer in defense of her unpopular proposal to double corporate subscription fees. The next sheet consisted of a counterproposal from two American academics, a superficially attractive prediction of how the magazine could be saved by selling advertising space, but a moment's glance at the figures told Loretta they were wildly optimistic; she simply could not imagine hard-nosed commercial organizations, department stores and airlines, jumping at the opportunity of advertising their products to a group of intelligent but for the most part impoverished academics. She moved automatically through the other items on the agenda, making an occasional mark in the margin, then felt she had done her duty and worked on her book for a couple of hours.

It was a brilliantly sunny day and as time wore on she was more and more frequently distracted by the antics of weekend boaters. At one point she heard shrieks, lifted her head and saw a teenage girl collapse into giggles as her boat bumped the bank and sprayed her companions with brackish water. Loretta watched them with envy, regretting the demise of her rowing boat and remembering that the oars, propped against the wall of her small garden shed, were all that remained of it. She began to feel a fool for working, struggling to reorder her thoughts on *Shirley* without even Bertie for company when everyone else was out having a good time. Her shoulders ached and she slipped off her chair, stretched out her arms and did a couple of the warm-up exercises she had been taught at the gym, her movements restricted by the risk of knocking ornaments off the mantelpiece or hitting her hand on the filing cabinet. When she had finished she looked at her watch and saw that it was only half past two, with the long hot afternoon stretching emptily before her.

She decided to walk into the city center and see if any of the bookshops were open, needing to buy copies of the *Frost in May* trilogy before she attempted to review Antonia White's diaries. Reviewing was always like this, she thought, fetching her bag and checking that her sunglasses were inside; you agreed to look at one book without realizing how long it had been since you read the author's other work. Loretta opened the front door, thinking she could read at least a bit of *Frost in May* on the plane to Paris, and stopped dead on the threshold. A lavish bouquet of summer flowers, enclosed in cellophane, completely covered the step.

There were Longine lilies, flawless and creamy as vellum, stargazers with orange stamens bursting from mottled pink flesh, half a dozen stems of an orchidlike flower whose name she knew but could not remember and three or four white roses. The bouquet was tied with a double bow of white ribbon—real satin, not the artificial kind favored by most florists these days—and Loretta bent with a sense of wonder to pick them up. It was an extravagant gesture on its own and her astonishment was compounded when she saw, underneath, a carrier bag from a smart shoe shop in Little Clarendon Street. Balancing the flowers in the crook of her left arm, she lifted the bag and heard the rattle of tissue paper inside, obscuring its contents.

Downstairs in the kitchen Loretta slid the flowers onto the table and opened the carrier bag. The tissue paper slid apart to reveal her jeans and T-shirt, neatly folded, and an envelope bearing her name and a scribbled sentence in ink of a different color. "Sunday, 8:45 A.M.," it said, "bell doesn't work. Please ring me about collecting dress, number inside." Loretta tore open the envelope, which contained a ten-pound note and a postcard reproduction of Rossetti's *Beata Beatrix*. Barely glancing at the familiar image, Loretta turned the card over and read in a neater version of the same script:

Dear Ms. Lawson,

So sorry about Friday night and for rushing off without seeing you—please give your friend the enclosed ten-pound note. Hope you didn't mind me borrowing your clothes, they've been washed and ironed. Apologies also for coming so early, I've got a lift to Dorset.

Yours,
Caroline Wilson

Loretta stared at the telephone number in the top right-hand corner of the card, almost comically dismayed. She had been certain that she would not hear from Caroline Wilson again—so certain that she had taken Bridget's advice and dropped the white dress off at the Oxfam shop in Summertown the previous afternoon. There was time to return to the shop the following morning, before Loretta set off for Paris, but would the shop simply hand it back? Even charities were shrewd these days, and the time was gone when designer dresses could be found for a fiver among the washed-out cardigans and C & A tat. Loretta grunted, threw down the card and turned to go upstairs when she remembered she had not looked out a vase for the blameless flowers.

The young man had a surly, uncongenial expression; there was something about him which suggested he was watchful, suspicious, even that he resented her looking at him at all. Loretta had a feeling he expected someone else, someone who certainly wasn't a woman, yet she was unsure whether his reaction would be hostile or erotic. She took a step back, deliberately distancing herself, yet his eyes continued to hold hers. His nose was bulbous, his lips fleshy, and it was easy to imagine his stubby fingers moving from the musical instrument they presently held to grasp a glistening fig from the table in front of him, squeezing it until the purple skin split and the jammy seeds spilled out.

Loretta nearly laughed out loud, recognizing the way in which her own suggestibility had colluded with the painter's intention. It was all to do with mood, with the brooding horror she had been trying to push to the back of her mind ever since Paula Wolf's body was discovered in the barn in Bridget and Sam's garden a week ago; why else should she be so affected by a picture she had passed without a second glance on previous visits to the Ashmolean? She leaned closer and peered at the inscription in small letters along the bottom of the frame to discover who had unsettled her so much.

Still Life with a Young Man playing a Recorder, she read, and the artist's name: attributed to Francesco (Cecco) del Caravaggio. Loretta's smile faded and she moved back, thinking of her discussion with Janet Dunne earlier in the week and wondering whose argument was validated by her unexpected reaction to the painting. The sinister undertones had been plain to her *before* she knew the identity of the painter, obviously a follower of the more notorious Michelangelo Merisi da Caravaggio, yet she was already looking at it with a fresh eye, reading even more sinister things into it. A recorder could easily double as a club, especially one as thick and heavy as Cecco del Caravaggio had chosen to paint, and the unidentified vegetable on the table, next to the straining figs, bore a marked resemblance to an exposed human brain.

"I wouldn't like to meet him on a dark night," said a voice somewhere behind her left shoulder, uncannily echoing Loretta's own thoughts. Red hair flashed past her as the police inspector, the woman whose name Loretta could never remember, bent to read the inscription on the frame. "Car-a-vagg-io," she said, pronouncing it with a hard *g* as though the name was unfamiliar. She straightened and moved back to stand next to Loretta. "Big place this; I've seen hundreds of Greek vases but not that picture your friend was raving about."

Loretta, who was astonished by the policewoman's presence in the museum, remembered her indignant questions to Bridget about what she had been doing on Tuesday—no, Monday— afternoon. "Are you—is this official?" she blurted out.

The Inspector, who had been glancing at pictures on the end wall of the gallery without much interest, turned to look at her as though she was mad. "Official?" she repeated.

"Well, I mean, aren't you on duty?"

The Inspector's eyes narrowed. "I got home at midnight last night after spending most of yesterday at the hospital interviewing a very distressed woman who was beaten unconscious just over a week ago. I came in at seven this morning and I don't suppose I'll get home before midnight tonight. All I've had to eat is a succession of sandwiches and a lot of canteen coffee. Don't you think I'm entitled to a short break?"

"Of *course*," Loretta said quickly, aware that the policewoman had raised her voice and people were looking at them. "I'm sure it must be terrible for you—no, I mean it. I didn't expect to see you here, that's all, in an art gallery."

"It's been recognized as an occupational hazard, stress. Everyone knows policemen retire early, but do you know how many of them actually get to the official retirement age? My first superintendent, he retired and set up his own security firm, he dropped dead at fifty-seven. *Fifty-seven.*"

"OK, you don't have to convince me." Loretta had been misled by the woman's smartly pressed suit and bright lipstick, but now she saw the taut skin below her eyes, the pallor of her cheeks beneath her tinted foundation. "Why don't I show you, if you're still interested, the painting Bridget was talking about? It's through here."

The Inspector pulled back her cuff and looked at her watch. "I don't know, I ought to get back to the station."

"It's the quickest way out, from here." Loretta took a couple of steps towards the far end of the Weldon Gallery, uncertain whether the policewoman would accompany her.

"Oh, well, as I'm here." They walked the length of the gallery, the Inspector enlarging on the theme of stress, exhaustion and their effect on efficiency. "I mean, it's macho culture; when I started you couldn't admit you were too tired to question somebody properly or you wanted to be sick after seeing a body. Which way here?"

They were in a wide, high hall with elaborate wall

hangings and a staircase rising to the second floor. "Those are the Raphael and Michelangelo sketches," Loretta said, gesturing with her right hand to a series of vertical glass cases. "The Pre-Raphaelites are up those stairs if you like that sort of thing, which I don't . . . The Piero's through here, at the far end."

Talking seemed to have tired the Inspector and she said nothing as they turned into another long gallery. Loretta mentioned one or two pictures as they passed, and pointed out a small bronze relief of a woman in a chariot drawn by two panthers. Finally she stopped and said: "This is it—*The Forest Fire*."

The policewoman leaned forward to examine a fat bird, a partridge or a grouse, which had launched itself from a tree and appeared to be taking deadly aim at a passing cow herd. Beside her Loretta admired the bears, a mother and her cubs, lumbering up a slope guarded by a lion in an attempt to escape the flames devouring the trees behind.

The Inspector said: "I can't see it myself, why she likes it so much. Why have they got human faces?"

"I suppose they're mythological. Don't you like the bears?"

"They're a funny color, aren't they? And those ducks—my aunt's got a set of plaster ones on her wall that look more lifelike."

Loretta smiled. "So has my mother. Shall I show you the way out?" She led the way through an antechamber, past the portrait of Elias Ashmole in full-bottomed wig and a coat of rose-colored velvet, to the great marble staircase which descended to the ground floor.

"I know where I am now," the Inspector said at the top of the steps. "No need to come down."

"I might as well, I think it closes quite soon." She

added hesitantly: "Are you having any luck with the van? The Transit?"

The Inspector shook her head. "Not my bit of the inquiry. There's a couple of DCs going through all the registrations in Oxfordshire but it's a long job—he may not even be local." She didn't seem to mind Loretta's question, and they walked companionably through the souvenir shop and out into the open air.

The Inspector stopped on the path, glanced back at the fluted marble columns and said thoughtfully: "Sometimes I wonder why I do this job." Her gaze traveled up the neoclassical façade to the seated figure with one arm upraised on the apex of the pediment. Loretta waited for her to say more but she merely sighed, and resumed her progress towards the short flight of steps leading down from the courtyard into Beaumont Street. The grass on either side of the path was neatly mowed and bright green, a monument to the efforts of the gardening staff and a wettish summer.

Loretta said: "Presumably it's worth it in the end. Especially in a case like this one."

The Inspector stared across the road, watching a limousine with a uniformed driver turn out of the garage of the Randolph Hotel into Beaumont Street. A fat man sat in the back, smoking a cigar. "How do you mean?"

"Well—you know. When it's someone who's attacked several women." There was a plaque fixed to the open gate, listing the museum's opening times in white letters on a shiny black surface. Loretta read: "Tue. to Sat. 10–4. Sunday 2–4. Closed on Mondays." She thought: Closed on Mondays?

"It'll all be forgotten in a week," the detective was saying. "Those coppers who caught Peter Sutcliffe, who remembers them now?"

Loretta wasn't listening to her. Bridget said she had

visited the Ashmolean on Monday afternoon, after lunch at Browns with Sam, yet there it was in black and white in front of her—the museum was closed on Mondays. Loretta narrowed her eyes, trying to think of an alternative explanation to the obvious one that she had caught her friend out in another lie. Nothing came, but the fib was so trivial and so pointless that Loretta could not imagine what was behind it.

A car squealed to a halt at the bottom of the steps, unmarked but giving itself away by the squawking of a police radio through the open windows. The passenger door flew open and a man in shirtsleeves leaped out, stopping abruptly when he recognized the Inspector.

"Ma'am," he exclaimed with a mixture of relief and urgency, "the boss says, can you come at once? He thinks we've got him."

The woman's eyes flickered as she assimilated this startling piece of news, and her whole body tensed. Seconds later she was striding down the steps, firing questions at the excited detective: "OK, Blady, where are we going? Does he know we're on to him?"

Blady hurried forward as the Inspector slid into the seat he had just vacated, briefing her in a voice too low for Loretta to hear. She hung back, thinking she had been forgotten, but at the last minute the woman paused and leaned out of the car. Her eyes glittering with anticipation, she said tersely: "Sorry, Dr. Lawson—you heard."

The door snapped shut, Blady threw himself into the back and the engine roared into life. The police car accelerated towards the traffic lights at the end of Beaumont Street, swung into the right-hand lane to avoid a tourist bus and veered left into St. Giles as the lights changed to green. It was gone before Loretta had time to think and she walked slowly down the steps, peering towards the Martyrs' Memorial as though she expected the car to rematerialize; it was like being in a cinema, she thought, on the edge of your seat, and suddenly the projector had broken down at the climactic moment. This time there was no point in waiting for the screen to flicker back into life and she turned away, keeping her head down as she skirted a party of American tourists arguing over the quickest route from Beaumont Street to the Botanic Gardens.

13

"HELLO," SAID BRIDGET IN AN ARTIFICIALLY bright voice, "you're talking to an answering machine but please don't hang up. If your call is urgent—"

Loretta cut her off in mid-sentence, seeing little point in adding to the two messages she had left the previous afternoon. The phone's digital display told her she had used up only ten pence of the pound coin she had fed into the slot and she took a piece of paper from her jeans pocket, punched in the number of the Oxfam shop in Summertown and asked whether the woman in charge of pricing secondhand clothes had come in yet. She hadn't and Loretta left another message about the white ball dress, pleading with the shop assistant to make sure no one sold it before she returned from Paris. Then she pressed the follow-on call button, trying to overcome her nerves and ring John Tracey. It was Monday, the Sunday journalist's day off, and Tracey would probably be at home; he might know no more than the two-sentence announcement she had heard on several news bulletins, a terse, legalistic confirmation that Thames Valley Police were questioning a man about the murder of an American tourist and a series of sex attacks on the Newbury-to-Oxford road, but he would certainly be able to find out more. Someone coughed noisily, reminding Loretta there was a queue to use the phone, and she hastily punched in Tracey's number, biting her lip as she listened to the familiar double burr of the ringing tone.

There was a click, another answering machine: "Hi, John Tracey speaking. I'm also taking messages for Terese McKinnon." Loretta blinked at this unexpected addition to his usual laconic greeting, the name meaning nothing to her. Tracey was droning on, giving the number of his fax machine at home and his direct line at the office, and when she finally heard the tone Loretta could think of nothing to say. She hooked the receiver back on its rest, abandoning her remaining fifty-four pence, and glanced up at the departures board. The boarding sign had come up against her flight and she hoisted the strap of her carpetbag onto her shoulder, making way for a choleric middle-aged man who brushed up against her in his eagerness to reach the phone.

Loretta headed for passport control, wondering about Terese McKinnon. She might be a stringer on a visit to London, Tracey did occasionally offer his spare room to foreign journalists, but Loretta did not think she had seen the woman's byline in the *Sunday Herald*. She handed her passport to an immigration official, waited while he gave it a cursory glance and joined the queue to have her hand luggage X-rayed. The security staff were as stony-faced as ever, reminding her of a trip to Amsterdam during the Gulf War when the sight of police with automatic weapons patrolling the passenger terminals at Heathrow had made her doubt the wisdom of her spur-of-the-moment decision to go away for the weekend.

"Thanks," she said, wasting the courtesy on an uncommunicative woman who shoved her bag towards her as it emerged from the X-ray machine. She began the long hike to the departure gate, stepping onto a moving walkway and speeding past returning holidaymakers with patchy suntans and T-shirts announcing they had spent the last two weeks in Corfu and loved every minute of it. Loretta disliked airports, the recycled air and the endless waiting, and she regretted having to spend her birthday in one; the morning's post was in her bag, half a dozen cards stuffed back in their envelopes after she opened them on the coach to Heathrow. Bridget had posted hers on Saturday morning, when she went to buy coffee, with a scribbled apology for failing to find something more suitable than a washed-out flower print, while John Tracey had either forgotten the date or was too angry to send anything.

In the departure lounge she found a seat in the nonsmoking section and snapped open her carpetbag. She had bought two papers at the airport bookstall, hoping they might contain more details than the *Guardian* about the man detained for questioning, but the *Independent*'s report was virtually word-for-word. The *Daily Telegraph* was more forthcoming, revealing that the suspect worked for a company based in Banbury but had previously been employed as a farm laborer on a large estate only three miles from Thebes Farm. Loretta felt a prickle of excitement, recognizing the unstated implication that the man's local knowledge might have extended to the layout of Bridget's garden; the *Telegraph* went on to report that the search for the dead woman's missing clothes and the murder weapon had switched from woods behind Thebes Farm to the estate where the suspect used to work, concentrating on a number of ramshackle outbuildings. These had been

238

searched before, a police spokesman admitted rather sheepishly, but extra manpower had been diverted to the area now it was considered central to the inquiry.

Loretta lifted her head, glancing round the departure lounge in search of a phone. She saw one on the wall, next to the ladies' loo, and was plucking up courage to try John Tracey again when an amplified female voice announced that her flight was ready to board. Loretta hesitated, wondering if there was time to leave a message on Tracey's answering machine, but a flight attendant was already collecting boarding passes. Feeling a slight sense of reprieve, she folded the newspapers, slid them into her bag and promised herself she would try Tracey again as soon as the plane landed in Paris.

A still photo filled the small screen, a line of armored vehicles rolling down a wide street. The voice-over was fast and urgent, so fast that Loretta was thankful she had been speaking French part of the day and her initial rustiness had worn off. She leaned forward to turn up the volume, then supported herself on her elbow on the hotel bed and listened to a report that Mikhail Gorbachev, contrary to reports yesterday, the first day of the Soviet coup, was alive and being held prisoner with his family at a resort in the Crimea. The screen switched to a picture of Boris Yeltsin, who was still holding out against the conspirators in the Kremlin, while a correspondent in Moscow phoned in a report about the response to Yeltsin's call for a general strike. The next item was a studio discussion with a French trade-union official who had once met the leader of the conspirators on a trip to Moscow; his French was guttural, more difficult than the Parisian accent of the anchorman, and Loretta's brow creased with the effort to understand. A single long ring from the phone startled her and she stuck out a hand to grab it.

"Yes? *Oui?*"

"Loretta? Is that you?"

"Bridget? How did you get hold of me?" She was expecting a call from John Tracey, in reply to the message she had left on his machine the previous evening, and she was astonished to hear Bridget's voice. "I mean, where are you ringing from?"

Instead of a straight answer Bridget burst into tears: uncontrolled, choking sobs which alarmed Loretta so much that she jerked forward to turn down the volume of the television. The curly telephone cord twisted itself round her arm as she returned to the bed and she struggled impatiently to extricate herself. "Bridget, what is it?"

Bridget tried to speak, broke down again and sobbed out unintelligible half-sentences. Loretta remembered an occasion when the situation had been reversed, when all that stood between her and imminent dissolution was Bridget's voice at the other end of a telephone line. "It's all right," she said quietly, "I'm here. Cry as long as you like."

It took a full minute for Bridget to regain control. "I'm sorry," she said weakly, and Loretta heard her blow her nose.

"What's happened? Can you tell me?"

"It's Sam. He knows about the baby."

"The baby?"

"I almost told you that day in the Duke of Cambridge, when we had that stupid row, but I just couldn't bring myself . . . I didn't want to admit it, even to you."

"What's wrong with the baby?" Bridget had had the usual test for Down's syndrome, the risk was higher because of her age, but she had assured Loretta that the

240

result was negative. Loretta thought of other conditions, spina bifida and anencephaly, and did not immediately register what Bridget was saying. Then she gasped: "Not the father? What do you mean?"

"It's not *his*." Ignoring Loretta's yelp, Bridget began to gabble: "It was when they did the first scan, I didn't know they could tell the age of the fetus so accurately, they took one look and said I must have got the dates wrong, it was more mature than they expected. Remember that time in February when we split up?"

"Yes, but—"

"That's it, that's when it happened, I've been over the dates a hundred times."

"But whose is it?" Loretta demanded unwisely. "Do you know?"

"Of *course* I know, I wasn't sleeping around. I went to a ghastly party in Headington and you know I don't normally drink that much but I was so depressed . . . I don't even remember leaving but next morning I woke up and there he was. I mean, I've never even fancied him. He *said* I invited him in, his wife was away at the time—"

"*Who?* Who are you talking about?"

"Stephen."

"Stephen Kaplan?"

"Yes."

"Oh, God." Loretta breathed out, letting her body sag on the hotel bed. She wondered how Bridget had thought she could get away with it, given the difference in their physical types—Stephen small, dark and wiry, Sam tall with straight blond hair. Blame it on recessive genes? "Does he know? Stephen?"

Bridget choked. "He just *laughed* when I told him. You know that old joke, with my brains and your looks . . . I was still sort of hoping I'd made a mistake, that he'd turn out to have used a condom or something. But he didn't."

"God," Loretta said again. She understood now why Bridget had insisted the baby would bear Sam's name—as though naming something had the power to alter its essence. "How did Sam find out? You didn't *tell* him?"

"Course not." She added, bewilderingly: "It was the estate agent."

"What?"

"The hospital sent a letter saying all the tests were negative and giving the new date when it—when the baby's due. Some idiot put the old address on the envelope, Woodstock Road, and it's been sitting there ever since. The agent sent it on last week, after she showed Professor Lal round. It came this morning. I was on my way to the hospital and Sam thought it might be urgent. He was waiting in for the plumber, one of the loos isn't flushing properly since the police messed about with the drains."

"Where are you now?" asked Loretta, trying to assimilate all this information. "At home?"

Bridget was silent for a moment. Then she said in a small voice: "I'm at your place. I forgot to give you back the key. I didn't know where else to go."

Loretta pictured the note she had left on the kitchen table, next to an unopened tin of Felix, for the neighbor who came in to feed the cat. She had scribbled down the date and time of her return flight, and the name and telephone number of her hotel, just in case of emergencies.

Bridget drew in her breath and said: "He hit me, Loretta. Well, slapped me."

"*Slapped* you? Are you all right?"

242

"Yes, I ran out to the car. He came after me, he banged on the window and shouted about a divorce."

"What do *you* want?"

"I don't know. Oh, Loretta."

"You're sure he didn't hurt you?"

Bridget sniffed. "My cheek hurt for a while but it's all right now."

Loretta glanced at her watch. "Look, I'm going to ring the airline and see how soon I can get a flight. It's too late to get back tonight, but maybe tomorrow—"

"Thanks, Loretta. I didn't want to ask."

"Don't be ridiculous. Bridget, you don't think he'll come after you?" A slap wasn't fatal, it hardly turned Sam into a wife-beater, but distance doubled her anxiety. She gave an involuntary glance at the bathroom door, as though someone might be lurking in there.

"I haven't turned the lights on at the front. I mean, I'm not scared of him or anything, but I thought I'd sleep in your room if that's all right."

Loretta's stomach contracted. "There's a torch under my bed, you can use that on the stairs." She did not add that it was heavy and made of rubber, purchased after a spate of burglaries in Southmoor Road. "Listen," she said, "put the phone down and I'll try the airport. I'll call you back as soon as I can."

"Can't I ring you? What if it's Sam?"

Loretta sighed and wished she had a more up-to-date answering machine, one with call-vetting. "I'll let it ring twice, put the phone down and ring again so you'll know it's me. All right?"

"All right."

"Have you eaten anything?"

"A slice of toast this morning. I'm not hungry."

"Have a look in the freezer while I ring Charles de

Gaulle. What about Mrs. Mason? Does she know you're there?"

"Someone came in this evening to feed the cat. He was lying on your bed with me and he went racing off downstairs. I don't think she realized I was here."

"I'd better speak to her as well. Go and get something to eat and I'll see about this flight."

It took Loretta longer than she anticipated to get the right number for the airline, to find someone who could deal with her request and to establish that there was no way of swapping her return flight on Thursday afternoon for one the following morning. Instead she had to buy an expensive single ticket for Wednesday afternoon, paying by credit card and not thinking about how she would find the money when the bill arrived next month. The television was still flickering silently when she finished, the specially extended news bulletin having given way to an American film, and she turned it off before dialing her own number in Oxford.

"Bridget? It's all fixed. I should be home tomorrow evening about seven. Did you find something to eat?"

"Yes, it's in the oven. It'll be ready in five minutes."

"Try not to worry. I mean, we'll sort something out." This was well-meant but not entirely honest; Bridget had dealt a bitter blow to Sam's self-esteem, and Loretta did not think he was a very forgiving person.

"Loretta? I was watching the news before you rang and they've charged him, that bloke they arrested on Sunday. Apparently they found her case in his loft."

"In his loft? They said that on television?"

"No, I knew already. A couple of reporters rang last night, Sam told me when he came to bed." Bridget suddenly sounded very tired.

"And does he drive a blue van?"

"Yes. He works for a wine warehouse in Banbury."

"Wine? I thought it was supposed to be something toxic."

Bridget sighed. "There's an advert on the side, some wine called Explosif."

"Never heard of it."

"It's Algerian or something."

"Like Red Infuriator?"

"What's that?"

"They sometimes have it at Bottoms Up."

"I suppose. Listen, Loretta, the timer's just gone off. Can I tell you the rest tomorrow?"

"Of course. Bridget?"

"Yes?"

"What happened at the hospital this morning? How's your blood pressure?"

"Down a bit, or it was." She sounded close to tears again. "Don't worry, they've given me plenty more tablets."

Loretta lifted the phone back onto the bedside table and went to the open window, gulping in the dusty night air. She felt queasy, her stomach churning as though she had eaten something bad even though she had gone to one of her favorite restaurants in Paris. Her room was on the top floor of the hotel, at the back, and if she stood to one side she could see the twin towers of Nôtre Dame; the view across the rooftops calmed her, gradually dispelling her mental image of Bridget eating by torchlight in Oxford. Lights were coming on in uncurtained windows and in the distance she could make out a fire escape at the back of an apartment block, its sharp contours blurring as it zigzagged down into darkness.

Somewhere a woman began to sing, imitation Piaf, every note a throbbing vibrato. It could be a recording but Loretta thought not, picturing the singer moving from table to table in the outdoor café in the Rue des Grands Degrés, accompanying herself on a guitar. She listened for a while, motionless by the open window, until the song reached its melancholy conclusion and was received with a polite spatter of applause. A breeze ruffled the muslin curtains and she drew them across, bending to turn on the table lamp as she went to the chair where she had left her Filofax lying open.

Rose Earhart, the Australian friend she had arranged to meet for dinner the following evening, lived in a tiny flat off the Boulevard Rochechouart. Loretta dialed the number and was unsurprised when the phone was answered by another answering machine. Rose was self-employed, a film editor who worked for subsistence wages on low-budget films, and she had warned Loretta she was putting in long hours to finish a movie by a Senegalese director.

"Rose," Loretta said tiredly, "I'm so sorry but something's come up and I have to go back to England." She hesitated, wanting to say more but held back by feelings of protectiveness towards Bridget, even though the two women did not know each other. "It's too complicated to explain just now," she added, "but I'll write when I get home. I'm really sorry about tomorrow night." She pressed down the rest, dialed 0 for reception and began to explain, in halting French, that she would have to check out the following morning and would like to settle her bill—the French word escaped her for a moment—she would like to settle her *addition* as soon as she had finished breakfast.

The arrivals lounge at Terminal One was large and bare, with two fast-moving queues for EC passport-holders and a much slower one for other nationalities. Loretta took out her passport and checked her watch anxiously, thinking she might just catch the 5:30 coach to Oxford if she was lucky. She joined the shortest queue, shuffling along behind an Italian woman with upswept blond hair and a chunky gold necklace until the line came to an unexpected halt. Loretta tutted, stepped sideways to see what the hold-up was and groaned when she saw the man behind the desk questioning two Asian men. They had old-style blue passports, the precursor of Loretta's shiny red one, and the younger man was turning out his pockets, searching for something. Loretta watched them uneasily, wondering whether she should volunteer to help.

"Your passport, please. May I see your passport?"

Loretta turned, not entirely certain that the remark had been addressed to her. The speaker was a man in a dark jacket, not in uniform but unquestionably official. Loretta stared at him and said: "Me? Why?"

He plucked the passport from her hand, scrutinized the unflattering picture taken in a photo booth and snapped it shut. "All right, Dr. Lawson, would you come this way?"

"Where to?" Loretta hung back, glancing at her fellow passengers in the hope of finding a sympathetic face, someone whose support she could enlist. She was out of luck: the blond Italian was flipping through the pages of *Oggi*, oblivious to what was going on, and the French couple behind her were preoccupied with a crying infant.

"There's nothing wrong with my passport," Loretta protested, following the man in the jacket only because she wanted it back. "I mean, where are you taking me?"

He ignored her, leading the way to an unmarked door in the side of the terminal building. Rapping loudly on the door with one hand, he thrust the passport at her with the other and walked away. The door swung inward and Loretta hesitated on the threshold, repelled by the gray, institutional furniture and the acrid fumes of cigarette smoke. Two black lines, roughly parallel, snaked across the floor, as though an unconscious body had recently been dragged across it; Loretta's fertile imagination immediately began filling in the details, a drug courier collapsing under interrogation as a condom packed with cocaine burst in her stomach, the chaos in the room as customs officers tried ineffectually to revive her. At that moment a door opened on the far side of the room to admit a man and a woman, both of them familiar, and any notion that she had been stopped on a customs matter evaporated from Loretta's head.

"Dr. Lawson." The Inspector greeted her in a tired, cheerful voice, coming round the table to shake her hand. "Sorry to grab you like this but it is important. Good flight?"

Her grip was tense, contradicting the matter-of-factness of her greeting, and she had the restless, exhausted look of someone feeding on high levels of adrenaline. Loretta said nervously: "What is this? What's going on?"

The other detective coughed, turning his head aside, and Loretta recognized the young man she had seen on Sunday afternoon, outside the Ashmolean.

"Sit down, Dr. Lawson." The policewoman gestured vaguely towards the chairs and waited for Loretta to move. "Please," she added, pulling one out herself.

After a slight hesitation Loretta said, "OK," and let her carpetbag slide to the floor. She perched on the edge of a chair, hardly aware how uncomfortable it was, and faced the Inspector across the table. "I'm sorry," she said, "I've forgotten your name."

"Queen," said the policewoman. "Stella Queen. And this is DC Blady."

Loretta nodded, feeling slightly less at a disadvantage. "OK," she said again, "are you going to tell me what this is about?"

Instead of answering, Inspector Queen patted the pockets of her suit jacket and frowned. "My cigarettes . . ."

Blady produced a gold packet and she took one, looking interrogatively at Loretta. Loretta shook her head and she returned the packet to its owner, leaning sideways as he struck a match and lit her cigarette. She leaned back in her chair, visibly relaxing as she inhaled, and was silent for a moment.

"Just one thing," she said unexpectedly, "before we start. Why did you change your flight from Paris, Dr. Lawson? I gather you weren't expected home till tomorrow?"

The room was airless, without windows, and Loretta could feel the smoke insinuating itself into her hair. She put a hand up and touched it, as though she could protect it from the pollution. "Just a work thing," she said cautiously, not wanting to admit the real reason. "Bridget's asked me to stand in for her next term, while she's on maternity leave, and there isn't much time to fix it up. I said I'd come back early if I could."

To her surprise, Inspector Queen was immediately alert. "So you've fixed up to see Dr. Bennett? When? Tomorrow?"

Loretta felt a ripple of alarm. "Why? Has something happened to Bridget?"

"Such as, Dr. Lawson?"

Loretta moved anxiously in her chair, feeling the metal surround quiver under her weight. "I've no idea, it was you who said—why don't you just tell me what's going on?"

There was a distant rumble, the sound of a wide-bodied jet taking off. Inspector Queen stubbed out her cigarette on a cheap tin ashtray which already held several butts and looked directly at Loretta. "Bridget Bennett has been missing since lunchtime yesterday," she said calmly. "I have half a dozen officers checking with her friends and colleagues—"

"What?"

"—but so far we've drawn a complete blank. She seems to have disappeared off the face of the earth, which isn't all that easy for a pregnant woman. If you have any information about her whereabouts, any idea at all where she might be, you should tell us now. I have a WPC stationed outside your house—"

"Outside *my* house?"

Inspector Queen said revealingly: "We couldn't get in because your neighbor's visiting her sister in High Wycombe and her son's a bit—not all there. He says he doesn't know where she keeps your key."

"This is ridiculous," Loretta interrupted. "Who says—what makes you think Bridget's missing?"

Inspector Queen glanced sideways at her companion. An unspoken message passed between them and he said casually: "Mr. Becker admits they had a row yesterday lunchtime. He says she went off in her car, she didn't say where she was going, and no one's heard from her since."

Loretta appealed to the Inspector: "*Sam* reported her missing? Is that what you're saying?"

"Not exactly," Inspector Queen hesitated for quite a long time. "Dr. Lawson, I have to tell you that at ten thirty this morning I went to Mr. Becker's office on Osney Island and arrested him on suspicion of murder."

"*Murder.*" Loretta shook her head disbelievingly, her own suspicions about Sam the previous evening shrivelling like punctured balloons. She said, putting off the moment when she had to admit she knew perfectly well where Bridget was: "I don't like him, I'm not going to pretend I do, but I'm sure he wouldn't harm Bridget."

"No one's accused him of harming his *wife*, Dr. Lawson. Mr. Becker is being held on suspicion of murdering Paula Wolf."

"Paula Wolf?"

They stared at each other in mutual incomprehension. Loretta felt an urge to laugh, a horrible reflex she had experienced once before after a minor car accident in Banbury Road. She cried out: "What? I don't understand."

A tray stood on the table between them, with a jug of water and two scratched plastic glasses. Inspector Queen pushed it towards Loretta, asking rather nervously whether she wanted a drink. Loretta waved it away, unaware that the color had drained from her face and she was hyperventilating. "It was in the *Guardian* this morning," she protested. "I read it on the plane. You've already charged someone; it gave his name and everything."

The Inspector's mouth tightened and her eyes focused on a point somewhere beyond Loretta's right shoulder. She said without emotion, as though reading from a prepared statement: "David John Coombes has been charged with one offense of attempted murder arising out of an incident on the A34 in 1989. Further charges are imminent, but he is no longer a suspect in the inquiry into the death of Paula Wolf."

"He isn't? You mean she didn't get into his van?"

"She did, but he says he lost his nerve. All the other attacks were at night and he picked on women who'd broken down. He always parked far enough away so they couldn't get his registration number. He says he made some excuse and dropped her off, though he may

251

have tried something on and she got away. *Something* must've happened, because she was in such a hurry she left her bag behind." She held out her hand for the cigarettes, slid one out of the packet and waited for Blady to light it, her eyes not leaving Loretta's face. "To get back to Dr. Bennett, we don't—we have no reason to believe she's in any danger."

The words should have been reassuring but Loretta sensed an undercurrent, an unspoken "but" which would shortly render them meaningless. She waited and eventually the Inspector added, through a cloud of smoke: "Mr. Becker has actually been quite frank with us, he's admitted knowing Miss Wolf in America and . . ." She hesitated, thrown off course by Loretta's sharp intake of breath. "And that he had, um, an intimate relationship with her."

"Intimate relationship? You mean an affair?"

Inspector Queen pushed back her chair and crossed her legs. "Of sorts; according to Mr. Becker it didn't last very long. If it hadn't been for the phone numbers—"

"What phone numbers?"

"In her—well, it's not really a diary, there are dates but she seems to have used it mainly to copy out bits of the Bible. Her brother had it with him when he arrived this morning. My—the officer who was here to meet him recognized Mr. Becker's number straight away, the CES number, that is. They found it in her bedroom, with her clothes and stuff, but naturally they had to ask God before they decided to show it to us." She looked cross for a second, the shadow of her irritation with the Imitators of Christ clouding her face. "Otherwise there was nothing to link them. Mr. Wolf says she turned up out of the blue at Christmas, she didn't say where she'd been when she got out of jail—never mentioned Mr. Becker or anything about the clinic."

"The clinic?"

Inspector Queen finished her second cigarette, leaned forward to stub it out and glanced at her watch. "To cut a long story short," she said briskly, "Miss Wolf used to work at a clinic near Boston, one of those posh private places you read about. You know, Liz Taylor's always in and out of them."

Loretta remembered a newspaper photograph of a very overweight Elizabeth Taylor arriving by car at the Betty Ford Clinic. "What on earth was Sam doing there?"

"Not the same one. This one's got a funny name, Mount Minnows . . . Mr. Becker's a bit vague about why he was there, but it seems to have been something to do with a computer virus."

Loretta was astonished. "You can't *catch* a computer virus."

"I didn't say you could. This company he worked for in Boston, apparently they sacked someone and he got his own back by messing up the computer. Mr. Becker says it took him months to sort out, he was working evenings and weekends—I don't know enough about it to give you chapter and verse. Anyway, when he finished he booked himself into this Mount Minnows place for a rest, met Miss Wolf and—" A phone rang in the inner room and she turned her head. "Get that, will you, Blady?"

He nodded, levered himself away from the wall and disappeared into the inner room.

Loretta said: "But why did she follow him to England? And it's hardly a motive for killing someone, an old girlfriend turning up. Bridget's hardly . . . we're not talking about a couple of sixteen-year-olds."

Inspector Queen's face closed up and she said awkwardly: "Mr. Becker hasn't confessed to killing her, Dr. Lawson."

"He hasn't? But you said—"

"As his lawyer pointed out, he does have an alibi for that Thursday afternoon—unlike your friend Dr. Bennett. He admits hiding the body in the barn, he's not denying that, but he claims he only did it to . . . he says he was protecting his wife." She ignored Loretta's outraged exclamation and hurried on: "Mr. Becker says he got home at the usual time that evening and there they were in the dining room, Dr. Bennett and Miss Wolf— her body, that is. Someone was coming to supper and he couldn't think what else to do, he never intended to leave the body in the sheep bath—"

"Stop! This is *ridiculous*."

Inspector Queen looked slightly affronted. "He does say it was self-defense—Miss Wolf attacked Dr. Bennett, there was a struggle and Miss Wolf fell and hit her head on the corner of the mantelpiece. If you remember, it's stone—"

Loretta gasped: "He's saying they *fought* over him? That pathetic male fantasy?"

"I assume the thought uppermost in Dr. Bennett's mind would have been to protect her baby," Inspector Queen said reprovingly. "According to her brother, Miss Wolf was in a very emotional state before she left, he'd been trying to get her to see a doctor. When she just disappeared like that he was half convinced she'd gone off and killed herself. He thinks it's highly unlikely she knew Mr. Becker was married. Or, more to the point, that his wife was pregnant."

"What do you mean, more to the point?"

"We knew from the post-mortem that Miss Wolf had recently given birth—had a baby. Till this morning we had no idea who the father was, or that the child was stillborn."

"*Stillborn,*" Loretta breathed.

Inspector Queen rattled on: "Mr. Becker swears he didn't know he'd got Miss Wolf pregnant; he only slept with her two or three times and he assumed she was on the pill. Especially with her working in the clinic."

Loretta closed her eyes and leaned back in her chair, pressing hard against the metal crosspiece. She heard a door open, Blady saying "ma'am" in an excited voice, and the scrape of the Inspector's chair as she went to join him. A moment later Loretta opened her eyes and saw Blady watching her, his hand rising to his mouth with what she took to be another cigarette until she realized it was actually a stick of chewing gum.

"Dr. Lawson?" Inspector Queen returned from the inner room, closing the connecting door behind her. "Where and when are you supposed to be seeing Dr. Bennett?"

"Um, I said I'd ring her when I got back."

"Does your answering machine have a remote-control device?"

"What?"

Inspector Queen made an impatient sound. "One of those things that sends a tone down the phone line. In case Dr. Bennett has left a message for you."

"No." The lie was automatic, even though the device was in the bag at Loretta's feet. "I mean, I haven't got it with me."

"Pity. Now about your luggage. If you tell Blady what it looks like, he'll collect it on the way to the car."

Loretta looked down at her watch. "The coach—"

"Sorry, but I need to listen to your answering machine." The Inspector hesitated. "Look, Dr. Lawson, I've just been talking to one of the forensic team I sent to St. Frideswide's College. There was a bit of argy-bargy, the porter wouldn't let them into Dr. Bennett's room till he'd spoken to the warden, but I won't bother you with all that. The point is, there was a cassette tape in her desk—a Madonna tape, is that right, Blady?"

"Yes, ma'am. *Like a Prayer*."

"Pardon?"

"That's what it's called, ma'am."

"Oh." She frowned and turned back to Loretta. "Anyway, the point is, Paula Wolf's fingerprints are all over it, Dr. Lawson."

"I don't *believe* you."

Inspector Queen ignored her. "She's got a cassette player in her car, hasn't she? I expect she listens to it on her way to work."

"Yes, but—"

"We thought it was suspicious, both cars being so clean inside, hers and Mr. Becker's. He said it was a special offer at the garage they use, a good clean inside and out when you have it serviced, but the manager says you have to pay extra. Fortunately for us this tape got moved from Dr. Bennett's car before—she must've taken it to work without realizing Miss Wolf had picked it up."

She waited a moment, watching Loretta's face as she assimilated this information, then said: "Dr. Lawson, if you're ready? We're wasting time."

Loretta got up, reaching automatically for her bag and gripping the handle more tightly when Blady moved to take it from her. Inspector Queen was already at the door, holding it open, and as soon as Loretta passed through into the arrivals lounge the two detectives formed up on either side of her as though she was under arrest. They were waved through passport control, attracting curious looks from passengers whose flights had arrived in the three-quarters of an hour since Loretta was extracted from the Paris queue. In the baggage reclaim area, the number of her flight was still up on a board, overlooking a creaking carousel on which two pieces of luggage, a scruffy holdall and a musical-instrument case, circled endlessly.

The Inspector said doubtfully: "Yours?"

"No."

"You travel light."

Loretta spotted the phones, off to her right. "Can I make a phone call?"

"Who to?"

She walked on. "Doesn't matter." She had not really expected them to allow her to make a call unsupervised but she could feel panic rising, sweat staining the underarms of her shirt even though it was not a particularly warm evening.

"Green channel here?"

"Mmm," she said, sleepwalking past a row of customs officials. She did not even notice that the Italian woman from her flight had been stopped and searched, her belongings spread out on a table like items in an extremely upmarket jumble sale. The woman lifted her head from repacking, recognized Loretta and muttered something sympathetic in Italian; Loretta ignored her, oblivious of anything but the fact that she was leading the police straight to Bridget.

The Italian shrugged. "OK, please yourself, *va fanculo*," she muttered, and went back to folding a pair of peach satin cami-knickers.

257

14

"WHAT WERE YOU DOING IN PARIS? HOLI-day?"

Loretta, who had been staring out of the car window at the familiar flat countryside between Christmas Common and Oxford, barely moved her head. "Conference," she said, hoping the Inspector would take the hint.

"In Paris? Where's the Police Federation meeting this year, Blady? Scarborough?"

He half turned from the front seat. "Don't know. Sorry, ma'am."

Inspector Queen was silent for a moment but the approach of Oxford seemed to be making her nervous. She smoothed her skirt out over her knees and re-marked: "I've often wondered what you *do* at these conferences, academics."

"Discuss things."

"But do you really do anything you couldn't do on the phone? Presumably you've all got computers and fax machines these days. I mean, who pays?"

"I do."

"Not your college?"

This was absurd enough to jerk Loretta out of the

fearful speculation which had absorbed her for most of the journey from Heathrow. She imagined Bernard Shilling's face if she put in an expenses claim for attending a meeting of the *Fem Sap* editorial collective and replied, more sharply than she intended: "No, certainly not." The car sped past a motorway sign giving advance warning of Exit Eight, the turn-off for Oxford, and her heart responded with a fast, jerky beat which left her slightly out of breath.

She reluctantly accepted that the cassette tape, with its incriminating fingerprints, belonged to Bridget. Sam was uninterested in pop music, he had never heard of k. d. lang and was politely bored when Loretta and Bridget reminisced one evening about bands they had seen in the early seventies—the Who, Led Zeppelin, Fairport Convention. In any case he had a portable CD player, Loretta had seen it at his flat in Norham Gardens, whereas Bridget quite often took her old Walkman to work. Loretta could easily picture her bumping down the cobbled street in front of St. Frideswide's in her Astra, singing along with Madonna as she turned into the small college car park and pressing the "eject" button so she could take the tape with her. It was harder to imagine Paula Wolf in the front seat of Bridget's car, fingering the plastic cassette case; Loretta's idea of the dead woman was based on the drawing which had appeared in the *Guardian*, that two-dimensional image in which life was so obviously extinct.

There were phones at intervals along the A34; Loretta had used one to ring Joe Lunderius just after Christmas when she was held up by road works on the way home from a two-day conference at Southampton University. Paula *could* have phoned Thebes Farm from there, after she got out of the blue van, although there was no obvious reason why she should have tried Sam's

259

home number rather than his office. Then it occurred to Loretta that Paula might have mixed up the two numbers; a foreigner, particularly one who had just had an unpleasant experience, would not necessarily recognize the slight difference between the two codes. If Paula was distressed, incoherent even, it might explain Bridget's willingness to go and pick her up without fully understanding who she was, or her connection with Sam. Loretta had no sooner thought of this explanation than she recoiled from it, unconsciously lifting one of her hands in a gesture of rejection. She did not believe Sam's version of events for a minute, it was a malicious fiction designed to deflect suspicion from the more obvious suspect, himself, *and* punish Bridget for her deceit over the baby.

In that case, nagged a dissident voice, why had Bridget asked Loretta to supply her with an alibi for the very Thursday afternoon Paula Wolf arrived in England? Loretta recalled Bridget's anger when she refused to lie on her behalf, to say they had met for lunch and walked on Port Meadow. There was also, insisted the unwelcome voice, the small matter of the computer log; she had forgotten the technical term Tracey used, but it showed Sam quietly working in his office throughout the afternoon. If it wasn't Bridget who went to Paula's rescue, who was it?

The big car slowed on the approach to the A40, waiting for a gap in the busy evening traffic. Loretta nibbled her lower lip, picking at a piece of loose skin until it peeled away and left a tender patch. She thought about Bridget's reaction to the discovery of the body, her spectacular bout of vomiting in the garden at Thebes Farm, and told herself such a display could not have been put on; Bridget was a hopeless actress, a creature of impulse whose responses sometimes embarrassed

260

and even irritated her friends. As for the cassette tape, such a small, portable object hardly proved anything—it could have been lying around at Thebes Farm when Paula arrived, innocently picked up by Bridget a few days later, after the murder.

"Dr. Lawson?" Inspector Queen touched her lightly on the arm as they approached the Headington roundabout. "What's the best route to Jericho? Marston Ferry Road?"

"Mmm." Loretta glanced at her watch and was astonished to discover it was only twenty past seven; they had done the journey in record time. Several years ago, when she lived in Islington, she had learned a relaxation technique at a yoga class which she now tried to put into practice, unsuccessfully attempting to regulate her breathing.

"Your neighbor comes in to feed the cat, is that right?"

"What?"

"Mrs.—the woman two doors down."

"Mrs. Mason."

"She looks after him when you go away, that's very convenient."

They passed the Cherwell School on their right, pulling out to overtake a slow-moving van.

"I prefer dogs myself," Inspector Queen prattled on as they reached the junction with Banbury Road. "Big ones like Labradors, I haven't got any time for those yappy little things. Though with the hours I have to work . . . My sister's got a cat, a big tabby. What color's yours?"

"Gray." Loretta didn't bother to point out that the Inspector had almost fallen over Bertie on the stairs when she came to the house the previous week.

"And the canal isn't a problem? I suppose cats don't like water, do they?"

"No."

"One of our divers got Weil's disease from the canal. You know, that thing you get from rat's urine. He was off for months."

The lights changed and they crossed Banbury Road. Loretta glanced north at the solid Edwardian villas leading up to the Summertown shops; everything looked so ordinary, a young Chinese woman in jeans crossing the road, an elderly woman carrying a Yorkshire terrier, the yappy kind of dog Inspector Queen had just disparaged. Loretta's fingers closed on the door handle, responding to her unformed wish to escape from the car, and the Inspector gave her a sharp look.

"Left here?" said the driver at the end of Moreton Road, only the second time he had spoken since they all got into the white Rover.

"Yes. And then right into Polstead Road or St. Margaret's, it doesn't matter which." Loretta shrank into her corner, trying to remember whether the police needed a warrant to search a house. If she made enough noise opening the front door, made it clear she was not alone, maybe Bridget would take the hint and hide—although it was hard to imagine a pregnant woman squeezing under a bed or concealing herself in the narrow wardrobe in the spare bedroom.

"Sorry?" she said, turning her head.

"I asked how long you've lived there, Southmoor Road."

"Oh, three years."

"And you don't mind commuting to London?"

"I don't go every day. Not this one," she added hastily, seeing that the driver was about to take the first turn into Southmoor Road, "there's a one-way system."

Without acknowledging her advice he changed up a gear, drove on a hundred yards and turned into Southmoor Place. The short road ended in a T-junction and the car halted while the driver peered at a carelessly parked Volvo which overhung the junction by a yard.

"The way people park," said Inspector Queen, and the car inched round the corner, steering a narrow course between the Volvo and an old Citroën parked opposite. The driver cruised along the street, keeping an eye on the numbers, and bumped up onto the pavement behind Loretta's green Golf.

"That's yours, isn't it? You're lucky it hasn't been pinched, they love those GTIs at Blackbird Leys."

Loretta ignored her, too busy trying to spot Bridget's maroon car. As the engine died she gave up looking and leaped out, her keys already in her hand as she hurried round the Rover to her front gate. She heard the Inspector call her name, glanced up the street to see a uniformed policewoman getting out of a parked car, and bolted up the path, throwing open the front door and dropping her carpetbag as she got inside.

"Bridget," she called in as loud a whisper as she dared, "Bridget, where are you?" She looked fearfully back at the front door, wondering why the detectives hadn't caught up with her, and saw that her abandoned carpetbag was preventing them from opening the front door.

"Hang on, ma'am, something's in the way," said Blady's voice and Loretta took advantage of the delay to move further down the hall, straining for the least sound of occupation on the upper or lower floors. She heard nothing, neither footsteps nor the creak of a floorboard, and she almost cried out in the hope that Bridget had gone out, that what she was listening to was the eerie silence of an empty house.

263

"Dr. Lawson? What's going on? What's the hurry?" Inspector Queen strode down the hall to confront Loretta, angry and suspicious.

She turned. "Um, nothing. The answering machine's in there." She pointed through the open door of her study, then swung round, her heart pounding, as she heard a noise from the kitchen. Loretta and the Inspector stood very still for half a minute, their eyes fixed on the bend in the stairs, and Loretta almost laughed out loud when the gray cat appeared, tail high and grumbling volubly about her three-day absence.

"Bertie." Loretta scooped him up, held his sturdy body against her chest and gently unhooked his claws from the thin fabric of her shirt. She said inanely: "Who's a good boy then?"

Inspector Queen rolled her eyes upwards and stepped into Loretta's study. "In here, you say?"

Loretta followed, carrying the cat. She was aware that Blady was behind her, close enough to feel his breath on her neck, and she moved swiftly out of range, hurrying across the room to her desk where the green message light blinked at her in the artificial dusk created by the lowered blind. The cat squirmed and she allowed him to slip from her arms, chewing her lip again as she leaned forward to raise the blind. The evening sun filled the room with a rosy glow but Loretta was in no mood to admire the effect, worried now in case Bridget had phoned with a message about her current whereabouts.

"Ready?" she asked, turning to the Inspector, and was just in time to see Blady slip out of the room. She sighed, thinking there was little point in challenging the legality of the search, and pressed the "message play" button on the answering machine. From the time the tape took to rewind she guessed there were half a dozen messages on the machine, although the first two or three should be safe enough, left over from earlier in the week. The machine beeped and a deep, slightly familiar American voice began to speak.

"Loretta, this is Dolores del Negro calling from Berkeley on Monday morning. I guess it's Monday evening your time. I got your message Friday and I was hoping to catch up with you today. Maybe if I leave my home number you can call me there. Talk to you soon."

Inspector Queen frowned and tapped her foot as the American woman dictated a long number, hesitated and then repeated her work number in case Loretta did not have it to hand.

The machine beeped and someone coughed into the tape. "Hello, Laura, it's Jenny, just ringing to say happy birthday. I did get you a card but Anthea's got chicken pox and now Kate's starting it as well, you know how it is. I expect you're out having a lovely time, and if I don't hear from you I'll try again later in the week. Bye."

"My sister," Loretta explained as Jenny finished speaking.

"Hello? Hello? This is L. D. Taylor, electrical repairs . . . your radio's ready if you'd like to collect it. It's half past two on Tuesday and if you get this message today we're open till five thirty. Thanking you."

"Loretta?" Christopher's voice, very agitated. "I know you're not home, I thought you might have left your number in Paris . . . Could you wait a moment, please, can't you see I'm talking? Sorry, Loretta, all hell's broken loose here—the cops just took Sam away, they said something about *murder*. OK, in a *moment*—I have to go, Loretta, call me as soon as you get home."

Inspector Queen said: "News travels fast."

The tape wound on. "Hi, er . . . this is John Tracey.

Listen, Loretta, I'm supposed to be getting a flight to Moscow but those wankers at the embassy are messing me around about a visa ... I just got a call from a freelance in Oxford and your mate's husband, Boris Becker or whatever he calls himself, apparently he's been arrested. I called the cops and all they'll say is he's helping with inquiries but it doesn't look good. Um, it's Wednesday morning by the way, eleven ... ten past twelve."

The answering machine beeped and Loretta closed her eyes, half expecting to hear Bridget's voice. Instead she heard Tracey again, more hesitant this time: "Loretta, it's me, I'm still at the office. I called him back, the freelance, and this DC he knows says they've got half of CID looking for Bridget. Christ, I wish you wouldn't disappear like this—ring me as soon as you get in, OK? I don't want you doing anything stupid. The Moscow trip's off, by the way, you can get me at the office or I'll call you later." The machine beeped twice and began to rewind.

"John Tracey, doesn't he work for one of the Sunday papers? How do you know him?" Inspector Queen sounded suspicious.

"I used to be married to him." Loretta leaned forward and pressed the "store" button so the messages would not be erased.

Blady appeared in the doorway. "Nothing, ma'am."

"Nothing at all? No note?" The Inspector glanced at Loretta.

"I went through the post, it's on the kitchen table."

"What about upstairs?"

"No, ma'am."

The Inspector's shoulders sagged; all the animation went out of her and she looked drained, middle-aged. She stared into space for a moment, her eyes half-

266

closed, then said tiredly to Loretta: "Will you be here for the rest of the evening, Dr. Lawson? You're not going out?"

Loretta shrugged. "I suppose."

"You'll ring us if you hear from Dr. Bennett?"

Loretta said nothing.

"You do know the penalties for obstructing the police?"

Loretta lost her temper. "For God's sake, why don't you leave me alone? You grab me at the airport, force me back here, search my house—what more do you want? Blood?"

Inspector Queen flushed, but she kept her temper. "Blady," she said curtly, nodding towards the door. "I'll see you outside." She folded one arm across her chest, supporting her chin on her clenched fist, and remained in this contemplative position until they heard the front door close. Then she lifted her head and looked directly at Loretta.

"You won't help her, you know. Not by doing anything stupid."

Loretta turned away, walked to her desk and stared out of the window.

"Where do you think she can hide? She's pregnant—there's the baby to think of."

Loretta breathed heavily, struggling against tears.

"She needs medical treatment, I've talked to the hospital. You're not doing her any favors, her or the baby—"

"Get out."

"Dr. Lawson—"

"Get out."

To her surprise, the policewoman did not argue. Loretta heard her move to the door, pause as though she wanted to say something else, then walk down the hall to the front door. She waited until she heard footsteps on the path, the clang of the gate as it opened and closed, then snatched up the phone. Her hand was trembling so much that she misdialed, gasping with frustration as she attempted John Tracey's direct line at the *Sunday Herald* a second time. Behind her the cat leapt onto a filing cabinet and let out a series of yowls, furiously demanding attention, but she barely heard him.

"Come on, come *on*. That's not John Tracey, is it?"

"No, I was passing his desk. Rosie, has John left? Sorry, love, you've missed him."

Loretta pressed down the rest and tried Tracey's home number. It rang three or four times and then the machine answered: "Hi, John Tracey speaking. I'm also taking message for Terese McKinnon."

"Oh, *God*," Loretta moaned as he listed his other numbers, unable to contain her impatience. "John, it's me, it's"—she looked at her watch—"it's ten to eight on Wednesday evening. Oh, God, where *are* you? Ring me as soon as you get in, I've got to speak to you—" She swallowed air, choked and put the phone down.

There was a noise in the hall and she ran to the front door, almost tripping over the cat who followed and entangled himself in her legs. She seized the sheet of paper lying on the mat, read the first line of a flyer advertising an itinerant knife-sharpening service and crumpled it into a ball. In her study the phone rang and she ran to answer it, her heart pounding.

"Laura? You sound out of breath—is everything all right?"

"*Jenny.*" Disappointment flooded through her and her one thought was to get her sister off the line. "Can I ring you back? I'm sorry, I can't explain—"

"You sound *awful*. What's happened?"

"Jenny, I can't talk now."

"Hang on, Laura, I am your sister, if something's wrong—"

"*Please*, Jenny." Loretta could hardly believe that Jenny, who was usually preoccupied with her own domestic concerns, was suddenly and inopportunely offering sympathy. "I'm expecting a call and I'll ring you tomorrow. Bye."

She replaced the receiver, breathed out heavily and wondered what on earth to do next. Tracey might not ring for hours; he often ate out in the evenings instead of cooking for himself, or he might even have got his Russian visa and be on his way to Moscow. She ran through a mental list of the people she could ring— Christopher Cisar, Audrey Summers, various friends of Bridget in Oxford—but decided she didn't know any of them well enough to tell the truth. Anyway, she didn't want to block the line in case Tracey arrived home and found her message. She stood irresolute, drumming her fingers on the desktop, horribly frustrated by her inability to act.

The phone rang again and she snatched it up. "John?"

"No—it's me."

Loretta let out a yelp. "*Bridget*. Where are you?" A thought occurred to her and she said rapidly: "No, don't say. They may be—it's not safe." She knew nothing about phone-tapping, whether it took days or hours for the police to get a warrant, but she didn't want to take the risk. "Oh, God, Bridget, the police were waiting for me at Heathrow, they've only just left. I don't know how to tell you—"

"I *know*. I played back the messages on your machine."

"You what?"

"Christopher, then John Tracey . . . I knew they'd think of you and I just ran."

Loretta's relief at this news was swiftly replaced by anger. She blurted out: "Where *were* you that Thursday? What are you trying to hide? Don't you trust me?"

"Loretta, *stop*." Bridget began to cry. "I'm so frightened and I don't know what to do. You've got to help me."

"All right, wait a minute." Loretta tried to think clearly. If Bridget had left the house at lunchtime she could be anywhere—the other end of the country. What they needed was a code, a way of conveying information which would mean something to the two of them but give nothing away to an eavesdropper.

Bridget seemed to be thinking along the same lines for she suddenly said, in a calmer voice: "Remember Professor Lal, Loretta? I'm at his house."

"Professor who?"

"Professor *Lal*."

"No, I don't think—" Comprehension dawned and she said triumphantly: "Yes, I do, I've got it. I'm on my way." In a hasty attempt to throw any listeners off the scent, to mislead them about where she was going, she added: "It'll take me, what? A couple of hours?"

"A couple of hours?"

"Oh, never mind."

"What do you mean, a couple of hours?"

"Oh, God, forget it." She would be able to explain the subterfuge face-to-face in a matter of minutes. "Look, I'm leaving now, OK?"

"OK. Loretta, come round the back, won't you? I daren't open the front door."

The line clicked and Loretta put down the phone. She hurried into the hall, knelt by her carpetbag and removed her purse and checkbook. She opened the purse and took out a wad of notes, pulling a face when she saw that most of them were useless French francs; Bridget would need cash, but there was no time to waste on finding a cash dispenser. Two minutes later she was ready to leave, her purse transferred to a small shoulder bag and no clear plan in her head beyond getting to Bridget's side. She opened the front door, started down the path and froze: there, parked three or four car lengths up the street, was a police patrol car. The house was still under observation; Loretta turned and darted back inside, appalled that she had not foreseen this complication. She stood in the hall, trembling and uncertain whether she had been seen. Thirty seconds, then a minute, passed without incident and she began to relax, turning over the problem of how to get out unobserved. The house formed part of a short terrace, with no access to the road apart from the front door; there was a row of semis further down Southmoor Road and she briefly considered a route over her own garden fence and those of her immediate neighbors until she came to a house with a side gate.

She looked down at her jeans, thankful that she was dressed for such an excursion, but her face clouded when she realized that her plan would still bring her out in view of the police car. She put a hand up to her face, close to despair, and moved into the study to ring Bridget and explain the hold-up. Her hand was actually on the phone when she heard a loud splash from the bottom of the garden, lifted her head and saw a man and a woman exchanging places in a rowing boat. Loretta watched for a moment, let out a loud exclamation and ran from the room, clattering down the stairs and hurling herself through the kitchen and dining room to the French windows. The key was in the lock, a piece of carelessness on her part for which she was

271

heartily grateful, and she took the steps up to the lawn two at a time, careering across the grass and coming to an abrupt halt on the landing stage.

"Hey," she called after the rowing boat, which was now pulling sedately northward. "Hey, can I have a lift?"

The man who had taken over the rowing stared at her, oars in mid-air. "You talking to me?"

"*Yes*. Please, can you turn back?"

There was an agonizing moment of indecision while the man leaned forward to consult his girlfriend, then he dipped an oar into the water and began to turn the boat.

"Thanks," said Loretta, scrambling aboard. "I'll get out at the bridge." She crouched in the middle of the boat and smiled encouragingly over her shoulder at the oarsman as he pushed off.

"That your house?" asked the woman.

Loretta nodded. "I'm having a bet with a friend," she improvised, "he's walking to the bridge and I said I could get there quicker by boat."

"Oh." The woman accepted this unlikely explanation without question and Loretta remained where she was, clutching the sides of the boat, until the bridge came into sight.

"You can let me off here," she cried, rocking the boat and almost losing her balance in her eagerness to reach dry land. She stumbled onto the towpath and made for the bridge without a backward glance, congratulating herself on the ease with which she had outwitted the watchers in Southmoor Road, and broke into a fast trot as she crossed the canal into Aristotle Lane.

15

LORETTA PAUSED AT THE END OF FRENCHAY Road, looked over her shoulder to make sure she wasn't being followed and turned left into Woodstock Road. She walked quickly but not too fast, anxious not to draw attention to herself, and started wildly when a cyclist shot past, ringing her bell and calling: "Hi, Loretta!" The rider was twenty yards up the road by the time Loretta recognized the loud voice and flying hair of Lucy Wilkes, a bright but lazy sixth-former whose parents had sent her to Loretta for extra tuition in English before her A levels. Loretta waved belatedly and allowed Lucy to dwindle to a speck before she turned into a front garden concealed from the road by a high hedge. There was no car in the drive but the garage door was firmly closed and Loretta guessed Bridget's car was inside. She made for the narrow passage between the garage and the white-painted house, hardly noticing the familiar acrid smell which drifted over from a nearby factory when the wind was in the right direction. Stepping out onto the paved area behind the house, she observed the garden long enough to notice that the grass was knee-high, then

273

tiptoed past the drawing room window to the conservatory.

She tapped on the glass. "Bridget? *Bridget?*"

Nothing happened for a moment, then the door from the dining room opened and Bridget appeared. She unbolted the conservatory door, stood back to allow Loretta inside and then threw herself into her friend's arms with such force that Loretta nearly toppled backward. She held Bridget close, thinking again how thin and vulnerable she was, and almost at once Bridget dropped her head onto Loretta's shoulder and began to sob. It was a desperate, inhuman sound, even worse than the bout of crying Loretta had listened to on Tuesday night, on the phone from Paris, and she felt helpless in the face of so profound a grief. She stroked Bridget's hair, murmured loving words and felt behind her with her free hand for the handle of the conservatory door; the last thing she wanted was a curious neighbor coming round to see what the commotion was—not even Audrey Summers, whose house adjoined Bridget's.

"Come on," she said gently, sliding an arm round Bridget's shoulders and guiding her towards the dining room. "Let's get inside." The garden wasn't overlooked, it was long and bounded by trees, but she didn't want to take any chances. The dining room was dark, most of its natural light stolen by the conservatory, and Loretta felt for the light switch only to discover that the power was turned off. She peered round the room, which she had not seen since Bridget moved out, and repressed a shiver at its shadowy emptiness. There were lighter patches on the wall where pictures had hung; and a corkboard full of postcards, photographs, seminar lists and programs from the Phoenix cinema. Loretta remembered a picture of herself and Bridget drinking champagne on the grass at St. Frideswide's, celebrating the publication of Loretta's biography of Edith Wharton. It had been taken by a friend of Bridget's whose name Loretta could not remember although she clearly recalled Bridget thrusting the camera at him with a stream of confusing instructions on how to focus it; they were both amazed when it came out so well.

"Has all the furniture gone?" she asked uneasily, peering through the open door into the drawing room.

Bridget sniffed and moved away from Loretta's supporting arm. "There's a bed upstairs and a couple of chairs. The man who cleared the house didn't want them, so I just left them."

"Let's go up, then. It'll be safer, anyway."

Bridget led the way through the drawing room, into the dark hall and up the stairs. The remaining furniture was in a small back bedroom, west-facing so there was still enough light for them to see each other. The single bed, now stripped down to its faded mattress, brought back more memories for Loretta; she had slept in it often when she lived in London, driving up to Oxford for parties or just to spend a weekend with Bridget. A thick paperback lay on the bed, face down and open, as though Bridget had been trying to read, and Loretta looked at the title from force of habit: *Villette*.

Bridget pushed the book aside and climbed heavily onto the mattress, curling her legs under her and leaning back against the wall. Loretta lowered herself into an old armchair and tried to make herself comfortable; she gave up, drew it nearer the bed and lifted her head.

"Oh, my God," she blurted out, "your *face*."

Bridget raised her hand and touched the livid bruise under her left eye with her fingertips. "I told you he hit me. It looks worse today than it did yesterday. You scared me," she went on, "saying it would take you two hours. I thought you'd misunderstood, or there was another Professor Lal who lived in Birmingham or somewhere."

Loretta shook her head. "I was trying to make them think you were miles away—if anyone was listening, that is."

Bridget said bitterly: "I wish I was. Loretta, what did they say, the police? Why do they want *me*? Has he told them I knew about the body, is that it?"

Loretta said nothing, her hands closing on the wooden arms of her chair.

"Say *something*, Loretta."

"It's—it's much worse than that."

"How do you mean worse? I've been thinking about it all day, it's been going round and round in my head. He must have told them I knew she was there, he's getting his revenge, the bastard." Her voice rose: "I'm married to a murderer and I'm having another man's baby—how could it be worse?"

Loretta stared at her, fearing another bout of hysterical weeping. She glanced down at her watch, anxious about time, and said cautiously: "You really think he's capable of it, killing someone?"

"After yesterday I'd believe anything. You weren't there, Loretta—if I hadn't locked myself in the car I don't know what would have happened."

"But you said—on the phone you said it wasn't much, just a slap."

Bridget lifted her hand again, lightly touching the contours of her face. "I didn't want to worry you. I knew you'd see for yourself when you got back. I thought you'd help me find a solicitor, someone who knows about . . . battered wives." Her lips turned down, distancing herself from the expression.

"All right, but—Bridget, you still haven't told me. Where *were* you that Thursday?"

"Not *that* again. I met Stephen in the King's Arms. I had to ask him about—you know. Whether he used a condom."

"Why on earth didn't you tell the police?"

Bridget shivered and pulled down her skirt to cover her knees.

"Are you cold?"

"A bit."

"Here, have this." Loretta stripped off her green jacket and held it out.

Bridget hesitated, glancing towards the window, where a faint red glow above the trees marked the approach of night, then draped Loretta's jacket over her shoulders. "Thanks. What about you?"

Loretta was wearing the same thin cotton shirt she had traveled in. "Don't worry about me," she said, rolling down her sleeves and folding her arms across her chest.

"I didn't want them talking to Stephen," Bridget went on. "He seemed to think it was a huge joke and I was *terrified* Sam would find out. You know how thick some of those cops are."

"What about the rest of the afternoon?"

Bridget said impatiently: "I just walked around. Stephen was going to London, he had to catch a train at two something, and I wandered round the shops for a while. Retail therapy," she added with the ghost of a smile, "though it doesn't really work when you're pregnant. I tried on a couple of dresses in Monsoon—"

"Did you buy anything?" Loretta asked eagerly, thinking there would be a record of the transaction.

"No." Bridget placed a hand on her stomach. "I got fed up with that after a while and . . . actually, I walked over to your place. If you'd been in I'd probably have told you the whole story but by the time I saw you—the next day, wasn't it? By then I'd decided to keep quiet, it didn't seem fair to Sam."

"Then what?"

"You're as bad as the police, Loretta. I can't *prove* any of this, you know, it wouldn't have helped if I had told them. I walked round to Aristotle Lane and on to Port Meadow—it was a sunny day and I sat by the river for a while. I wanted to think it all through before I went home . . . It's ironic, isn't it? If I hadn't got pregnant I wouldn't have married him, then it turns out it isn't even his child."

"You wouldn't? I thought you were crazy about him."

Bridget shifted on the bed, stretching her legs in front of her as though the weight of her stomach was too much for them. "Oh, I was—in a way. I mean, I had doubts but . . . you know what it's like when you're in love, you try to make everything fit. I'm thirty-nine, Loretta, how many unattached men are there when you get to our age? It was so great at first, not just the sex, though that was brilliant. He had this attitude to life—you know, very Harvard Business School."

"What?"

"Sort of, this is what you want, this is what you have to do to get it. Very practical, optimistic. All sorts of things seemed possible all of a sudden."

"Overcontrolled, you mean."

"Maybe, but I didn't see it. I knew *you* didn't like him."

"I thought he was cold."

"Yes, but not in bed. Not at first. Then he asked me if I'd ever been tied up."

"*What?*" Loretta jerked forward.

"And I did have a fantasy about it, lots of women

278

do." She added defensively: "Haven't you read Nancy Friday?"

"Yes, but fantasies are one thing. Acting them out is another."

"Please, Loretta, this is hard enough without you lecturing me. I let him tie me up a couple of times—well, I enjoyed it. It felt ... dangerous but he kept saying I was really in control, that I was the powerful one because I'd chosen to let him do these things to me."

"Oh, God," groaned Loretta, half aware that Bridget had said something similar very recently. "Designer S & M. You didn't really fall for that stuff?"

Bridget turned her head away.

"Go on, I might as well hear the rest of it."

"That time in February, when we split up—"

"Yes?"

"I couldn't bring myself ... I know *you*, you'd have wanted to see the bruises."

"What do you mean?"

"You know," she said quietly. "He went too far."

"Bridget, for God's sake, you're telling me this and you *married* him?"

"He did apologize, he said it only happened because he had too much to drink, he didn't realize ... It never happened again and he started talking about getting married. Then I found out I was pregnant."

Loretta lay back in the low chair. "I don't believe this. You of all people, falling for a line like that."

"You can talk. Only last week you were thinking of going back to John Tracey."

"Not for long."

"Loretta, you've never been pregnant. I didn't want to be a single mother and I couldn't face another abortion." She lifted a hand and wiped a tear from the corner of each eye.

"Oh, I'm sorry." Loretta went to sit beside Bridget on the bed, taking her free hand. "You're quite right, who am I to judge?" Bridget's hand was icy and Loretta rubbed it between her own. "You really are cold, aren't you? Have you had anything to eat?"

"This morning. Some of that horrible muesli."

"We'll have to stop on the motorway. You'd better stay in the car and I'll bring you something."

"The motorway? Where are we going?"

Loretta looked at her watch. "You know that phone on Woodstock Road, next to the playing field? I'm going to ring Christopher and ask to borrow his car. I daren't call from here—"

Bridget seized her arm. "Loretta, you still haven't told me. What's he saying? That I helped him hide the body?"

Loretta squeezed Bridget's hand. "He says . . . he says it was an accident but you killed her."

Bridget choked, gagged and half fell off the bed. She blundered out of the room, across the landing and into the bathroom where Loretta, scrambling to follow, saw her retch into the lavatory bowl.

"Bridget," she said, going to kneel beside her. Bridget's lips were rimed with bile and Loretta pulled a tissue from her pocket to wipe it away. "I'm sorry," she murmured, dropping the soiled tissue into the toilet. "Try not to think about it." She fell back on her heels and added despairingly: "What a *stupid* thing to say. Come on, lean on me."

She guided Bridget back to the bedroom, helped her to lie down on the bed and covered her with the thin linen jacket. "God," she said, "it really is cold in here. Listen, Bridget, this is what we're going to do. I'm going out to the phone; if Christopher isn't in I'll try Janet. I could rent a car but the police—"

280

"What about yours?"

"I had to leave it. They were watching the house."

"How did you—"

"It's a long story. You know that hotel I stayed in last summer, in Northumbria?" She saw that Bridget's eyes were half-closed, her face alarmingly pale in the gathering dust. "Bridget, are you all right?"

"Mmm."

Unconvinced, and terrified by the prospect of having a sick fugitive on her hands, Loretta began to gabble: "It's women-only, I stayed for a week and the woman who runs it was so nice. I'm going to take you there and as soon as you're settled we'll get a really good lawyer. John'll know someone. Bridget? Bridget, did you hear me?"

Bridget rolled over onto her back and Loretta's jacket slipped to the floor. "I didn't do it. You do believe me, don't you?"

Loretta covered her up again. "Of course."

"Who was she? I mean, why did he kill her?"

Loretta bit her lip, worried about wasting time. "He met her in a clinic, did he ever mention it to you?"

"What sort of clinic?"

"I don't know. He said—he told the police some story about working too hard; I wondered if he had had a breakdown and didn't want to admit it. Apparently she worked there and they had some sort of affair. I really don't know the details."

"When? When was this?"

Loretta thought about Paula Wolf's pregnancy, the stillborn baby she had given birth to that summer. "Last year," she said, working back, "sort of August, September."

Bridget murmured, closing her eyes: "He never said."

Loretta looked at her watch and was horrified to see

281

it was twenty past nine. "Will you be all right here while I go and phone?"

"Yes. Don't be long."

"I won't." Loretta went to the door, thought of something and turned back. "They found a tape in your desk, a Madonna tape—her fingerprints were on it. It's not like Sam to listen to Madonna."

Bridget groaned and lifted a hand to her forehead. "What're you talking about, Loretta?"

"A cassette tape. In your desk. With her fingerprints on it."

"I left some tapes in his car. When I drove over to see Mum. When my starter motor went."

"Last month?"

"Please, Loretta, I feel awful."

Loretta remained where she was for a moment, staring at the hunched figure on the bed. The sun had set and the room was in near-darkness, Bridget's face and arm lighter shapes on the opaque oblong of the bed. "I won't be long," she said and turned to go downstairs.

She was on the last step when the phone rang, echoing eerily in the empty hall. It was on the woodblock floor behind the front door and Loretta stared at it, one hand going out to grasp the newel post. It rang and rang, and when Bridget called out from the floor above Loretta turned and exclaimed, "Shhh!", as though the person at the other end might hear them. The phone stopped abruptly, in mid-ring, and she waited, listening to the sudden silence. There was no way of knowing whether someone—Inspector Queen or Sam Becker— had hit on the house as a possible refuge for Bridget, or whether it was merely a wrong number.

"Bridget, I'm off," Loretta called, and eased open the front door. She slipped out, thankful for the cover of the high hedge, and hurried across the gravel to the open gate. The phone was a couple of hundred yards up Woodstock Road and she walked jerkily, preoccupied with all the questions she wanted to ask Bridget: whether she had seen anyone she recognized in the city center after leaving Stephen Kaplan or on Port Meadow, although the water meadows were such a vast tract of land that Loretta didn't hold out much hope. There was also the matter of Sam's alibi, which still looked unbreakable—

Loretta caught her breath as she reached the phone, remembering that she had started to question Christopher Cisar about computer logs on Friday evening. The conversation was almost immediately interrupted by the appearance of John Tracey, but she now realized what had prompted her inquiry: months before, in the spring, she had been sitting in another restaurant in Oxford, bored to tears, as Bridget encouraged Sam to give a step-by-step description of an attempt to steal information from the main computer at CES and the brilliant strategy he had devised to block it. His account was far too technical for Loretta to follow but it was obvious he knew the system inside out; if there *was* a way of tampering with the log, he would know how to do it. Loretta opened her purse, snatched a twenty-pence piece and punched Christopher's number into the phone, bursting with questions. She listened anxiously to the ringing tone, willing him to be in, and it wasn't until she heard his voice that she remembered the much more urgent problem which had brought her out to the phone in the first place.

"Christopher," she gasped as he recited his telephone number, "it's me, Loretta."

"Hi, I've just talked to your answering machine. Where are you speaking from?"

"Woodstock Road. Christopher, I need your help."

"You haven't been home?"

"Yes, but I can't talk now. I need to borrow your car."

"My car?"

"I wouldn't ask if there was any other way. *Please,* Christopher."

"Hold on, Loretta. You know Sam's been arrested?"

"*Yes.* Can you bring it now?" She gave him the address of Bridget's house and added: "Park it in the drive and leave the keys in the ignition. Don't come to the door. I don't want to involve you, not more than I can help. I'll get it back to you somehow, it might take a couple of days—"

"Loretta, what in hell's going on?"

"*Trust* me, Christopher."

"We have to talk."

"*No,* the less you know the better."

"I don't like the sound of this, Loretta, but you win. I'm on my way."

Loretta replaced the receiver and began to walk back down Woodstock Road, trying to work out a route to Northumbria in her head. A new stretch of the M40 had opened earlier in the year, joining Oxford and Birmingham, but she couldn't remember whether it intersected with the M1. She hoped there would be an up-to-date map in Christopher's car; there weren't any services on the M40 so she would not be able to stop and buy one. Panting, slightly out of breath from anxiety and the unfamiliar exertion, she turned into Bridget's drive and slipped into the dark passage between the house and garage. The conservatory door was unlocked and she let herself into the house, calling to Bridget that she was back. There was no reply but when she went upstairs Bridget was there on the bed, fast asleep. Loretta tiptoed out of the bedroom, thinking she might as well sleep until Christopher arrived with the car. He lived in Boar's Hill, the other side of Oxford, and she wasn't sure how long it would take him to drive round the ring road. She tried to remember what sort of car he had, something big and quiet but she was hopeless at makes; in any case, one car was pretty much the same as another unless he drove an automatic.

She used the loo, flushed it and ran her hands under the cold tap. A sliver of soap, dry and cracked, lay in a pretty Victorian soap dish, presumably left behind by mistake, and she managed to work up a little lather. There was no towel and she fished in the pocket of her jeans for a tissue, the last of the handful she had removed from the hotel bathroom in Paris that morning. As she dried her hands she heard the crunch of tires on the gravel, dropped the tissue into the loo and ran to the top of the stairs. Relief flooded through her, wiping out her earlier resolve not to speak to Christopher, and she took the stairs two at a time, muttering under her breath.

Much later, obsessively replaying the evening's events in her mind, Loretta tortured herself with the charge that she had known, a split second before flinging open the front door, that it was not Christopher's car which had sounded on the gravel. It had arrived too quickly and she thought—although she was not absolutely convinced of this—that she had heard two car doors slamming rather than one as she reached the bottom step. But the realization came too late and she could only stare in horror as the two detectives, Blady and an older man, approached the house.

Blady said: "In there, is she?" and waited for Loretta to move out of his way. She fell back, saying nothing, and he pushed open the door to the drawing room. "There any lights in this place?" She heard him feel for the switch, try it and swear under his breath. He turned to her and said roughly, "Come on, Dr. Lawson, you're only making it worse for yourself."

Still Loretta said nothing. She could not see his face but she could feel his irritation as he moved round the dark hall, trying one door after another—the downstairs lavatory, a walk-in cupboard, the kitchen. She wondered, briefly, where the other man had gone, then heard him call to Blady from the back of the house.

"Stay with her," Blady ordered as the older man emerged from the drawing room. He ran lightly upstairs and gave a shout of triumph, and almost immediately there was an answering shriek from Bridget.

"Leave her *alone*," Loretta cried, dodging round her captor and pounding up the stairs. "For God's sake, she's *ill*." She arrived in the small room as Blady identified himself and began to caution Bridget, pushing past him and kneeling beside her terrified friend.

"I'm sorry," she exclaimed, cradling Bridget in her arms, "I'm sorry, I'm sorry." To her alarm Bridget began to shake, gasping for breath and uttering words which made no sense.

"Get a doctor," Loretta ordered, rounding on Blady. "Next door, Dr. Summers—go *on*." He hesitated and Loretta struggled to her feet, holding Bridget's hands tightly to prevent her from falling sideways. "If she goes into labor—"

Blady shot out of the room, calling downstairs to his colleague: "Bill, can you go next door and get the doctor?" He reappeared, demanding to know which side Dr. Summers lived.

"There," snapped Loretta, pointing at the party wall—a useless gesture in the darkness. She heard voices in the hall, what sounded like the beginning of

286

an argument, then Christopher called: "Loretta? *Loretta?*"

"Up here."

She heard him coming up the stairs. Blady went to meet him and demanded: "Who are you?"

"Christopher," she cried as he ignored Blady and came into the room. "Oh, thank God! Bridget's collapsed and these cretins don't seem to understand. I'm scared she's going into labor."

"Shit. Why are there no lights in this place?"

"The electricity's turned off."

"Lay her down on the bed. That's it. Can you support her head?"

Between them Loretta and Christopher got Bridget into a more comfortable position, her head in Loretta's lap. She moaned and thrashed about, not seeming to know where she was, and Loretta peered up at Christopher, unable to distinguish his features. "What's keeping them?" she asked anxiously and Christopher went to find out.

"Apparently the doctor isn't home," he said a moment later. "Don't panic, they've called an ambulance. Loretta, what is going on here? You didn't tell me those guys were *police*."

"Please—not in front of Bridget."

Christopher sat down in the low chair which Loretta had occupied before she went to the phone. "How's she doing?"

"I don't know, I hope it's just shock ... Have you got a handkerchief?"

Christopher passed it across. Loretta pushed Bridget's hair back from her brow and wiped sweat from her forehead. Her mouth was open and she was dribbling, making a damp patch on Loretta's jeans. "She's so hot,"

287

Loretta murmured, dabbing at Bridget's mouth. "I don't know why she's breathing like this."

Christopher leaned forward and felt for Loretta's other hand. She clutched his, holding it tightly while her ears strained for the distant wail of a siren. "God," she muttered, "when will they come?"

They sat in silence in the small bedroom, the only sounds Bridget's uneven breathing and the voices of the detectives, talking quietly in the hall below. Suddenly Christopher released Loretta's hand.

"Did you hear that?" He moved to the door and said with obvious relief: "It's OK, I can hear the ambulance."

A moment later the house was full of noise, doors slamming and people talking downstairs. A torch beam shone into the room, illuminating the unhappy tableau on the bed, and a female voice asked redundantly: "Is this where she is?"

Christopher moved to the window so the ambulancewoman could reach the bed, where she knelt to take Bridget's pulse.

"She's six months pregnant," Loretta explained. "Her blood pressure's too high and she just seemed to collapse. Is she going to be all right?"

"Where was she when this happened?" The ambulancewoman gently lifted Bridget's arms, checking for broken bones. "Did she fall?"

"No, she was already on the bed. She hasn't had anything to eat all day and she's been taking tablets—I don't know what sort."

"All right." The ambulancewoman stood up, went to the top of the stairs and shouted: "Ted! Can you bring the stretcher?"

"Bridget," Loretta whispered, bending over her, "they're going to take you to hospital but don't worry,

I'll come. I'll be with you." Bridget grunted and Loretta had no idea whether she had understood.

The ambulancewoman reappeared, followed by her male colleague, and they began the painstaking task of maneuvering Bridget onto the stretcher, out of the room and down the stairs. Loretta went with them, hovering nervously and earning a mild rebuke from Ted for getting in their way. At the bottom of the stairs she waited to follow them to the ambulance but a hand gripped her arm and a woman's voice said: "Dr. Lawson, I'm afraid you'll have to accompany us to the station."

Loretta shook herself free, feeling no surprise at the presence of Inspector Queen. "Leave me *alone*," she snapped. "I'm going with Bridget."

"I'm sorry, Dr. Lawson." The Inspector sounded genuinely regretful but it did not stop her beckoning to a burly male detective.

Christopher stepped forward into the patch of light shining into the hall from a street lamp. "Would somebody tell me what's going on here?"

"Who are you?"

"Christopher Cisar."

"Inspector Stella Queen, Thames Valley CID. I interviewed you at the party."

Christopher shrugged this aside. "What are you guys doing here?"

"I'm here to arrest Dr. Bridget Bennett on suspicion of murder—"

Loretta cried out, stepping back and colliding with Christopher, who put his arms around her.

"—of the murder of Paula Wolf, but in view of her medical condition I'm going to allow her to be taken to the John Radcliffe Hospital." She nodded to Blady. "You go with her. I'll come up as soon as I've sorted this lot out."

Blady climbed into the back of the ambulance and the woman closed the doors from the inside, calling in a businesslike voice: "Right you are, Ted." The engine rumbled and the reversing lights came on, signaling that the driver was about to edge backwards in an arc towards the garage.

"Dr. Lawson." In an expressionless voice Inspector Queen began to recite the formal words of the caution, familiar to Loretta only from films. Halfway through, the ambulance trundled forward to the gate, paused to turn into Woodstock Road and switched on its siren. Inspector Queen went on speaking, mouthing inaudible words like a TV with the sound turned off. Loretta gasped, covered her face with her hands and started to sob.

POSTSCRIPT

Southmoor Road
Oxford
25 November 1991

Dear John,

A courier has just arrived with your package and I'm so grateful. I tried ringing you at the *Herald* but they said you're on your way to Zagreb. Call me as soon as you get back, I've got so much to tell you. First thing is Bridget's had her baby, a girl. Six pounds two ounces and she's called Jessica Elizabeth Bennett. They let me into the prison hospital on Friday to see them both; Bridget was exhausted but quite well.

I can't thank you enough for the stuff from Boston. You do realize this nurse you interviewed, the one who used to work at the Mount Minos clinic, has given Sam a motive? No wonder he didn't want anyone turning up in Oxford who knew the real reason he was there, especially someone as upset and unstable as Paula Wolf. Is there any chance of us getting to see the clinic records? I'm not clear from your notes whether he agreed to go there specifically to avoid prosecution or whether the police decided not to charge him anyway. It's a pity the doctor who runs the place isn't more cooperative, I don't see what he's got to hide. On the other hand America's such an open country, the Freedom of Information Act and all that, and I wonder if there isn't a legal device for getting hold of them?

I know you didn't have time to track down the ex-girlfriend, the one he put in hospital, but if you've got her name I could have a go on the phone. Of course, as you say, if she didn't want to give evidence against him in spite of what he did she may not be willing to talk to us either, but it's worth a try. I'm having a similar problem with Bridget, she's extremely reluctant to mention the S & M thing in court, even though it does indicate a history of violence. Obviously that's why Sam thought he could get away with it, the women he beat up are too embarrassed to talk about it. Did he *really* use a whip? Fortunately we've got photos of Bridget's face immediately after she was arrested (and a doctor's report), and when she hears what you've found out she may change her mind.

You say Paula helped him escape from Mount Minos, which certainly doesn't *sound* as though he was a voluntary patient. Is there any way of finding out what happened after they got away, i.e., between mid-September and him arriving in Oxford in November? I suppose he dumped her soon after but I do wonder how he got a job in England so quickly.

Bridget's solicitor is still trying to find a computer expert who'll say Sam could have altered the log; a friend put me on to a couple of people who've explained how it could have been done, but Sam's clever and there isn't any actual proof. All we need is someone who's able to stand up to cross-examination and cast doubt on Sam's alibi in the jury's mind, because I've saved the best news till last. I was in the building society two weeks ago, paying my mortgage, and I happened to look up and see a video camera—that thing they have in case of armed robberies. I suddenly thought, lots of shops have them these days, and I came back to Southmoor Road and had a look at the list Bridget gave me (the first time I saw her after she was remanded, I got her to write down every shop she went in that Thursday afternoon). It took me three mornings to go round them all and I got quite demoralized—some of them reuse their videos almost immediately. But I kept at it and I've found two that don't—a bank in the center and a shop in Little Clarendon Street. The first sighting is at two twenty-eight, about half an hour after she left Stephen Kaplan, and the second is three seventeen, when she was on her way to Southmoor Road. She only went into one shop on the way back to college to pick up her car, no luck there, but she remembered seeing a film crew in the High Street. I racked my brains to think who it might be, I called all the obvious places like the local BBC newsroom and drew a complete blank.

Then I went into the English department at Fitzroy last week and someone happened to mention *Inspector Morse*. I rang up the TV company who make it, found a really helpful woman and asked if they had been filming in Oxford that day. They had, and they let me go up on Thursday and look at what they shot. Bridget's actually in the film, thank God she wasn't the face on the cutting-room floor, and you can quite clearly see her crossing the road. The scene was filmed between four and four thirty, the producer thinks four fifteen is the likeliest time. Of course we can't *prove* she didn't rush back to college from Little Clarendon Street, pick up her car, drive home, take Paula's call, go and pick her up from the A34 (the police have found Paula's prints on a phone four or five miles south of the ring road), take her home and bash her on the head—but I did the round trip with Bridget's solicitor and it took us an hour and three-quarters.

We've just been notified of the trial date, it's been set down for mid-February. I know you can't write anything before then, but do you think the paper will let you cover it, just in case anything goes wrong? Bridget's solicitor will be delighted with this stuff you've dug up, I'm so grateful, but you never know with a jury. I hardly dare think of it, Bridget and I haven't talked about it at all, but a murder conviction does still carry a mandatory life sentence. One other piece of news, by the way—they've finally agreed to drop the charges against me, aiding and abetting a fugitive or whatever it was. Bridget told them I was about to take her to hospital when they arrived, and of course she very nearly did lose the baby.

I hope you have a good trip to Zagreb. If you ran up any expenses in Boston, phone calls and so on, let me know and I'll send you a check. Ring me as soon as you get back—I'm at St. Frideswide's on Mondays and Wednesdays, London on Tuesdays and Thursdays, and at home on Fridays.

Love and thanks from Loretta

JOAN SMITH

Published by Fawcett Books.
Available in your local bookstore.